LORDS & LADIES CHRISTMAS

Be whisked away to Regency England with three delightful Christmas stories from three hugely talented authors.

Nicola Cornick
"...seduces her readers with her vividly portrayed descriptions of the Regency era, wicked wit, sensual emotion and intense romance."
—*Cataromance*

Lyn Stone
"...masterfully blends excitement, humour and emotion."
—*Romantic Times Magazine*

Julia Justiss
"...has a knack for conveying emotional intensity and longing."
—*All About Romance*

Nicola Cornick is passionate about many things: her country cottage and its garden, her two small cats, her husband and her writing, though not necessarily in that order! She has always been fascinated by history, both as her chosen subject at university and subsequently as an engrossing hobby. She works as a university administrator and finds her writing the perfect antidote to the demands of life in a busy office.

A painter of historical events, **Lyn Stone** decided to write about them. A canvas, however detailed, limits characters to only one moment in time. "If a picture's worth a thousand words, the other ninety thousand have to show up somewhere!" An avid reader, she admits, "At thirteen, I fell in love with Bronte's Heathcliff and became Catherine. Next year, I fell for Rhett and became Scarlett. Then I fell for the hero I'd known most of my life and finally became myself." After living four years in Europe, Lyn and her husband, Allen, settled into a log house in north Alabama that is crammed to the rafters with antiques, artifacts and the stuff of future tales.

After publishing poetry in college, **Julia Justiss** served stints as a business journalist for an insurance company and editor of the American Embassy newsletters in Tunis, Tunisia. She followed her naval officer husband through seven moves in twelve years, finally settling in the piney woods of East Texas, where she teaches French. 1997 winner of the Romance Writers of America's Golden Heart for Regency, she lives in a Georgian manor with her husband, three children, and two dogs, and welcomes letters from readers. Reach her at 179 County Road 4112, Daingerfield, TX 75638, USA or www.juliajustiss.com

A Regency Lords & Ladies Christmas

Nicola Cornick

Lyn Stone

Julia Justiss

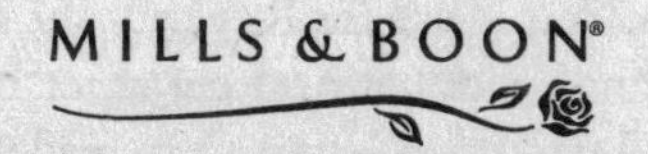

First published in Great Britain 2006 by Harlequin Mills & Boon Limited, Eton House, 18-24 Paradise Road,Richmond, Surrey TW9 1SR

The Season for Suitors and *The Three Gifts* were originally published in the USA in the *Christmas Keepsakes* anthology.
Christmas Charade was originally published in the USA in the *Gifts of the Season* anthology.

ISBN-13: 978 0 263 855081
ISBN-10: 0 263 85508 2

102-1106

Printed and bound in Spain by Litografia Rosés S.A., Barcelona

CONTENTS

THE SEASON FOR SUITORS 9
Nicola Cornick

CHRISTMAS CHARADE 131
Lyn Stone

THE THREE GIFTS 249
Julia Justiss

Dear Reader,

When I think of a Regency Christmas I think of the family celebrations described in Jane Austen's letters – ice-skating, carolling, impromptu dancing, playing charades and sitting around a roaring log fire telling stories. *In The Season for Suitors* my hero, Sebastian Fleet, has forsaken the pleasures of a family Christmas after a terrible tragedy. Can Carla Davencourt, who has loved Seb for years, open his heart to the comfort and joy of the Christmas season?

This story is especially for all those readers who wrote to me after Seb first appeared in my books and asked when he would have a story – and a love – of his own.

I wish you all a very happy and peaceful Christmas season.

With love from

Nicola Cornick

PS Don't miss my first single title Regency historical. *Deceived* is a tale of love, desire, betrayal and redemption… Coming from M&B Books in the UK in March 2007.

The Season for Suitors

by

Nicola Cornick

Chapter One

THE LETTER arrived with his breakfast.

It was written in an unmistakably feminine hand and it smelled faintly of jasmine perfume.

Sebastian, Duke of Fleet, was not pleased to see it. Letters from ladies, especially those that arrived early in the morning, usually presaged bad news. Either some misguided woman was threatening to sue him for breach of promise, or his great aunt was coming to stay, and he welcomed neither.

"Perch, what is this?" the Duke asked, tapping the parchment with his finger.

His butler continued to unload the breakfast from the silver tray, placing the coffeepot at an exact degree from the cup, and the milk jug at the perfect angle from both. Perch was a butler of precision.

"It is a letter from a lady, your grace."

The duke's brows drew together in an intimidating frown. He had spent much of the previous night at Whites; both the drink and the play had been heavy, and this morning his mind was not very clear. At least he had had the sense to reject the amorous advances of one of London's latest courtesans. He had had no wish to wake up with her painted face beside him.

He had an unwelcome suspicion that he was getting too old for drinking and debauchery, a superannuated rake. Once he started to wear a wig and use face paint to cover the ravages of age, he would have to ask Perch to shoot him.

He pushed aside the dispiriting thought. Without the wine and the gambling and the women there was little left for him, except a rambling old mausoleum of a house that, on this December day, was particularly difficult to heat. Indeed, his hot water bottle had burst in the night, adding another unpleasant dimension to his night's slumber.

"I *perceive* it is from a lady," he said coldly. "I simply wondered which lady was attempting to communicate with me?"

Perch's expression suggested that his master might consider breaking open the seal in order to find out, but after a moment he answered him.

"The letter was delivered by a man in the Davencourt livery, your grace."

The duke reached thoughtfully for the coffeepot and poured for himself, then he slid his knife under the seal, scattering little bits of wax across the table, where they mixed with the crumbs from the toast. Perch winced at the mess. Seb ignored him. What benefit was there in being a Duke if one could not scatter crumbs as one pleased? After all, he attended to his ducal responsibilities in exemplary fashion. He had improved the family seat at Fleet Castle, he was generous to his tenants, he had even been known to attend the House of Lords if there was a particularly important debate taking place. His days were perfectly ordered—and damnably boring. Life was hard when one had done everything there was to do.

He unfolded the letter and looked at the signature.

Yours sincerely, Miss Clara Davencourt.

He was aware of rather more pleasure than seemed quite appropriate. He had not seen Clara Davencourt for almost eighteen months and had not known she was currently in London. He sipped his coffee, rested the letter on the table and swiftly scanned the contents.

Your Grace…

That was rather more formal than some of the things Miss Davencourt had called him during their last encounter. Arrogant, conceited and rude were the words that sprang immediately to his memory.

I find myself in something of a dilemma...

Seb's blue eyes narrowed. The combination of Miss Davencourt and a dilemma was sufficient to strike dread into the strongest constitution.

I find that I need some paternal advice...

A smile curled the corner of Seb's firm mouth. Paternal advice, indeed! If Miss Clara Davencourt had deliberately set out to depress his pretensions as the most notorious rake in Town she could not have done a better job. He was only twelve years her senior and had not begun his life of dissipation at so young an age that he was qualified to be her father.

My brother is preoccupied with affairs of state and all the more suitable of his friends are unavailable at present, which only leaves you...

Seb winced. The minx. She knew how to deliver a neat insult.

I therefore have no alternative than to beg your help. If you would call at Davencourt House at the earliest opportunity I should be most grateful.

Seb sat back in his chair. Calling on young ladies in order to play the role of paternal confidant was so foreign to him as to be ludicrous. He could not imagine what had possessed Clara even to ask. Of course, he would not comply. It was out of the question. If she needed advice she should be sending for a female friend, not the greatest rake in London.

He glanced out the window. The winter morning looked crisp and bright. There was a dusting of frost on the rooftops. There were so many possibilities for a clear Yuletide morning. He could go riding. He could go to Tattersalls and spend more money on horses. He could go to Whites and read the paper, chat with his cronies, drink some more fine brandy. He yawned.

He could go to Collett Square and call upon Miss Clara Davencourt.

It would be something to do. He could teach her that summoning rakes to one's drawing room was in every way a poor idea.

He folded the letter and slid it into his pocket. Draining his coffee cup, he stood up and stretched. He was aware of a most unfamiliar feeling, a lifting of the spirits, a sense of anticipation. He took the stairs two at a time, calling for his valet as he went.

MISS CLARA DAVENCOURT was sitting in the library of the house in Collett Square, listening with a quarter of an ear while her companion, Mrs. Boyce, read to her from the *Female Spectator.* She checked the little marble clock on the mantelpiece. The Duke of Fleet would surely have received her letter by now.

She wondered when he might call. Then she was struck by the thought that perhaps he might not call at all. Given that they had parted on the worst possible terms eighteen months before, she supposed it was quite possible he would not wish to see her again. She fidgeted with the material of her skirt, smoothing away imaginary creases. Seb Fleet was a rogue, but on this occasion that was what she needed. A gentleman simply would not do.

Clara wrinkled her nose slightly as she recalled their last meeting. She had called Fleet a callous, coldhearted scoundrel when he had rejected her admittedly unconventional but honest offer of marriage. It had taken all her courage to propose in the first place, and to be turned down had been a dreadful blow. In her pride and unhappiness she had told him that she never wished to see him again so she could understand if he chose not to respond to her plea now.

"The Duke of Fleet, ma'am." Segsbury, the Davencourt butler, was bowing in the doorway. Clara jumped. Despite the fact that she had been half-expecting him, she felt shock skitter along her nerves. Mrs. Boyce jumped, too. She dropped the newspaper and her hand fluttered to her throat. Clara noted the pink color that swept up her companion's neck to stain her cheeks, and the brightness that lit Mrs. Boyce's eyes. She bit her lip, hiding a smile. She had seen Sebastian Fleet have this effect on many ladies, no matter their age.

The duke was bowing to Mrs. Boyce and smiling at her in a way that made the woman's hands flutter like nervous moths. Clara watched with a certain cynicism. Charm was as effortless to Fleet as breathing.

Nevertheless, as he turned toward her she could not quite repress the flicker of awareness that he kindled inside her. She had assured herself that the previous eighteen months had taught her indifference where the Duke of Fleet was concerned. Now she knew that she lied.

It was impossible to be indifferent to Sebastian Fleet. He was a big man, both tall and broad, and his command of any room and any situation appeared natural. Despite his size he moved with a nonchalant grace that compelled the gaze. Clara reminded herself not to stare. She dropped her eyes to the embroidery that rested in her lap. She hated embroidering and would leave the material sitting around for months with absolutely no work done on it at all, but at a time like this it was a useful subterfuge.

Fleet was standing before her now. She could see the high polish of his boots. She resisted the urge to look up sharply. Instead she raised her chin slowly, composedly, every inch a lady of quality.

His eyes were very blue and lit with a devilry that told her more clearly than words that he was remembering their last meeting. Her heart thumped once with a mixture of nostalgia and relief. Now, she was sure, they could behave as mere acquaintances.

She saw the look in his eyes and amended the thought. She was far too aware of his physical presence to be comfortable with him. She felt her color rise and silently cursed him. He had taken her hand although she had not offered it. Neither of them were wearing gloves, and his fingers were warm and strong against hers, sending a shiver along her nerves.

"It is a great pleasure to see you again, Miss Davencourt." He held her hand for a moment longer than was quite respectable. A rakish smile curved his firm mouth. "I was afraid we might never meet again."

Clara cast her gaze down. "I regret there was no other course open to me, your grace."

The Duke's smile grew. He turned to Mrs. Boyce. "I wondered whether I might have a little time alone with Miss Davencourt, ma'am? We are old friends."

For a moment Clara thought her companion was so swept away by Fleet's charm that she was actually going to agree. Then the happy light died from Mrs. Boyce's eyes. Clara had impressed upon her many times that she was not to leave her alone with any gentleman, least of all a certified scoundrel. This, the one time Clara *did* wish to be left alone, was the first occasion on which Mrs. Bryce had remembered what her duty entailed.

"I am sorry, your grace, but that would not be in the least proper of me."

Mrs. Boyce sat up straighter, looking fully prepared to take up residence on the gold sofa until the Duke had departed.

It took more than a mere refusal to stop Seb Fleet. "I had actually intended to take Miss Davencourt driving, ma'am," he said. "It is such a beautiful day."

Mrs. Boyce's face cleared. "Driving! Oh, I see. Well, in that case there can be no objection. Nothing untoward could possibly take place in a curricle."

Fleet smiled broadly. Clara knew with an instant's insight that he was thinking of all the disreputable things that *could* happen in a curricle. No doubt he had indulged in them all at one time or another. But he spoke quite gravely.

"I assure you that Miss Davencourt will be completely safe with me, ma'am. I view her in a strictly paternal fashion."

Clara cast him a demure, sideways glance, which he met with his bland blue gaze. She had hoped that her reference to his paternal advice in the letter would vex him, since he had spent so much time at their last meeting telling her that he was too old for her.

"Then I shall fetch my cloak," she said, dropping a slight curtsey. "Thank you, your grace."

The flash of amusement in Fleet's eyes told her that he was not fooled by this show of meekness. She felt his gaze follow her out and almost shivered under the cool blue intensity of it.

She kept him waiting only a few minutes and he was openly appreciative when she rejoined him in the hall.

"It is a rare woman who does not take an hour over her preparations, Miss Davencourt."

"I was concerned not to keep your horses waiting in the cold, your grace," Clara said, with an expressive lift of the brows.

"Rather than not wishing to inconvenience me? I take the snub, but your concern for my team is still admirable."

Clara gave him a little smile and accepted the arm that he offered. He handed her up into the curricle, tucked a thick rug about her and offered her a hot brick for her feet. Despite the chill of the day she felt snug. Fleet leapt up beside her and took up the reins. Clara noticed immediately that they did not travel with a groom and prayed that Mrs. Boyce had not observed the fact from her vantage point behind the drawing room curtains. It certainly made matters easier for her, for she wished to have no eavesdropper on their conversation; on the other hand it also made her a little nervous. She could not expect standard decorum from Fleet. In fact, she never knew what to expect from him. That was half the trouble.

"I confess I was a little surprised to hear from you, Miss Davencourt," Fleet said with a quizzical smile, as he moved the horses off at a brisk trot. "The terms of our parting left me in no doubt that you wished never to see me again."

Clara smiled back with dazzling sweetness. "You are quite correct, your grace. As I intimated in my letter, only the direst need led me to contact you. I hoped that out of the friendship you have for my brother, you would agree."

Fleet sketched an ironic bow. "And here I am, Miss Davencourt, at your service. How comforting it must be to know that you may appeal to my sense of honor and know that I will respond immediately."

Clara's lips twitched. "You are all generosity, your grace." She looked up and met the intense blue of his eyes. "I hope," she added politely, determined to get the awkward part out of the way as soon as possible, "that we may put the past behind us. I am older and wiser now, and you—"

"Yes?"

"You, I suspect, are exactly as you were two years ago."

Fleet inclined his head. "I suspect that I am."

"So we may understand each other and be friends?" Clara finished.

There was a pause before Fleet spoke, as though he were weighing her words and found them lacking in some way she could not quite understand. "If you say so, Miss Davencourt," he said slowly.

He shot her another look. Clara felt her nerves tingle. She had always known Sebastian Fleet to be shrewd; those members of the ton who declared the duke to be nothing more than an easygoing rake did not understand him at all. The sharpness of mind behind those cool blue eyes had been one of the things that had attracted Clara to him in the first place. But she should not be thinking on that now. Dwelling on his attractions was foolish. She was no longer a green girl of one and twenty to fall in love with the most unobtainable duke in society.

The breeze ruffled Seb Fleet's dark golden hair, and he raised a hand absentmindedly from the reins to smooth back the lock that fell across his forehead. Contrary to both fashion and common sense, he wore no hat. The very familiarity of his gesture jolted Clara with a strange pang of memory. They had been in company a great deal together at one time but it was illusory to imagine that they had ever been close. Fleet had squashed that aspiration very firmly when he had rejected her proposal of marriage. No one ever got close to Sebastian Fleet. He did not permit it.

She knew she should not raise old memories but Clara had never done as she should. "When I proposed to you..." she began.

Fleet's brows snapped down in a thoroughly intimidating way. "I thought we were not speaking of the past, Miss Davencourt."

Clara frowned. "I would like to say my piece first."

Fleet sighed with resigned amusement. "I was under the impression you said your piece when we parted. *Arrogant, proud, rude, vain* and *self-satisfied* were all epithets I took to heart at the time and have not forgotten since."

"And," Clara said, "I imagine you have not altered your behavior one whit as a result."

"Of course not." Fleet flashed her a glance. "Naturally I was flattered by your proposal but I made it clear I am not the marrying kind."

"Being too much of a rake."

"Precisely."

"I thought it was worth asking you anyway," Clara said, with a small sigh.

Seb smiled at her, a dangerously attractive smile. "I know," he said. "It is one of the reasons I like you so much, Miss Davencourt."

Clara glared at him. "You like me—but not enough to marry me."

"You are mistaken. I like you far too much to marry you. I would be the devil of a husband."

They looked at each other for a moment. Clara sighed. She knew he liked her, which was half the trouble. They liked each other very much and it was a perilous form of friendship, forever in danger of toppling over into forbidden attraction.

Fleet turned the conversation decisively. "Tell me what I may do to help you, Miss Davencourt."

Clara hesitated. "I suppose it was unorthodox of me to write to you."

Fleet glanced at her. There was a smile in his eyes. "In so many ways. Most young ladies, particularly with the history that is between us, would think twice before pursuing so rash a course."

They had turned in to the park. It was too cold a morning for there to be many people about, but

Clara found it pleasantly fresh, if chilly. Autumn leaves and twigs, turned white with frost, crunched beneath the horses' hooves. The sky was a pale, cloudy blue with faint sunshine trying to break through. Clara's cheeks stung with the cold and she burrowed her gloved hands deeper under the fur-lined rug.

Fleet slowed the curricle to a pace that required little concentration and turned his head to look at her directly. "Perhaps," he added dryly, "you will satisfy my curiosity when the time is right?"

Clara's throat was suddenly dry. Feeling nervous was an unusual experience for her.

"I have a proposition for you." Clara looked at him out of the corner of her eye. He was starting to look a little exasperated.

"You are dissembling, Miss Davencourt," he said. "Could you be more specific?"

Clara swallowed hard.

"I need a rake," she said bluntly, "so I sent for you."

It was impossible to shock the Duke of Fleet. He was far too experienced to show any reaction to such a statement. After a pause, he said, equally bluntly, "Why do you need a rake?"

Clara drew a deep breath. "I need a rake to teach me how to outwit all the other rakes and scoundrels," she said. "I used to think I was up to all the tricks that a rogue might play, but I am sadly outwitted. I was almost abducted in broad daylight by Lord

Walton the other day, and at the theater Sir Peter Petrie tried to back me into a dark corner and kiss me. If I am not careful I shall find myself compromised and married off to save the scandal before I have even realized it. It is intolerable to be so beset!"

Fleet gave a crack of laughter. "You are a sensible girl, Miss Davencourt. I cannot believe you unable to depress the pretensions of the worst scoundrels in town! Surely you exaggerate?"

"Sir, I do not," Clara said crossly. "Do you think I should be asking you for help were it not absolutely necessary? Now that I am an heiress, matters are threatening to get out of hand."

"How thoughtless of your godmother to die and leave you so much money," Fleet said sardonically. He dropped his hand lightly over her gloved ones. "If only you were not so pretty and so rich, Miss Davencourt. You have become irresistible!"

Clara turned her shoulder to him. "Oh, I should have known better than to ask you for help! You always laugh at me. But you know it is true that one is seldom the toast of society if one's parents are poor."

Fleet's grip tightened for a moment and she looked up to meet his eyes. "I do understand," he said. "Your situation is not so different from being a duke subject to the wiles of matchmaking mamas and their daughters. You would be astounded at the number of young ladies who have twisted their ankles outside the portals of Fleet House," he added ruefully. "The pavement must be unconscionably uneven."

Clara stifled a giggle. "I do recall that you are unsympathetically inclined toward twisted ankles. When I sprained mine that day we had the picnic at Strawberry Hill you refused to believe me, and I was left to hop back to the carriage!"

She thought Fleet looked suitably contrite. "I apologize. That was very uncivil of me."

Clara sensed a moment of weakness. "So you see the difficulty I face," she said, spreading her hands in a gesture of pleading. "Will you help me?"

The weakness had evidently been an illusion. Fleet gave a decisive shake of the head. "Certainly not. This is nothing more than a blatant attempt to trap me into marriage."

Clara was outraged. Her lavender blue eyes flashed. "I might have known you could not disabuse yourself of the idea that I might *still* wish to marry you, your grace! Despite everything I have said you cannot believe yourself resistible! Of all the arrogant, conceited, vain and self-satisfied *old* roués!"

There was a look in his eyes that suggested he admired the spirited nature of her outburst—but it was clear that the word "old" had stung him.

"That is most unfair of you," he said. "I am only three and thirty. Hardly in my dotage!"

Clara gave an exaggerated sigh. "Let us ignore your tragic obsession with age for a moment, your grace.

The whole point of what I am asking is for you to teach me how to outwit a rake, not fall into his arms. You need have no concerns that I intend to importune you. I have no romantic feelings for you whatsoever!"

There was a heavy silence between them. The horses had slowed to a standstill beneath the bare branches of an oak tree as Seb Fleet turned his full attention toward her. Despite the cold air, Clara felt a fizzing warmth inside her that was not merely irritation. Under his slow and thorough scrutiny the color rushed to her face in an even hotter tide. Breathing seemed unconscionably difficult.

"No feelings for me," he drawled. "Can that be true?"

"No," Clara said, gulping down a breath. "I lied. I feel exasperated and infuriated and downright annoyed and you are the cause of all of those feelings."

"Strong emotions indeed."

"But not of the warmer sort." Clara evaded his gaze and picked at the threads of the tartan rug. "I have everything I desire in life at the moment. Why should I wish to marry anyone, least of all you?"

She saw the flash of something hot and disturbing in his eyes and added hastily, "Do not answer that! It was a rhetorical question!"

"Of course." Fleet's smile was wicked. "I doubt that you would appreciate my answer anyway."

"Very likely not. It is bound to be improper."

"What do you expect when you are talking to a rake? You cannot have it both ways, Miss Davencourt."

Clara sighed sharply. "Which is exactly why you would be the perfect person to help me," she said. "You are an out-and-out rogue. When we met, you took my hand before I was even aware of what you were doing. You charmed my companion into giving you time alone in my company. Those are precisely the things I wish to learn to avoid."

Fleet shook his head. "The answer is still no, I am afraid."

"Why?" Clara felt indignant.

"Because, my very dear Miss Davencourt, it would not serve," Fleet said. "You may not have realized it—" he turned toward her and his knee brushed against hers "—but I am behaving very much against type in refusing your request. Your average rake would accept, with no intention of keeping matters theoretical and every intention of seducing you."

Clara looked at him skeptically. "You actually claim to be acting from honorable motives?"

"The very purest, I assure you. But then, I am no average rake."

Clara did not need to be told. Sebastian Fleet was not average in any way. The languid arrogance, the dangerous edge, the sheer masculine power of him—all of these things made him exceptional. She shivered deep within her cloak.

To ask him to help her had been a reckless idea from the first; she recognized that. But her need had been genuine. She had been under siege and she was tired of it. She was also very stubborn.

"Can I not persuade you otherwise?" she begged. "I am not asking you to escort me about town, merely to tell me those dangerous behaviors to guard against."

She saw him shake his head decisively.

"To do so would be extremely perilous, Miss Davencourt. I might forget I was a gentleman and a friend of your brother and act on instinct. And I do not mean a paternal instinct."

Clara looked into his eyes. The instinct was there, masculine, primitive, wholly dangerous. She felt her senses spin under the impact of his gaze. She knew that he wanted to kiss her. Right here. Right now. He had never pretended he did not find her attractive. She knew that had their circumstances been different he would have tried to seduce her without a qualm.

He had been ruthlessly open with her in the past, telling her he intended never to marry, did not wish for the responsibility, and that he was incapable of being faithful. It had been her disillusion and disappointment that had led her to rail at him for not being the man she had wanted him to be. And now he was rejecting her again, albeit for a very different proposal, and once again she could recognize his reasons and even appreciate them, in a way.

She cleared her throat and made a little gesture of acceptance. "Very well. I understand what you are saying and…I admire your honesty."

His eyes opened wider with surprise and then, echoing her thoughts, he said, "It is no difficulty to admit I find you very attractive, Miss Davencourt. I would have the most dishonorable intentions toward you if matters had fallen out differently."

He sighed, picked up the reins and gave the horses a curt word of encouragement. The curricle picked up speed.

It was a moment or two before Fleet broke the slightly uncomfortable silence between them. "Do you truly intend never to marry?"

Clara raised her brows. "I cannot say never, but for now I am very happy as I am."

"It would be a tragic waste for you to remain single."

Clara felt a sharp stab of anger then that he could appreciate the qualities that might make her a good wife—for someone else.

"I doubt you are a good judge of that," she said. The words came out more sharply than she had intended and, although his face did not register any emotion, she sensed he was hurt. He did not pursue the point, however, and once again a silence fell.

She was on the point of apologizing when he said abruptly, "You are genuinely happy as you are?" There was an odd note in his voice. "By which I mean to ask if you truly have everything you wish for?"

Clara ignored the small voice that told her she had everything she wished for *except him.*

"Of course," she said firmly. "I have my family and my friends and plenty to occupy myself. I am very happy." She fixed him with a direct look. "Aren't you?"

She saw him hesitate. "Not precisely. Happiness is a very acute sensation. I suppose you could say I am content."

"Content." Clara thought about it. There was a comfortable feeling to the word but no high excitement about it. "That is good."

"It is good enough, certainly." Fleet had turned his face away from hers and as a result she could not read his expression. He was difficult to read at the best of times, with that bland blue gaze and those open features. He appeared to be straightforward when in fact the reverse was true. Frustration stirred in her at how opaque he was, how difficult to reach. But then she had no reason to try to reach him. She had tried before and been rebuffed. She reminded herself that no one ever got close to the Duke of Fleet. This difficult friendship was as good as she would get. She had to decide whether it was worth it or not.

"If your rakes and fortune hunters are causing such a problem, I would suggest that you appeal to your sister-in-law, Lady Juliana, for help," Fleet said, breaking into her thoughts. "I doubt there is a rake in town who can out-maneuver her."

Clara shook her head sadly. "That would be the

ideal solution but Juliana is entirely engrossed with the babies at present. That was really why I contacted you. We are to go to Davencourt for Christmas in a couple of weeks, but until then I imagine I am very much left to fend for myself."

"With the help of the redoubtable Mrs. Boyce, of course."

"Yes, and you have seen how much use she is!" Clara laughed. "I love her dearly but she conceives that she will have failed in her duty if she does not marry me off, and so makes a present of me to every passing rake and fortune hunter. I believe they view me as the ideal Christmas gift."

Fleet looked at her. His blue gaze was warm enough to curl her toes.

"I can imagine why, and it is nothing to do with your money."

Clara raised her chin.

"Since you are not to give me the benefit of your theoretical experience, your grace, I refuse to permit you to flirt with me. Rather I suggest you take me home." She looked around. "Indeed, I have no notion where we are!"

The path was narrow here and wended its way through thick shrubbery. Even in winter the trees and bushes grew dark and close overhead, enclosing them in a private world. It was a little disconcerting to discover just how alone they were in this frosty, frozen wilderness.

Fleet was smiling gently. "Take this as a free piece of advice, Miss Davencourt," he said. "Always pay attention to your surroundings. The aim of the rake will always be to separate you from company so that he may compromise you."

He put up a hand and touched one gloved finger lightly to her cheek. Her gaze flew to his as the featherlight touch burned like a brand.

"And once he has you to himself," the duke continued softly, "a rake will waste no time in kissing you, Miss Davencourt."

For what seemed like an age they stared into each other's eyes. Clara's heart twisted with longing and regret. Could he look at her like that if he did not care for her? He would deny it of course. Lust was easy for him to admit, love impossible.

Her body ached for him with a sudden, fierce fire. His presence engulfed her. She felt shaky, hot with longing. She raised her hand and brushed his away. Her fingers were not quite steady.

"Your point is well made, your grace." Her voice was husky and she cleared her throat. "I shall guard against that possibility."

Fleet's hand fell and he straightened up in his seat. Clara breathed again, a little unevenly.

"Take me home," she said again, and there was more than a little entreaty in her voice.

They came out from under the trees and joined the main path. A gentleman on a very frisky bay rode past, touched his hat to Clara and bowed slightly to Fleet, then pirouetted away with a fine display of horsemanship.

"Coxcomb," Fleet said.

His face was set in grim planes, the line of his mouth hard. Clara's sore heart shrank to see it.

The next barouche to pass them contained a gentleman and two painted ladies, who smiled and ogled in their direction, the gentleman in particular giving Clara a thorough scrutiny through his quizzing glass. Fleet cut them dead.

"Friends of yours?" Clara enquired politely.

"Not of the type that I would acknowledge when I am escorting you." Fleet paused perforce to avoid several young blades who had deliberately blocked their path in order to pay their respects to Clara.

"Walton, Jeffers, Ancrum and Tarver," Fleet said, when they had moved on. "I begin to see your difficulty, Miss Davencourt." He paused. "Perhaps if people see me squiring you about, that may dissuade the gazetted fortune hunters from pursuing you."

"I doubt that will dissuade anyone," Clara said. "It is well known that you have no intention of marrying, your grace, so it is more likely to encourage them if they think that I am prepared to spend time with a notorious rake."

Fleet cast her a look. "Nevertheless, Miss Davencourt," he said slowly, "perhaps I could help you."

Clara looked hopeful. "You have reconsidered?"

Fleet shook his head. "Not at all. I will not teach you about rakes. That would be foolhardy. But as it is only for a few weeks I *will* act as your escort while you remain in town and keep the gentlemen from troubling you." He smiled. "All in the most perfect and irreproachably paternal fashion, of course."

There was a thread of steel beneath his courteous tone, as though he would brook no refusal, and it brought Clara's chin up in defiance.

"Pray, do not conceive it to be your duty to help me, your grace," she said sharply. "I would detest the thought that I was a burden to you."

Fleet smiled a challenge. "If I cannot help you in one way, why not accept my assistance in another, Miss Davencourt?" he said persuasively. "I will protect you from unwanted attention and, since you have no wish to marry, I shall not be getting in the way of any gentleman you would consider a genuine suitor."

Clara bit her lip. In some ways it was a tempting proposition since it would free her from the odious attentions of insincere suitors. In other ways, though, his suggestion was sheer madness. To spend time in Fleet's company would only remind her of all the things she had loved about him, all the things she could not have. The cure had been hard enough last time. To invite trouble again now was plain foolish.

"No," she said, unequivocally.

Fleet shrugged and her heart shrivelled that she meant so little to him one way or another.

"Very well, then." His tone was careless. "I shall take you home."

Chapter Two

FLEET REFUSED to leave Clara at the door as she would have wished, but escorted her into the hall. There was high color in her face, both from the cold air and from their quarrel, and she refused to meet his eye. Her chin was raised and her whole body was stiff with haughtiness. Fleet found it amusing, provocative and downright seductive. He wanted to kiss the hauteur from her lips until her face was flushed with passion, rather than pride. He wanted to feel that voluptuous body softening, responding, under his hands. He shifted uncomfortably. He had always wanted Clara Davencourt in the most simple and fundamental way. It was unfortunate he simply could not have her and he had to learn to live with that. Under the circumstances it was probably the most foolish idea to offer her his escort and he should be grateful she had turned him down. He was uncomfortably aware that it had been the interest of Tarver and Walton and half a score others that had made him wish to keep her close. Allowing Miss Clara Davencourt to arouse his possessive instincts was a mistake. For that matter, allowing her to arouse any instincts at all was totally unsafe.

Lady Juliana Davencourt was in the hall, which broke the rather difficult silence between them. Juliana was dressed in an old striped gown and Fleet, remembering the wayward widow of the past, would never have believed she could have anything half so frumpish in her wardrobe. She was cradling a tiny baby in each arm and looked up with a smile as they came in at the door. Fleet thought she looked young and vibrant and alive with happiness. It was most odd. He had known Juliana Davencourt since she was a debutante, had once even thought that her particular brand of cynicism might be the perfect match for his, yet here she was transformed into someone he barely recognized. And why was she carrying the babies herself? Surely Davencourt was rich enough to employ a dozen nursemaids? This modern trend toward caring for one's children oneself made him shudder.

"Sebastian. How delightful to see you again!" Juliana did not offer him her hand, for which he could only be grateful since he was certain it was not clean. She turned to Clara, drawing them both with her into the warmth of the library, where a fire burned bright in the grate. Clara removed the enveloping cloak that she had been wearing, affording Fleet the opportunity to admire the luscious curves accentuated by her fashionable gown. It was all that he could do to keep his mind on the conversation.

"Did you enjoy your drive?" Juliana asked.

"Yes, thank you, Ju," Clara said. "I think it will snow later, though. It is most unconscionably cold. How is little Rose's croup this morning?" She had taken one of the babies from her sister-in-law with a competence that both beguiled and appalled Fleet. He watched as the child opened its tiny pink mouth in an enormous yawn, then gave an equally enormous burp. Its eyes flew open in an expression of extreme surprise. Clara gave a delighted laugh.

"She is taking her food well enough, it seems!"

Fleet watched as Clara raised a gentle finger to trace the curve of the baby's cheek. She was smiling now, her face pink from the nip of the chill air outside, her hair mussed up by the hood of the cloak, escaping in soft curls about her face. Fleet stared, unable to look away. Something tightly wound within him seemed to give a little. He felt very odd, almost light-headed. It was as though he was seeing Clara in a different way and yet the revelation made her appear even more seductive. Clara with her own child in her arms…

Then he realized that Juliana was addressing him, and had been doing so for some time. He had no idea what she was talking about.

"We would be very pleased, Sebastian, although if you felt that you could not we would understand…"

"Of course," Fleet said automatically, forcing his gaze from Clara. "It will be my pleasure."

"You will?" Juliana sounded pleased, relieved and surprised at the same time. "But that is wonderful! Martin will be delighted!"

It was her tone that helped to focus his thoughts. What had he agreed to do? Juliana sounded far too excited for this to be a simple dinner invitation. He looked up to meet Clara's quizzical blue gaze. "You have surprised me," she said slowly, "but I, too, am delighted, your grace."

She gave him a smile so radiant that Fleet felt shaken and aroused. The fire seemed extremely hot and he was feeling very odd. He wondered if he had caught an ague.

Clara dropped a kiss on the baby's forehead.

"I think it is appropriate for your new godfather to hold you now," she murmured, moving towards him.

Understanding hit Fleet in a monstrous wave of feeling. He had just agreed to be the baby's *godfather!* He cast a terrified look at the little bundle Clara was holding out to him. Juliana was approaching in a flanking maneuver, murmuring something about him taking a seat so he could hold both babies at once. Both babies? Had he agreed to be godfather to the *pair* of them? He opened his mouth to protest, then closed it again, aware of the enormity of the situation in which he found himself. He could not in all conscience back out of the arrangement now. Juliana and Clara were both looking at him with shining eyes; it made him feel like a hero. He would have to wait until later—get Martin Davencourt alone over a glass of brandy, explain he had made a mistake, had thought he was being offered something much simpler, like a cup of tea or an invitation to a ball. He was certain he could sort the matter out, but in the meantime he would have to play along.

He sank into the big armchair before the fire and sat as still as a statue while the infants were placed in his arms. If he moved he might drop them. Worse, they might vomit on his coat of blue superfine. He had heard babies were prone to do such things although he had never been near one in his life.

They smelled faintly of a milky sickness that turned his stomach, and yet at the same time they were the softest and sweetest things he had ever touched. He lowered his nose gently and sniffed the top of Rose's head. She moved a little and made a small mewing sound. The other baby opened his eyes suddenly and stared at him. He realized he did not even know the boy's name.

"What…" His voice had come out huskily. He cleared his throat. "What is his name?"

"Rory," Juliana said. She was smiling. "They are called Rory and Rose."

Fleet looked down on the tiny bodies nestling close. He felt as though they had fastened their little hands about his heart and were squeezing tightly. A whole wash of emotions threatened to drown him.

He had to escape, and quickly. He looked at Juliana, then Clara, in mute appeal.

"Well, I..."

"You have done very well for a first attempt," Clara said, sounding like his childhood nanny, "although you do look utterly terrified."

To his inexpressible relief, she lifted Rory from his arms. Once Juliana had retrieved Rose he was free to stand, although his legs felt a little shaky. He made somewhat blindly for the door as though he could smell the fresh air and freedom.

"Thank you for the drive, your grace," Clara called after him. "Shall we see you tonight at Lady Cardace's Snow Ball?"

Fleet stared at her, trying to work out if he had heard the question correctly. He did not want to find himself accidentally agreeing to be godfather to yet more children or to something even more terrifying. He saw a tiny frown touch Clara's forehead at the length of time it was taking him to answer.

"Had you not been invited?" she inquired.

"Yes." Fleet took a grip on himself. "Yes, I shall be there."

Clara gave him another of her melting smiles. Much

more of this and he would be quite undone. Clara and the twins between them had unmanned him.

"Good," she said. "I shall look forward to seeing you tonight."

FLEET TURNED the horses toward home. Some of the light seemed to have gone out of the day. Clara's vivid personality had set the air between them humming with life. Without her, everything seemed more dull and grey. He dismissed the thought as fanciful. It was simply that the weather had turned. Dark clouds were massing on the horizon, promising snow. The wind was sharper now, with a cutting edge. Despite the fact that he told himself it was just the effect of the weather, he found he missed Clara's warmth.

He remembered the twins with a shudder. He was not cut out to be anyone's godfather. He was scarcely an example for the younger generation. If it had simply been a matter of presenting suitably large gifts on birthdays and Christmases then he might have fulfilled the requirements, but he was depressingly aware that the role of godfather asked much more of him. It was a pity—Clara probably thought more highly of him now than she had ever done in their acquaintance. That should not be permitted to sway him, however. He did not seek her good opinion. Nevertheless, it would be a shame to lose it so swiftly.

The snow was starting to fall. In London it fell with

sooty edges, to lie in a dirty slush on the streets. For a moment he recalled the pure brightness of Fleet in the snow, the way the icicles hung from the branches and the river froze over in intricate icy patterns and the snowdrifts lay ten foot deep in the lee of the hedges. He ached to be there.

The panic was rising in his throat, as it sometimes did when he thought of Fleet in the winter. He dashed the snowflakes from his eyes and tried to think of something else. The twins... No, that was a bad idea. His panic heightened. Suppose something happened to Martin and Juliana? If he did not rescind his role as godfather he could conceivably end up with the care of two small children. The images crowded his mind. Babies crying, nursemaids fussing around... By the time he turned in to the stables at Fleet House he had got as far as redecorating one of the bedrooms as a nursery. He handed the curricle over to the grooms, hurrying inside, away from his fears.

The house was warm and quiet. The day's newspapers were waiting for him in the library. He sat down, but instead of picking up the *Morning Post* his hand strayed idly toward the bookcase. His eyes fell upon an ancient copy of Sterne's *Tristram Shandy* and he picked it up without thought. The book fell open at the title page, where there was an inscription in childish letters:

Oliver Fleet.

He shut the book with a sudden, violent snap that raised the dust from the pages. It had been about this time of year that his brother's accident occurred. He hated Christmas. He had never passed the holiday at Fleet since Oliver's death.

He settled back in his chair. The silence was almost oppressive. He could hear the brush of the snow against the windowpane. It was nine hours until Lady Cardace's rout. Then he would see Clara again. He tried not to feel too pleased and failed singularly. He liked Clara Davencourt immensely and that was his weakness; he found her hopelessly seductive and that was his danger. With her corn-gold hair, huge blue eyes and voluptuous curves, Clara was ridiculously pretty and the embodiment of every masculine fantasy in which he had ever indulged. He suspected he was not the only gentleman to have had such musings, but he was fairly certain he was the only man who admired Clara for the shrewd intelligence that lurked beneath her charming exterior. She had a sharp mind, and most men would dislike that; Seb Fleet adored it. He loved their conversations. Such admiration had proved his downfall two years before when he had nearly fallen in love with her.

He must guard against falling in love with Clara Davencourt now. He had no desire to marry and he could not have her any other way. And yet the day did seem darker without her presence. He had an unnerving feeling that he was lost in some way and

Clara was the only one who could save him. Total foolishness, of course. The business with the infant Davencourt twins had affected his judgment. He would regain his calm with strong coffee and the *Morning Post*. And when he saw Clara Davencourt that evening she would be just another debutante. A pretty debutante, a rich debutante, but like all the other pretty little rich girls. He rang for the coffee. He reached for the paper. But he could not banish Clara from his mind.

THE SNOW WAS ALREADY a foot deep by the time the Davencourt carriage turned onto the sweep in front of Cardace House that evening. The glare of the lanterns was muted by the swirling flakes and the guests were hurrying within to escape the bracing cold.

"Our slippers will be soaked," Juliana grumbled, gingerly accepting Martin's hand to help her down onto the damp red carpet that led up to the door. "If it were not that this is the most important ball of the season and I am on tenterhooks to see what Lady Cardace has in store for us, I would rather be curled up in the library at home with a cup of hot chocolate and a good book!"

Clara shivered as the icy wind found its way beneath her cloak and raised goose bumps on her arms. Her evening gown was so flimsy it felt as though the wind were cutting through it like a knife. She hoped Lady Cardace's arrangements for her guests included both a hot drink and a roaring fire. There was nothing worse than a cold ballroom in winter.

Lady Cardace was the leading hostess of the Little Season, and invitations to her Snow Ball were the most eagerly sought tickets of the year. Each winter she arranged something truly original and each year the lesser hostesses would copy her, driving Lady Cardace to ever more outrageous forms of entertainment the next time.

"Ah," Martin said, looking about them as they hastened into the house, "I think this year's theme is the traditional Christmas. How charming!"

They surrendered their coats to a footman and accepted the hot cup of negus proffered by another servant. Clara gratefully inhaled the richly alcoholic fumes and warmed her hands on the crystal glass. Lady Cardace had exceeded herself this year. Sprays of holly and mistletoe adorned the ballroom walls, the deep green of the leaves contrasting richly with the red and white berries. The ceiling was hung with clouds of white gauze and sparkling snowflakes, a huge fire glowed behind the grates at each end of the hall, and the orchestra was already striking up for the first dance of the night. From the refreshment room wafted the enticing scent of a richly warming beef soup. Martin immediately headed in that direction to fetch a bowl for each of them.

Despite the festive atmosphere, Clara felt blue-devilled. It was nearing midnight and a surreptitious first—and second—scan of the ballroom told her the Duke of Fleet was not in attendance.

She glanced about her a third time, taking pains to conceal the maneuver. It seemed that every other accredited member of the ton was pressed into Lady Cardace's mansion. The evening was a dreadful crush. But the only man Clara secretly wanted to be crushed against was absent.

She wished now that she had not written to Sebastian Fleet. She had managed perfectly well without seeing him for the past eighteen months. Now she had stirred up those old feelings once again and a part of her ached for his presence.

"You look as though you have chewed on a piece of lemon peel," Juliana said, slipping her arm through Clara's and guiding her toward the rout chairs at the end of the room. "It is Sebastian Fleet, I suppose. You never quite managed to cure yourself of that affliction, did you, Clara?"

Clara bit her lip. She had not realized her preference for Fleet's company was still so obvious after she had spent so much time and effort in trying to appear indifferent. But Juliana's eyes were kind so Clara shook her head ruefully and admitted the problem. "I fear not. I have tried, but I cannot help my feelings."

"Ah, feelings." Juliana's lips curved into a smile and Clara knew she was thinking of Martin. "What a blight they can be. No, there is absolutely no point in fighting how you feel."

"I thought," Clara said, "that you disapproved of my tendre for the Duke of Fleet?"

"I did," Juliana said cheerfully. "I do. One cannot approve of Fleet. He is too old for you, he is too experienced and he is too much of a rake."

Clara sighed. She knew Juliana was right, but in some deep and stubbornly instinctive way she believed that she was the right woman for Sebastian Fleet. She had always believed it, but his rejection of her had made her falter and question her conviction.

"I do not wish you to be hurt, Clara," Juliana said. "Fleet has had years of practice in keeping intimacy at bay. I understand because I did the same thing myself."

"And Martin helped you to see that it need not be so," Clara reasoned.

"That is true. But that does not mean the same thing will happen for you." Juliana touched her hand briefly. "I am sorry, Clara. I want to help you—to save you the hurt." She shot a glance over Clara's shoulder. "Fleet is here now. Do you need a little time?"

Clara cast one swift glance toward the door then shook her head rapidly. "I am very well. I know you only mean to help me, Ju."

Juliana nodded and squeezed her arm, then they both turned to watch the Duke of Fleet approach. There was a prickle along Clara's skin, a mixture of fear and anticipation. He looked so autocratic, so easily in command.

Fleet had bumped into Martin in his journey across the room. Clara observed that Martin had managed to forget the refreshments. No doubt he had been distracted by some political discussion and had completely forgotten his original errand. She shook her head slightly.

The two men were coming toward them, deep in conversation. Juliana was beaming with a smile of warm pleasure as her husband approached her and Clara felt a pang of envy that she could not repress. She longed for such intimacy with Sebastian, but that was much more than he was prepared to give her.

Even so, she was scarcely indifferent to him. There was something about the way he moved that made the breath lock in her chest. She could swear her knees were trembling a little.

The duke had seen her now. He had also apparently noticed that a couple of gentlemen were hastening toward her, determined to get there before he did. A smile touched the corner of his mouth. The expression in his blue eyes made Clara feel ridiculously hot and bothered. She felt as though his gaze were stripping her naked. Damn the man. How could he work such mischief across a crowded ballroom?

Fleet had caught up to the two young men, Lords Elton and Tarver, and had diverted them from their original course toward Clara by grasping their arms, bending to have a word in their ears and then sending them packing in no uncertain terms. Clara's lips thinned. Though she had not particularly wished to be importuned by either Elton or Tarver, nor had she a need for Fleet to play the high-handed protector. Especially when she had earlier rejected his offer of help.

Fleet was upon them now. He bowed, first to Lady Juliana, then to Clara.

"How do you do, Lady Juliana, Miss Davencourt? It is a pleasure to see you this evening."

A faint smile curved Juliana's lips. "Thank you, Fleet. How pretty of you. Now, I sense you want something. How may we help you?"

Clara could sense Fleet watching her. She turned away and pretended a complete lack of interest. Surely there was some fascinating event occurring on the other side of the dance floor that she could focus upon.... Fleet took her hand. Her pulse jumped. He was smiling, very sure of himself.

"I was hoping you would grant me the pleasure of a dance, Miss Davencourt."

Lady Juliana was looking pointedly at their clasped hands. Fleet let go of Clara and she gave him a look of limpid innocence.

"I beg your pardon, your grace, but I do not dance this evening."

Both Fleet and Juliana looked startled.

"You do not dance tonight!" Fleet sounded thoughtful and not in the least put out. "How very dull for you to attend a ball and not indulge in the dancing."

Clara smiled. "I have no wish to indulge with you, your grace. You must forgive me. Pleasant as it is to see you, I told you earlier that I was not in need of your escort."

She sensed both Juliana's amusement and Fleet's chagrin, although he did not permit any expression to mar his features. Instead, he turned to Lady Juliana.

"If you were to recommend me as a suitable partner, ma'am, Miss Davencourt might be persuaded to relent."

Clara's lips twitched. She had to concede that it was clever of him to try an approach through Juliana but she was fairly certain her sister-in-law would not let her down.

Juliana laughed. "I cannot recommend you as suitable in any way, Fleet, at least not to a respectable young lady."

Fleet gave Clara a rueful smile that nevertheless held a hint of some other, more disturbing emotion in its depths. It promised retribution.

"Then if you will not consider me suitable, Lady Juliana," Fleet continued, "pray take pity on me."

Juliana flicked an imaginary speck from her skirts with disdainful fingers. "Pointless to appeal to my sense of pity, Fleet. You know I have none."

"I know your husband intends to dance with you, Lady Juliana," Fleet said, watching Martin finish his conversation with an acquaintance and make haste to join them. "A pity that Miss Davencourt denies herself—and me—a like privilege."

Juliana's whole face lit up at the sight of her husband. "When you are married, Fleet, then you may have the privilege of dancing with your wife. For now it is Miss Davencourt's right to deny a suitor if she chooses and she is weary of rakes. I suggest that you nurse your disappointment in the card room. Clara?"

Clara inclined her head. "Lady Juliana is in the right of it, your grace. I shall bid you good evening."

Fleet bowed gracefully. "Then I shall take you at your word. Good night, Lady Juliana, Miss Davencourt."

He went without a backward glance.

Clara watched him go. The lowering thing was that he radiated such indifference. She wished she had not given in to the childish impulse to thwart him. It was not that she wished to dance with either Lord Elton or Lord Tarver, but she had wanted to make that choice for herself. Once Fleet had dismissed them and presented himself as substitute she had vowed to reject him.

"A word of warning," Juliana said, turning back to Clara for a moment as Martin urged her toward the dancing. "Do not make a habit of playing these games with the Duke of Fleet. He *made* the game when you were still in the schoolroom."

"I think Clara was quite right to turn Fleet down," Martin said unexpectedly. "He can do nothing to enhance a lady's reputation."

"No, dear," Juliana said with an affectionate smile, "but as usual you have no notion of what is really going on." She led her spouse away to join the set that was forming for the quadrille.

He made the game...

Clara shivered a little. Fleet had told her that very morning he was no ordinary rake. She must be mad.

Everyone else was dancing and Clara realized she was the only girl left sitting out. It was not something that happened often, but whatever Fleet said to Elton and Tarver had evidently made the rounds, for although plenty of gentlemen were looking in her direction, none were making any move to engage her. How exceedingly annoying. Clara's exasperation with the Duke of Fleet grew stronger. Some of the debutantes were smiling behind their fans, clearly delighted the prettiest girl in the room was partnerless for once. Clara gritted her teeth. She would not stay to be laughed at. She would have to make a strategic retreat to the ladies' withdrawing room.

It felt like an unconscionably long time that she lurked in the shadows, pinning and repinning her silver brooch, tidying her already immaculate hair and smoothing her dress. Eventually she was so bored she could bear it no longer. She stalked out into the corridor wondering whether Juliana and Martin had concluded their dance and would provide her with some company.

The corridor was dark and quiet. Sprigs of holly

and mistletoe adorned the walls here, as well, between the flaring lanterns. There was a scent of pine and citrus in the air, a smell so nostalgic of Christmases past that Clara paused for a moment and breathed in the heady scent, smiling. She was thinking of Christmas at Davencourt, when a door on her right opened abruptly and the Duke of Fleet stepped out directly in front of her.

"At last," he said. "I have been waiting for you."

SEB FLEET HAD BROKEN both his resolutions for the evening within two minutes of stepping inside Lady Cardace's ballroom. His plan to tell Martin he had changed his mind about being godfather to the twins fell at the first hurdle when his friend greeted him with such delight that Fleet found himself unable to disappoint him. He might have despised himself for such sentimental weakness—it was an affliction that he had not suffered previously—but then he caught sight of Clara and all other thoughts fled his mind.

Clara had long ago ceased to wear the white muslin of the very young debutante and tonight she was in a gown of delicate pale green. It swathed her soft curves with the sort of cunning elegance that accentuated rather than hid the body beneath. Her fine, blond hair was swept up to reveal the tender line of her neck. She was smiling at something Juliana was saying. She looked radiant; Fleet felt it like a punch in the stomach. He vaguely remembered that he had resolved to avoid Clara that evening.

He had stopped, stared, and barely been able to conceal from Martin the fact that he was profoundly, outrageously, attracted to his sister. Then he had seen Elton and Tarver heading in the same direction with seemingly much the same thoughts as his own, and had ruthlessly stepped in to tell them that he was Miss Davencourt's escort that night unless they wished to challenge his right. Neither of them had done so.

He felt an almost uncontrollable compulsion to kiss her, to claim her, before the assembled company. The impulse appalled and excited him more than any other emotion he had ever experienced. Only the thinnest shred of self-control prevented him. Public response to such behavior would be to hound him into marriage or be cast out. So his desire for Miss Clara Davencourt would remain unslaked. Except...

Except that he could not resist. Part of a successful rake's strategy, of course, was cold calculation. He needed to be in control at all times. Seb Fleet had lost his control where Clara Davencourt was concerned. And now he had her where he wanted her.

Clara had stopped dead when she saw him. In the second it took for her to recover from her surprise, Fleet leaned one hand against the wall, pinning her between his body and the door.

This was dangerous and foolhardy, but he felt an

exhilaration that brooked no refusal. A strand of honey-colored hair had loosened from its clasp and lay against her cheek, heavy and smooth. He raised one hand to touch it and felt her jump. Her eyes were huge and dark in the shadows of the hall. When she spoke her voice was shaky and he felt a powerful rush of conquest.

"What do you mean when you say that you were waiting for me? You were playing cards."

Fleet shook his head. "I merely wanted you to think that."

There was silence between them. He kept her trapped between him and the door, so close he could feel the warmth of her body through the thin muslin of her gown. He leaned forward and brushed his lips against her ear. She jumped again and the response caused a jolt through his own body.

"Do not…" Her words were a whisper.

"I was intending to have you all to myself," Fleet said softly. "I knew you would not stay alone in the ballroom when you were devoid of admirers—what lady would expose herself to such humiliation? So I merely waited for you here."

He saw her expression change to anger.

"How conceited you are!" she exclaimed. "First you abandon me in the ballroom and then you presume you may pick up with me again whenever it suits you!"

Again she saw him smile. "I did not abandon you, Miss Davencourt. You rejected me."

She bit her lip. "Most gentlemen can comprehend a simple refusal, your grace."

"Alas, I have always been slower to understand than most." His breath stirred a tendril of her hair. The curve of her cheek was achingly sweet and the pure line of her jaw so tempting that he wanted to bury his face in its curve and breathe in the warm, feminine scent of her skin. His body tightened unbearably.

She turned her head slightly toward him. Their lips were no more than an inch apart now.

She whispered, "I have something to tell you, your grace."

Excitement kicked through his body. He could feel the caress of her breath against his cheek. She moistened her lips with the tip of her tongue and he almost groaned aloud to see it.

"You told me this morning that a lady should always be aware of her surroundings in order to thwart the evil plans of a rake." She raised her gaze to meet his. "I wanted to show you that I have taken you at your word. Good night."

He thought he had her trapped, but now he realized she had one hand behind her back from the very beginning of their encounter. Indeed, he could read the triumph in her eyes. There was the softest of clicks as the doorknob turned in her palm. She gave him a smile that was pure provocation, stepped back into the ballroom and closed the door gently in his face.

Chapter Three

SEB FLEET caught himself just before he slammed the palm of his hand against the panels of the closed door in sheer frustration. So, Clara Davencourt had out-played him for a second time that evening. He, on the other hand, had been taking his own game entirely too seriously. The constriction in his breeches told him just how desperately he wanted her. The physical ache was only matched by the aching disappointment of denial.

He shook his head slowly. He had been seduced by his own seduction. He had assumed he could outwit Clara and steal a kiss. But he wanted so much more from her; he could not pretend otherwise. He felt trapped between a rock and a very hard place.

"Are you all right, old fellow?"

Fleet straightened up. His host, Lord Cardace, had come out of the library further down the passage and was looking at him with concern and no little curiosity. He realized he must have looked very odd, half-slumped against the wall.

"I am very well, thank you, Cardace," Fleet said. "Just a trifle winded. The gout, you know. In my toes. Damnably painful when I try to dance."

Lord Cardace grimaced sympathetically. "The trials of age, eh, Fleet?"

"And of the bottle," Fleet agreed.

Cardace clapped him on the shoulder. "Then I'd find a seat if I were you. My wife has arranged for the mummers to entertain us. Can't abide all that old-fashioned singing and dancing myself and it's not for the old and infirm."

"Thank you for the advice," Fleet said with suitable gratitude.

He allowed Cardace to escort him with solicitude into the ballroom, then slipped away to the shelter of an alcove not, as his host assumed, to sit down and rest his aging bones, but to observe Clara without being observed. She was sitting between her brother and Lady Juliana in the demure pose of the perfect debutante. Fleet's lips twitched. She looked entirely composed. There was no hint that a few minutes before she had been within an ace of being ravished in a corridor by an out-and-out rake. The suitors were swarming around her again and Fleet felt the familiar wave of primitive possessiveness swamp him at the way the men were fawning, kissing her hand, whispering in her ear, smiling, toadying.

Until that moment, he had promised himself he would walk away. Clara Davencourt was not for him and well he knew it. He was full of good intentions. Then she gave her hand to Lord Elton to lead her into the dance, and a powerful wash of jealousy swept through Fleet. He started toward her.

One kiss. He would take one kiss and then he would leave her alone forever. He promised himself that.

He noted the precise moment she saw his approach. Her blue eyes narrowed with a disbelief she could not quite conceal. She caught her full lower lip between her teeth for a second before she turned aside to respond to something Elton was saying. The same honey-colored curl he had touched earlier in the darkness now curled in the hollow of her throat. She looked both fragile and determined. He could sense defiance.

Elton was no lady's champion. He saw Fleet approaching, turned pale, babbled something to Clara and shot away across the floor as though his coat were on fire. Clara turned on Fleet, ignoring the set that was forming around them, the curious ladies and gentlemen who had seen her abandoned before the dance even started.

"What on earth did you do to Lord Elton?" she hissed.

"I did nothing." Fleet was all innocence as he gained her side and took her arm.

"You know what I mean!" Clara's face was

flushed with annoyance. "You spoke to him earlier! What did you say?"

"I warned him not to pester you with his false protestations of affection."

Clara snorted. "So that you could pester me instead?"

"You injure me."

"And you infuriate me!" Clara's blue eyes flashed. "Twice now I have bid you good-night."

"I am sorry. I never retire early from a ball."

"Oh!" Clara let go of her breath on an angry sigh. "Your high-handed interference first left me without partners and now has me standing alone in the middle of a set."

"I would offer to dance with you," Fleet said, "but you have already refused me and I do not wish to put my fate to the touch again."

Clara gave him a dark look and turned to stride off the floor. Her back was ramrod straight, her entire figure stiff with outrage. She ignored the raised brows and titters of amusement.

Fleet followed. Clara was standing with her back to him. He put a hand on her arm, leaned closer and spoke for her ears only.

"Do not be too complacent about escaping me earlier. I shall kiss you before the night is out. I swear it."

He felt her tremble. She spun around to face him. Her gaze was uncertain now, but behind her eyes he saw the flicker of something else: she was intrigued against her will, unwillingly fascinated, tempted... His blood fired at the thought.

"I do not believe you," she said, summoning all her will to steady herself.

"Believe me," Fleet said.

He had timed the matter to perfection. There was a shout that the mummers were coming and then a tide of people swept them to the edges of the ballroom as the dance broke up. The door was flung wide and the mummers marched in to the beat of the drum. The orchestra took up the tune with gusto and the crowd shifted and split as the dancing started again. Gone was the decorous elegance of the waltz. This music was fast and wild and, for a moment in the flickering fire and candlelight, amid the boughs of holly and mistletoe, it seemed as though they were in a medieval hall surrounded by all the pageantry and joy of Christmas.

Fleet grabbed Clara's wrist and drew her into his arms. Her body was soft against his and she came to him without demur. Perhaps she imagined they were to dance, for the strains of the music filled the air, mingled with laughter and voices.

Instead he drew her into the shadowed darkness of the window recess. It was colder here. Snow brushed the panes and the reflection of the candlelight shone in the glass. Without another moment's delay he bent his head and covered her mouth with his.

She stiffened with shock, but only for a moment.

He felt her body soften against his, felt the instinctive response she could not hide. Her mouth opened beneath his and his mind spun even as a vise closed about his body, the desire he could barely control rampaging through him like wildfire.

He reined in his urgency and slid his tongue gently, caressingly, along the inside of her lower lip, teasing a response from her. He must be gentle; this was not the time and the place for anything else. She made a small sound in her throat at the invasion of his tongue and he was shot through with lust so hot and primitive he was suddenly within an ace of tangling his hand in her hair, and slamming her back against the cold stone wall to kiss her within an inch of her life.

The beat of the music was in his blood now, primeval and intense. His mouth crushed hers again, his tongue sweeping deep. He wanted her naked in his bed. He wanted to strip away the layers of clothing between them and take her with an urgency and desire that made no concession to gentleness. He had wanted her for such a long time. He had denied that need and now he could deny it no longer. "Clara…"

He said her name on a ragged whisper as his lips met hers for a third time. Her eyes were closed, the lashes a dark sweep against her cheek. Her lips were swollen from the ruthless demands of his. She was trembling.

So was he. His emotions were frighteningly adrift. The way Clara was clutching at his jacket to pull him closer, the taste of her, the fusion of sweetness and desire, kindled in him sensations never previously experienced. She was his and his alone; he would never let her go.

He pressed her closer to him, one hand coming up very gently to caress her breast. He could feel the nipple harden through the muslin of her dress against the palm of his hand. The heat ripped through him.

Their lips parted slowly, reluctantly, one last time and he felt as though he were losing something. He felt cold.

She was looking at him with such dazed sensuality in her eyes that his heart turned over. He could not speak. A moment later she blinked and her expression warmed from bemusement into anger.

"When I asked for your help this morning," she said sharply, "I was *not* requesting lessons in kissing."

Sebastian, shaken by the unexpected intensity of the experience and by achieving the one thing he had dreamed of doing for the past two years, was rocked back.

"You scarcely need lessons, my dear," he said. Did she not understand her own power? If she could do that to him with one kiss he shuddered to think what would happen when he took her to bed. *When?* He forced his wild thoughts to slow down. He would *not* make love to Clara Davencourt.

He looked at her again as the heat drained from his body and a shred of sense took hold. He had not given much thought to her reactions, being so wrapped up in his own. Now, scanning her face, he made a stunning discovery that sent his thoughts into turmoil again.

"That was your first kiss," he said slowly. He felt a little regretful. While he had been swamped with lust and thoughts of ravishment, she was experiencing something quite different. Something new. Something shocking. He should have guessed. He should have realized how important the moment had been for her. He shut his mind to the thought of how important it had been to *him*.

"Yes it was," she said.

Fleet was at a loss. He had taken greedily from her with no thought for her feelings. While he floundered, Clara had evidently regained full possession of her senses.

"Don't you dare say you are sorry," she said wrathfully.

Fleet smiled. "No. I'm not sorry." Her expression eased slightly. "It was nice," he added.

"Nice? *Nice!*" Clara took a deep breath.

He could see the hurt in her eyes. Nice was so bland a word for what had happened between them. Devil take it, how could he be making such a hash of this? He was supposed to be a man of the world. The trouble was that he was accustomed to dealing with women of the world, not inexperienced young ladies. He felt woefully out of his depth.

"Then I wish you a *nice* Christmas, your grace," she said, spun on her heel and walked briskly away.

SHE HAD BEEN KISSED for the first time. Thoroughly, expertly, ruthlessly kissed by a man who was a thorough, ruthless expert. She knew she should feel shocked or offended or both. The trouble was, it had been wonderful.

Clara curled up on her bedroom window seat and watched the snow falling. The clouds were breaking now, shreds of moonlight showing in the blackness, glittering on the white branches of the trees as the tiny flakes fell softly then finally ceased. It was very late and the city was quiet. Clara leaned her head against the cold pane and thought of Sebastian Fleet.

She supposed she had been in love with him from the start. That realization did not excuse her behavior but it certainly explained it. She should have slapped his face. Instead she had pulled him closer with a hunger that had startled her as much as it had no doubt astounded him. The experience had been like feast after famine, joy after long nights of loneliness.

She sighed, wrapping her arms about her knees and curling up tighter still. When he let her go she had realized what had been an earth-shattering experience for her was for him no more than a pleasant encounter with a pretty girl. The vast gap between the two of them—the experienced rake and the never-been-kissed debutante—had never seemed starker.

Now was the moment to accept the truth and relinquish her fantasy.

Sebastian Fleet would never love her as she loved him.

As she wanted to be loved.

As she *deserved* to be loved.

She pressed her fingertips to the cold glass. Outside the night was beautiful but frozen. The trees were still as statues. Above the trees swung a little star, glittering in the deep dark of the night, sometimes obscured by the scurrying cloud, sometimes shining bright, growing in strength.

Have hope.

Have faith.

Clara shook her head slightly. She slid off the seat and let the curtain fall back into place. The room was warm and quiet. She felt lonely.

"PERCH," the Duke of Fleet said, taking the pristine, pressed newspaper from the tray his butler offered, "would you be aware of those shops that sell Christmas gifts for infants?"

Perch's eyebrows shot up into his hair. "Gifts for infants, your grace?"

Fleet gave him a hard stare. "Nothing wrong with your hearing this morning is there, Perch?"

"No, your grace."

"Do you know the answer to the question?"

"No, your grace."

"But you could find out."

"Of course, your grace." Perch bowed. "Would you wish me to purchase something appropriate, your grace?"

"No," Fleet said absentmindedly, scanning the headlines, "I will do the purchasing myself. I merely need the direction."

"Of course, your grace," Perch said, "I shall see to it at once."

Fleet nodded, tucked the paper under his arm and headed toward the library. He wondered what Miss Clara Davencourt was doing this morning. He would not call in Collett Square to find out. After the fiasco of the previous night it was best to leave matters to cool. Looking back, in the frozen light of day, he wondered what on earth had possessed him. Before he had gone to the ball he had made a perfectly reasonable resolution to avoid Clara's company, which he had broken as soon as he had seen her. It was incomprehensible. He must have been drunk. He must have been bewitched. He must have been both bewitched *and* drunk at the same time. It must not happen again.

Even so, he knew that his behavior had been shabby. He should send her some flowers to apologize. Except that she would probably cut off the tops and return the stems to him. He smiled a little at the thought.

Two portraits flanked the entrance to the library.

They were of the previous Duke of Fleet and his Duchess. Sebastian rarely noticed them, for they were as much part of the fixtures and fittings of the house as a chair or a lamp. Now, however, he stopped and regarded the painted faces. His father looked noble, wrapped in scarlet and ermine and adorned with the ducal strawberry leaves. His mother had a gentler face beneath her coronet. Wise and kind, she had put the warmth into his childhood.

The huge ruby betrothal ring of the Fleets gleamed on her finger, alongside the simple wedding band. They were both in the vaults of his bank and there they would stay; it felt symbolic, somehow.

His mother had never really recovered from the loss of her youngest, Oliver. It was all wrong to bury one's child. Whenever he thought of the burden he had laid on his parents, he felt the same crushing cold. If he had saved Oliver it might all have been different, but he had failed.

He hurried into the library and sat down beside the fire. Perhaps it was time to rearrange the portraits in the house. A couple of landscapes might look attractive in the hall. At least there were no pictures of Oliver to haunt his waking nightmares.

There was a tap at the library door. Perch entered. "Hamley's Emporium is the best shop to purchase children's gifts, your grace," he said.

"Hamley's," Fleet said. "Excellent. I shall go there at once."

He felt a profound relief to be occupied.

IT WAS LATE when the knock came at the door of the house in Collett Square. Clara had been reading alone in the library in the big armchair in front of the fire. Martin and Juliana were attending a dinner party and Mrs. Boyce had gone to bed. Clara had fully intended to follow, but had become caught up in Miss Austen's *Sense and Sensibility* and stayed before the dying fire as the clock ticked past midnight.

She heard the knock and looked up, surprised anyone would possibly be calling at this time of night. She heard Segsbury's footfall across the floor, followed by the creak of the hinges and a low-voiced exchange.

"I regret, your grace, that there must have been some mistake. Mr. Davencourt and Lady Juliana are not at home...."

Your grace?

Clara sat bolt upright, her book sliding off her lap with a thud. Could this be Sebastian Fleet come to call at this hour? Impossible, unless he had arranged to take a glass of brandy with Martin and discuss the latest legislation going through the Houses of Parliament...

"It is no matter, Segsbury. My mistake, I believe." Fleet sounded distinctly ill at ease now. "If you would be so good as to give this to Mr. Davencourt. It is a Christmas gift for the twins."

There was a rustling sound. Clara's curiosity gave

her the excuse she needed. She opened the library door and went out into the hall.

"Miss..." Segsbury was as taken aback as a butler of his experience could be. "I apologize. I thought that you had retired."

"It is no matter, Segsbury," Clara said, with a smile. "Good evening, your grace."

"Miss Davencourt." Fleet sketched a bow. He did not smile at her. In the barely lit hall Clara could not read his expression, although she fancied his mouth was set in grim lines.

Her heart was tripping with quick, light beats. She had wanted to see Fleet again despite everything. She had been compelled in some way to force this meeting when she could have stayed quietly in the library and allowed him to go on his way. Now she wished she had not given in to that impulse. This hard-faced stranger was not the man she had wanted to see. Already he had distanced himself from her. Already the events of the previous night seemed like a fevered dream.

"If you will excuse me," Fleet said, "I was merely delivering this parcel." He gestured to the package now in Segsbury's hand. "It is a Christmas gift for your young nephew and niece. I hope I have chosen appropriately. It is a little difficult when one is not accustomed to shopping for children."

Clara felt a jolt of surprise. "You chose it *yourself?*"

A rueful grin touched Fleet's mouth. "I did."

"And you delivered it yourself, too. How singular!"

She saw his smile deepen and felt a jolt of pleasure inside. "Perhaps you could put the parcel somewhere safe, Segsbury," she said, "while I show the Duke of Fleet out."

Segsbury gave her a hard stare. He had been butler to Lady Juliana before her marriage and so was no stranger to unconventionality, but he had a very definite way of showing his disapproval of such inappropriate behavior. He looked at Clara for a long moment and she looked back steadily, then he bowed slightly.

"Very well, miss."

Neither Clara nor Fleet moved as Segsbury walked away with stately displeasure. The hall was quiet as his footsteps died away.

"I wanted to see you," Clara said.

"So it seems. It was not, perhaps, your wisest decision." Fleet's entire body was taut with what Clara assumed was anger.

"Last night—"

"Miss Davencourt, we really must *not* discuss this."

"Not discuss it?" Clara felt something snap within her. "What do you want to do instead, your grace? Sweep it under the carpet because it is difficult for us to face up to so inconvenient an attraction?"

"No," Fleet ground out. "What I want is to have you."

Clara felt a sudden, treacherous excitement. It

caught like a flare, blazing into shocking and sensual life. Fleet's eyes darkened with concentrated passion. He took one step forward, grabbed both her arms and his mouth captured hers, swift and sure.

Clara instinctively moved closer to him. All conscious thought fled her mind. Her arms went about him, fingers tangling in his hair. He tasted faintly of brandy and strongly of desire. The kiss grew frantic, then rough, almost brutal. The shock of it sent a blaze of feeling right to the center of Clara's body.

His impatient hands were already pushing aside silk and lace, and when he closed his hand over her breast, warm and hard against her bare skin, she gave a desperate moan as she felt her legs start to buckle. He half pulled, half carried her through the library door, slamming it shut behind them.

Then they were down on the rug before the fire and she was clutching at his shoulders. His tongue and teeth had replaced his fingers at her breast, and she squirmed and arched in quick delight to his touch.

She was shaking; so was he. Clara noticed it with astonishment, for surely this man was supposed to be an experienced rake. Yet he touched her with reverence as well as ferocious desire, as though he could not quite believe what was happening. The sense of power the thought gave her, the sheer unbelievable seduction of his hands on her body, roused a driving need.

His lips returned to hers with a passionate tenderness and urgency that inflamed her. He moved over her, throwing up her skirts, sliding a hand up her thigh, over the soft skin to find the hot, central core of her. Her body shivered like a plucked cord beneath his touch.

"Sebastian…"

She felt as though she were dissolving into some desperate pleasure, and when he moved down to meet her unspoken plea for release with the touch of his tongue against her most intimate place, the sensation was too hot and too sudden to resist. Her body was speared by so violent a delight that she rolled over, stifling a cry against his chest.

She could feel his arousal hard against her thigh but even as she reached blindly for him, intuitively knowing what was needed, he was withdrawing, wrapping his arms carefully about her. Although he held her close, she somehow knew he was putting distance between them. The pleasure and the astounding intimacy she felt turned cold and started to shrink.

"Clara… sweetheart…we must not…"

If Clara's thoughts had been clear, she would have noticed the harsh undertone in his voice, realized he was still trembling as much as she. Instead, she only knew that while her body still echoed with unfamiliar passion, Sebastian was trying to retreat, leaving her feelings too raw to bear.

"*We must not?* Sebastian, we already have!" Her

voice cracked, and she felt him hesitate then draw her closer against him. The warmth of his arms should have been reassuring but it was not, for it already felt wrong. She had opened herself body and soul to this man, had allowed him the most shocking and unimaginable liberties. Now, in return, she had received nothing but humiliation.

She stifled a little sob and hid her face in her hands.

"Clara. Do not..."

Sebastian gently helped her to her feet as she pulled her disheveled dress tight around her. When he would have drawn her down to sit with him on the sofa she resisted, deliberately choosing a chair that set her apart from him.

"I am sorry." This time she realized that he sounded wretched. "I should not have done it."

"*You* should not have done it?" Clara's fingers scored the arms of the chair. "Do not take responsibility for something that I wanted as much as you! Indeed, if you had not stopped me..." Her voice trailed away as she realized she would have given herself to him totally, without reservation. But even then he had not been so emotionally engaged as she. He had known what he was doing. And he had stopped it. She bit her lip to stifle her anguish.

"I should never have sent for you yesterday," she said tonelessly.

"No." His word was uncompromising. "And I should never have come to you."

"It took me such a long time..." Clara gulped. "I thought I no longer had such strong feelings for you."

He was shaking his head but said nothing. She felt desolate.

"What are we to do?" she said. She looked at him properly for the first time and her heart turned over at the misery and self-loathing in his eyes. "I know that you cannot offer me what I want, Sebastian."

He closed his eyes for a moment. The pain was etched deep on his face. "Clara, to make you a promise and then break it would be intolerable."

She knew what he meant. He did not wish to have the responsibility of loving her. He could not swear to be faithful to her for the rest of his life. She remembered what she had thought the previous night: he could not love her as she wished to be loved, as she deserved to be loved.

"So what do we do?" she said again.

He did not pretend to misunderstand her.

"About this perilous attraction between us?" He smiled faintly and Clara's heart clenched with a combination of misery and longing. "There is nothing we can do. You are not a woman I can have by any means other than marriage. I accept that." His voice was calm but there was an undertone of emotion that seared Clara. She knew he wanted her and wanted her desperately.

The words fell into the silence. Despite the warmth of the room, Clara shivered. A little while ago, a mere half hour perhaps, she would have believed she was truly a woman bound by convention. Now she had tasted passion and her body ached for it. It would be fulfilling, overwhelming, to make love with Sebastian Fleet. She had sampled desire and it made her hungry.

"Sebastian."

He read her tone and she saw the leap of fire in his eyes. He came to his knees by her chair, taking her cold hands in his. "Clara…"

For a long moment they stared at each other, but then Clara shook her head. "I cannot do it, Sebastian. If it were only for myself I…" She broke off, unable even now, after all that had happened between them, to confess to what felt such an unmaidenly desire. She looked up again and met his eyes. "But you would lose my brother's friendship and gain nothing but the censure of those who had been your friends."

"It would be worth it for you." The sincerity in his tone was beyond question. His hands tightened on hers. "It would be worth it and more, a hundred times over, to have you even for a little while…."

For a moment, Clara's world spun on the edge of a different existence. She was a woman of independent means. There was no one else she would rather marry. She could not imagine there ever would be, for she loved Sebastian Fleet with all the stubbornness in her character. Yet upbringing and principle ran so deep. To lose her good reputation, to lose her family and friends, all the things she had once taken for granted, and to gain what? Not Sebastian's love, for he had sworn himself incapable of that. What was he really offering her? A few months of bliss perhaps, but with everlasting darkness at the end.

He released her suddenly and stood up, turning away. "No, I know it would not serve. I could not ask it of you, Clara, even if you were willing. You are not the kind of woman who could be happy with such an arrangement."

He was right. They both knew it. Clara felt her spirits sink like a stone. So this really was the end.

"So what do we do?" she asked hopelessly, a third time.

"We do not see each other again. It is the only way."

Clara shook her head. "That will not suffice. We are forever in the same company. We cannot avoid it. It will be unbearable."

The shadows made the planes of his face even more austere. "Then I will go away."

"No!" The cry was wrenched from Clara. That she could not bear. Not to see him again would be painful enough, but to think that he had exiled himself because of her…

"Perhaps," she said, after a moment, "it will become easier in time."

"I doubt it." There was a smile in Sebastian's voice now. "Not when I cannot even look at you without wishing to kiss you senseless and strip all your clothing from you and make love to you until you are exhausted in my arms."

Clara made a small sound of distress, squirming in her chair with a mixture of remembered desire and unfulfilled passion. "Do not!"

"I am sorry." She knew he was not only speaking of what had happened between them. He was speaking of his inability to give her what she desired.

The library door opened with shocking suddenness. Both Clara and Sebastian spun around like a couple of guilty schoolchildren. Engrossed in their own passions and anxieties, neither of them had heard the front door open or the sound of voices in the hall, or footsteps approaching.

Segsbury, Juliana and Martin were all poised in the doorway. Segsbury looked genuinely startled to see the Duke of Fleet in the house a full half hour after the man's supposed departure. Juliana looked shocked and Martin merely furious.

Clara felt a bubble of hysterical laughter rising inside her. She was seated; Sebastian was standing a good few feet away. There was nothing remotely compromising in their demeanor. And yet she wondered what on earth was showing on their faces.

"A curious time of the night to be making calls, Sebastian," Martin said, and although his voice was perfectly pleasant it held a distinct undertone of menace. "Segsbury implied that you had brought some gifts for the children."

"I did." Clara saw Sebastian pull himself together with an effort. "Excuse me. As you say, it is late. I should be leaving."

For a moment it looked to Clara, frozen in her seat, as though Martin were not inclined to let his friend go so easily. Then Juliana drifted forward. "Dear Sebastian," she said, putting one hand on Fleet's arm, "how thoughtful of you to bring presents." She steered him toward the door and after a moment, Martin stepped aside, though there was still an ugly look in his eyes. "Segsbury will show you out," Juliana continued, "and we shall see you soon, I am sure." She relinquished his arm and Segsbury stepped forward, perfectly on cue, just in case the Duke had once again forgotten his way to the front door.

"This way, your grace."

Clara waited. Sebastian half turned toward her and Martin made an unmistakably threatening movement.

"Good night, Miss Davencourt," Sebastian said. There was nothing but darkness in his eyes. He inclined his head. "Davencourt, Lady Juliana..."

The library door shut with an ominous thud and Martin took a purposeful step toward her. Clara shrank in her chair.

"Martin, darling," Juliana said clearly, "I wonder if you might check on the nursery? I would be relieved to know that all is well."

Clara saw the tiny shake of the head that Juliana

gave her husband and, after a moment, to Clara's inexpressible relief, Martin went out. She was so thankful not to have to explain herself to her brother that she almost burst into tears.

"Oh, Ju!" She hurled herself into Juliana's arms and clung tight, careless of what her sister-in-law would think. And after a moment Juliana hugged her back fiercely, with no words until Clara had slackened her grip a little.

"I am sorry, Ju."

"Do not be." Juliana caught her hand and pulled her down to sit beside her on the sofa. "What happened, Clara?"

"He is to go away," Clara said, in a rush. "We think it is the only way."

"Yes," Juliana said quietly, "I think that may be true."

They sat for a moment in silence. "Perhaps you could go away for a little, too," Juliana said thoughtfully. "When your sister Kitty and Edward return to Yorkshire after Christmas."

"Yes," Clara said rapidly. "A change of scene. Perhaps that might serve."

"Clara—" There was anxiety in Juliana's voice now. "Forgive me, but did you... I mean, surely you did not..."

At another time, Clara might have laughed at her notoriously outspoken sister-in-law being so timid at confronting her. She shook her head. "We did not." She knitted her fingers together. "I would have given myself gladly to Sebastian tonight," she said, "but he was not so careless as I."

"Thank God," Juliana said, and there was a wealth of relief in her voice.

"I suppose so." Clara stood up. Her heart felt as bleak as winter. "I must go to bed. I am so tired. Thank you, Juliana."

Juliana's expression was sad. "If you wish to talk to me tomorrow, Clara, you will, won't you?"

"Of course." Clara managed a smile. "I love having you for a big sister, Juliana."

Juliana's answering smile was vivid and bright. "Thank you, Clara. I will see you in the morning."

As she went slowly up the stairs, Clara worried she would not be able to sleep, but when she finally came to lie down she was so exhausted that she remembered nothing from the moment her head touched the pillow.

There were no stars that night.

Chapter Four

SEB FLEET RAN DOWN the steps leading from his lawyer's offices and out into the cold street, pulling on his gloves as he did so. Today was a perfect, clear frosty winter's day with the air as sharp as a knife. It was the ideal day on which to leave London, the ideal way to remember the city, dressed in bridal white, its dirtiness hidden at least for a little beneath a blanket of snow.

It was two weeks since he had announced he was leaving England for an extended period of travel abroad. He had had no notion of the complexity of arrangements that would follow. Perch was attending to all the travel preparations, but Sebastian needed to settle his business affairs, from the authorizations needed to keep his estates running efficiently to a meeting with his anxious cousin and heir, who wished to know what would happen in the event of his untimely death abroad. It had reassured Seb to see Anthony, even if his cousin's thoughts were taking a morbid turn. It was good to know that with his passing, the Fleet succession would still be in safe hands. For half of Seb wished passionately for precisely that untimely death to which Anthony had alluded.

He felt trapped, and he hoped that different climes and fresh scenes might help him regain his perspective. All he had been able to think about in the fourteen days following his last meeting with Clara Davencourt was the sheer torment of wanting one thing and yet feeling incapable of gaining it. It was not so simple or so selfish as wanting Clara physically and being denied. He needed Clara in some deep sense that frightened him to analyze, and to tear himself away from her was to wrench out part of his soul. Yet to have her love and her trust felt such a huge burden and one of which he was not worthy. He would let her down; he would desert her. He could never meet her expectations or be what she deserved. The responsibility was too great and the image of Oliver was before him always. He had let Oliver die. He had let his parents down and caused them such a grief that could never be assuaged and he would never, ever, do that to another person again.

Sebastian had been walking with no fixed intention, so deep in thought was he. Now he found he had come out into the street by one of the pleasure gardens, the Peerless Pool. In summer it was the haunt of bathers who came to swim in the fresh spring waters. Now, the frozen lake was full of skaters. They circled beneath the high blue sky and their excited cries mingled with the cutting sound of skates on ice. The frozen branches of the lime and cherry trees seemed to catch the sound and send its echoes tinkling back.

Sebastian paused. It was a pretty scene and in the center of it skated a girl in crimson. He recognized Clara at once. She was surrounded by her family and friends. These were the very people with whom he would once have felt so comfortable. He found himself automatically moving to the marble steps that led down to the pool, then stopped. He had barely seen or spoken to Clara in the past fortnight, and to force himself on her party now felt awkward and wrong. Besides, now he looked more closely he saw that Lords Tarver and Elton were both in attendance, like twin ugly sisters waiting for Cinderella to choose between them. It made Sebastian feel ridiculously angry. Yet he knew that Clara might well be married by the time he returned from the continent and that he should feel relieved at the prospect. It was unfortunate that he was not even noble enough to want for her the thing that would achieve her greatest happiness. He did not want Clara enough to risk everything for her—the thought petrified him—and yet he did not wish her to find her happiness with anyone else. The tug of it was like an agonizing see-saw inside him. Risk all to gain all…he was so very close to it. And yet he turned aside to leave instead.

He almost missed it, had almost turned back through the gates where the doorman was still demanding his entry fee, when out of the corner of his eye he saw Clara fall. She had skated away from the others to the edge of the pool, where the ice ran beneath the branches of the bare trees. She was weaving her way under the trees, a snow queen all in red against the frosted white of the trunks. Then there was a harsh, horrible cracking sound and Sebastian saw the dark water run between the cracks in the ice, saw Clara clutch and miss the branch overhead, and did not wait to see more. He ran. The park keeper was still shouting for his money, unaware of the accident. The other skaters were still spinning and drifting on the other side of the pond. Sebastian scrambled down the bank, careless of the snow and the branches that tore at his coat and his face, and came down onto the ice near where Clara lay.

Someone else had seen now, and was shouting for help, but Sebastian reached her first. She was lying half on the ice and half in the icy water. She did not move. The ice cracked and shifted beneath his feet, but he ignored it. He caught a fold of her skirts and pulled fiercely.

"Clara!"

She moved then and tried to pull herself up out of the ice but it broke beneath her hands. He grabbed one flailing wrist. There was a pain inside him so immense and a panic so smothering that he could not speak. Her wrist was wet and he could feel his grip slipping. She was sliding from his fingers and he was powerless to stop her. There was an immense crack as the ice gave beneath her and she tumbled from his grasp. Seb saw the water close over her head.

The dark images that he had thought buried forever flashed across his mind with vividness. Oliver struggling against the ice, slipping away from him, disappearing from sight, his face white, his mouth open in a soundless scream… For a moment he was still with the horror of it and then he was lunging forward to seize hold of Clara before it was too late. His grasp met nothing but ice and air. He reached for her again and this time, to his inexpressible relief, he touched the material of her gown; he grabbed it and pulled. There was resistance, a ripping sound, and then her skirts were free of the clutching water and he was drawing her to him fiercely. They both tumbled backwards onto the snowy bank, Clara held tight in his arms. He pressed his lips to her hair and tried to pull her closer still, until she made a muffled sound of protest.

The others were arriving now, full of questions and anxiety. Juliana and Kitty plucked Clara from his arms and fussed over her. Martin was shaking his hand and saying something, but Seb was not sure what it was. He felt sick and shaken and afraid. Martin carried Clara up the bank. Seb could hear her protesting that she was quite well and he felt breathless with relief. They were calling for a carriage to take her straight home. Clara turned to look at him and held out a hand in mute appeal, but he turned away. He was too dazed to speak to her, both by what had so nearly happened to Clara and by the tragic memories it had stirred for him. He did not want her thanks.

The fuss and bustle gave him the chance to escape. He went to a nearby coffee house and, although he could see them looking for him out in the street, he stayed in his own dark corner until the last of their carriages had rolled away.

The coffee warmed him and gradually soothed his shaken emotions. He was able to force the fearsome images of the past back into the dark recesses of his mind where they belonged. Nevertheless, he knew that this was not the end. It could not be, now. For in those moments when he'd held her, he had confessed to Clara that he loved her. Not in words, perhaps, but in the expression in his eyes and the touch of his hands as he clutched her so fiercely to him; he had known it and so had she. And he knew she would seek a confrontation now, stubborn girl that she was. He would have to be ready.

CLARA CAME TO HIM that evening, as he had known she would. He could have gone to his club and avoided the confrontation but he planned to leave first thing in the morning, as soon as it was light, and so he settled upon a final evening at home. Now he knew it would be a final reckoning, as well. When he left, it would be with the truth between them. He would tell Clara about Oliver and explain once and for all why he was not worthy of her. He sat in his study with a glass of brandy untouched on the table beside him and he stared into the fire and thought of Clara. Who had he been fooling when he pretended not to care for her? She had stripped away all but the last of his defenses now. He loved her. He loved her desperately and he had done so for a very long time.

"When Miss Davencourt arrives, please show her into the study," he told Perch, and he was on tenterhooks as the clock ticked on toward midnight. Perhaps she had been injured more than he had realized; perhaps she had taken a chill. It might be better if they did not meet. He could slip away in the morning and ask Perch to arrange for a message and a bouquet of flowers to be sent, wishing her a speedy recovery....

"Miss Davencourt, your grace."

Perch was ushering Clara into the room. She looked a little pale but he was glad to see that she appeared otherwise unharmed. He was quick to set a chair for her.

"You should not have come out tonight," he said. "You sustained a shock. Were you injured? You might have caught a chill...." He realized that he was rambling like a nervous youth. There was a spark of amusement in Clara's eyes.

"I am very well," she said. "I came to thank you, Sebastian. You disappeared so quickly this afternoon."

Sebastian shrugged awkwardly. He was feeling very ill at ease. Before she had arrived, he had been confident he would direct their conversation. Now he was not so sure. The balance of power between them seemed to have changed and he did not know how to change it back.

"Does Martin know that you are here?" he asked. "After last night..."

A shadow touched her face. "No one knows. I slipped out when they thought I was asleep."

He felt a rush of amusement followed by a jolt of despair. That was his Clara, so stubborn, so determined to do what she felt was right. Yet she was not really *his* Clara at all. He was about to tell her so.

She sat forward in the chair, looking directly at him. "Do you still intend to leave for the continent tomorrow, Sebastian?"

He looked away. "I do."

Her face fell. The bright light had gone. "I was hoping that you might have changed your mind," she said. "We all wished to thank you properly."

He looked up and met her eyes so sharply that she flinched a little. "Was that why you came here, Clara?" he said harshly. "To thank me?"

"No." She dropped her gaze. A shade of color stole into her cheeks. "I came here to tell you that I love you."

Sebastian looked at her. Her eyes were clear and steady. She was the most beautiful thing he thought he had ever seen. He felt an immense admiration for her courage, followed by a choking wave of love and an even sharper pang of despair. How many women would have had the honesty to behave as she had done?

She was regarding him directly but he knew she was nervous. She moistened her lips with her tongue. A tiny frown touched her forehead at his silence.

"My dear." He cleared his throat. He sounded nervous. That was not good. He had to hide his feelings from her at all costs. "You know that I hold you in the greatest esteem."

She moved with a swift swirl of silk to kneel at his feet. She put one hand on his knee. "No you do not, Sebastian. You do not hold me 'in esteem.'" Disdain colored her voice. "You *love* me."

He moved to raise her to her feet. He could not bear this closeness.

"You and I will never be equal, Clara," he said, trying to make her understand. "You are too open and truthful—damn it, you are too *good* for me. I am jaded. My soul is old."

Clara smiled. It devastated him. "You are making excuses, Sebastian. Do you think I do not know? You are afraid to let yourself love me."

He knew she was right. He had been building barriers against her from the moment they met, instinctively knowing that her love could be his undoing. And now the thing he feared most had happened. He was undone. He had to make her leave him before he disintegrated completely. He could not explain to her about Oliver. That would bring her too close and he would never recover.

"You are in love with love, Clara," he said, struggling to keep his voice neutral. "For me there is nothing between liking and lust. Do not try to dress up my desire for you as something it is not."

There was a stubborn spark of anger in Clara's eyes now. "Why are you lying to me, Sebastian? What is it that you fear?"

He feared so much. He feared that he would offer her his love and she would then have the power to destroy him. But more than anything he feared taking responsibility for another life. He had failed once before when he had allowed Oliver to die. He could not risk that happening to Clara, his one and only love. He said nothing.

"I know you love me," Clara repeated. "I saw it in your face today at the pool. That is why I am here!" She spread her hands wide. "You have only to allow yourself to care for me and all will be well." Her tone was less forceful now, as his silence was starting to undermine her certainties.

"I do care for you," Sebastian said, "but I do not care for you enough." He hated himself for what he was doing. He could see the color draining from her face and the spirit leaching from her eyes, and knew how much he was hurting her. "I acknowledge that people can love each other with the sort of passion you describe," he said. He could barely hear his own false words over the desperate beating of his heart. "But I do not love you like that, Clara," he said starkly. "I do not love you nearly enough. It would not be fair to you to promise otherwise."

Clara scrambled to her feet. There was a blankness to her eyes. She stumbled a little, bumping clumsily into the small table on which stood his glass of brandy. He wanted to pull her into his arms then and never let her go, to comfort her and beg her forgiveness. He was too afraid to do it.

"Either you are lying or you do not know the truth," Clara said. She did not trouble to keep her voice from shaking and he loved her for it; he loved her for the strength of character that made artifice unimportant to her. "I was wrong when I called you coldhearted," she added. "Your heart is a desert, Sebastian, a dry, shriveled place where nothing can live, least of all love."

He could not look at her. He waited until he heard the soft patter of her footsteps receding and then he finally looked up. The face that looked back at him from the mirror was barely recognizable. He looked so haggard. He looked a broken man.

He had hurt Clara inexcusably. But he had succeeded in driving her away and protecting himself from the terrifying risk of loving and losing her. He knew that he should feel glad, but his heart felt like the desert that Clara had so accurately described.

"MISS DAVENCOURT? Miss Davencourt!" Clara was heading for the front door, hampered by the fact that she was blinded by tears. She tripped over the edge of the Persian rug, grabbed a table for support and almost toppled the priceless vase that rested on it.

"Miss Davencourt!"

Her arm was caught in a reassuring grip and she found herself looking into the face of Perch, the butler. She noticed, irrelevantly, what kind eyes he had. Then she also noticed that the door to the servants' stair was open and a row of anxious faces was peering at her from the gloom. Her curiosity was sufficient to overcome her misery for a moment.

"What on earth is going on?"

Perch steered her discreetly into the dining room, and the other servants trooped in silently. In the gothic shadowy darkness they lined up in front of her, candlesticks in hand, their expressions a mixture of hope and concern. Clara looked to the butler for enlightenment.

"Begging your pardon, Miss Davencourt," Perch said, "but we were thinking that you might have persuaded his grace..." He studied her face for a moment, shook his head and sighed. "No matter. Shall I procure you a cab to take you home, miss?"

The other servants gave a murmur of protest. It was clear they did not wish to let her go so easily without telling her their concerns.

"We thought you were to be the new Duchess of Fleet, ma'am," one of the housemaids, a girl with a round red face, said. "That's what Mr. Perch is trying to say. His grace has been sweet on you for as long as I've worked here."

Clara felt a rush of misery. She looked at their anxious faces and managed to raise a rueful smile. "Thank you, but I'm afraid I shall not be the next duchess."

"His grace must be mad," the hall boy whispered, rolling his eyes expressively. Perch shot him a warning look.

"We are very sorry to hear that, ma'am," he said. "We should have liked it very much."

Clara's desolate heart thawed a little. She looked at them all properly for the first time, from the brawny under-gardener to the smallest scullery maid and realized how extraordinary it was that they had all pinned their hopes on her. "I had forgotten," she said. "The duke is to leave on the morrow, is he not? Are you—" she hesitated "—will he be closing the house?"

A row of doleful nods was her answer.

"We are looking for new positions, ma'am. All except Mr. Dawson, his grace's valet. He travels abroad with his grace."

So, most all of them would be out of work as soon

as Fleet left for the continent, Clara thought. It was another consequence of his departure and one she had not even considered. She felt horribly guilty.

"I am sorry," she said.

"Not your fault, ma'am," one of the footmen said stalwartly. "His grace is a fine man but in this case his wits have gone a-begging, if you will excuse my saying so."

"His grace has a picture of you in his traveling case, ma'am," another of the maids put in, blushing. "I saw him pack it when he thought no one was watching."

There was a hopeful pause.

"I do not suppose, madam," Perch said weightily, "that you would be prepared to give his grace another chance?"

Clara looked at them all. "I have already given him several chances," she said.

Perch nodded. "We are aware, ma'am. What lady could be expected to do more?"

There was another rustle of disapproval from among the assembled ranks. Clearly they believed their esteemed employer had run mad.

"Unless you could think of a winning scheme," Clara said, "it is pointless. And even then I am not sure that his grace deserves it."

The housekeeper and several of the maids shook their heads. "Men!" One of the girls said. "Hopeless!"

"Get him at a moment of weakness," one of the

footmen suggested. "He'll admit to his feelings when he's in his cups."

The valet nodded. "That's true, ma'am. If we could get him drunk."

Clara stifled a laugh. "I am not certain I would want a man who has to be drunk to admit his love for me."

The housekeeper shook her head. "Begging your pardon, ma'am, we're thinking it was the business with Master Oliver that made him this way. Those of us who have been with the family for years saw it happen. The master changed. Terrible shock, it was. After that he turned cold."

One of the older housemaids nodded sadly. "Aye, such an affectionate little boy he was, but he blamed himself from that day forward."

Clara raised her brows. "Who was Master Oliver?"

The servants shuffled uncomfortably. "Master Oliver was his grace's brother," Perch said. "There was an accident."

"Drowned," one of the footmen put in. "Terrible business."

Clara was so surprised that she was silent for a moment. She had never heard of Oliver Fleet, still less that the duke had ever had a brother. He had never, ever mentioned it to her and, she was sure, not to Martin, either. But then, he was good at keeping secrets.

"I had no notion," she said. "How dreadful. I am so sorry."

The servants nodded sadly.

"His grace blamed himself. He has been as cold as ice ever since," Perch explained. There was a long silence before he continued.

"We know that you are too good for his grace, ma'am, being a true lady and generous to a fault, but if you could see your way to giving his grace—and the rest of us—another chance…"

The eagerness of their expressions was heartbreaking. Clara thought of the stories behind the faces, the families that depended on their wages, the fear of being without a job or a roof over their heads, the uncertainty of a servant's life. And yet it was not only that that had prompted them to throw themselves on her mercy. They had seen her come and go through Sebastian Fleet's life for two years and the sincerity of their regard warmed her.

"If you have a plan," she said, "I am prepared to listen to it."

Perch checked the clock on the mantel. "In approximately two minutes his grace will decide to go out to drown his sorrows, ma'am. We shall give him a few hours to become cast adrift, and then we will escort you to fetch him home." He looked around at his fellow servants. "We believe he will admit his feelings for you very soon, ma'am. His grace has almost reached the point where they cannot be denied."

There was a crash out in the hall. Everyone jumped at the sound of the library door banging open and Seb Fleet's voice shouting irascibly for his butler. He sounded absolutely furious.

"Perch? Where the devil are you, man? I want to go out!"

"Perfectly on cue," one of the footmen said.

Perch smoothed his coat and trod slowly towards the door, opening it and closing it behind him with his usual grave deliberation.

"You called, your grace?" Clara heard him say.

"I am going out," Fleet repeated. She thought he sounded murderous.

"Might one inquire where, your grace?"

"No, one might not, damn you! Fetch my coat!"

"May I then remind your grace that you are to travel at first light?"

Fleet said something so rude that one of the housemaids gasped and clapped her hands over her ears.

"Sorry you had to hear that, ma'am," the housekeeper whispered. "His grace is in a proper mood and no mistake."

Clara bit her lip to stop a smile.

The front door slammed. There was a long pause while they all seemed to be holding their breath, then Perch appeared once more in the doorway of the dining room.

"I've sent Jackman to follow his grace," he said. "We shall soon know where he has gone. Miss Davencourt—" there was a smile in his eyes as he turned to Clara "—may we offer you some refreshment while we wait?"

Chapter Five

Seb Fleet did not choose to drown his sorrows at Whites, but instead went to the Moon and Goldfinch, a considerably less salubrious place on the Goldhawk Road where he could drink himself to hell and back without anyone caring. Indeed, once the landlord had seen that his money was good he kept him so well-supplied with alcohol that Sebastian found himself by turns maudlin, then merry, then maudlin again in the shortest possible time. By three in the morning he had made several dubious new friends, turned down eager kisses from the landlord's daughter, and was comfortably asleep on the bar when he was shaken roughly awake. The door of the inn was open and a fresh burst of snow was swirling inside, pulling him from his welcome stupor.

"Sebastian! Wake up at once!" It was Clara's voice. Fleet groaned.

"This the missus, is it?" the landlord enquired affably.

"Not yet," Clara snapped.

Fleet shook the hair out of his eyes and tried to sit up. The room swam about him. His mouth felt like a cockpit. His eyes were gritty and his face was wet where he appeared to have fallen asleep in a pool of beer.

"You smell like a sewer," Clara grumbled. "Perch, Dawson, can you manage him?"

"Hello, my sweet love," Sebastian said with a slight slur, as his butler and valet struggled to lift him with all the finesse of a collier hefting a sack. He smiled at Clara as her cross-looking face swam before his eyes. He felt inordinately pleased to see her. He could not quite remember why, but he knew that earlier in the evening he thought he would never, ever see her again. Evidently he had been quite wrong. He struggled to remember the circumstances, failed completely, and lurched heavily against Dawson's side.

"How splendid that you are here, my darling," he called, as Perch and Dawson tried to maneuver him to the door. "I did not expect to see you." He staggered dangerously and almost knocked over the butler.

"Sorry, Perch. Don't know why you don't just leave me to sleep here."

"Yes, your grace." Perch sounded as though that was precisely what he would have done had he been permitted to have his way. "Miss Davencourt was concerned for you, your grace."

"Very wifely," Fleet observed. His head felt too heavy to think clearly. Here was Clara, turning his heart inside out again and making him feel as raw as an untried youth. He loved her so much that there was a lump in his throat at the thought of it. It was dreadful that she should see him this way. He must look terrible. He smelled. He was a disgrace. And yet she was still here, despite everything, and he really did not have the will to resist any more.

"I am not certain it is the proper thing for you to be here, Miss Davencourt."

Clara smiled. "I am here to discover if you love me, Sebastian."

"Love you?" Fleet asked. The question seemed so absurd that he started to laugh. "Of course I love you! I love you so much it breaks my heart."

"Excellent," Clara said. "You are drunk, of course, so that may make a difference. Will you still love me when you are sober?"

"Of course I will." Fleet squinted, his head lolling against Dawson's shoulder. "'Course I will! I love you to perdition, you little fool! Why do you think I keep trying to make you go away?"

"Hmm. It lacks something for a declaration, I think," Clara said. "I shall not propose to you again, however. A lady has her pride."

"Marry me," Fleet said. He tried to get down on his

knees but Perch and Dawson held him up. It was probably best they did; he had a feeling that once he was down there he would never stand again.

"We shall talk about it in the morning," Clara said. "Now please be quiet, Sebastian, and get into the coach."

Fleet stumbled to the door, encouraged on his way by the profuse thanks of the landlord. The cold air sobered him somewhat and the falling snow on his face restored him to an unwelcome sense of reality. Clara was waiting patiently while Perch and Dawson hauled him into the carriage. She accepted Perch's hand up with perfect composure and settled herself opposite him, wrinkling her nose delicately at the combined scent of beer and tobacco.

"Clara," he said again, as the door shut on them. "This is no escapade for a lady. You really should not be here."

"If you were not here then neither should I be," Clara said calmly, wrapping the rug about them both. "I was worried about you, Sebastian."

Fleet pressed a hand to his aching brow. "I do not want you to worry about me!" The words came out almost as a shout and Clara put her gloved hands over her ears. "How many times do I have to explain this? This is exactly what I was trying to avoid!"

"It seems to me," Clara said, ignoring him, "that you have not permitted anyone to care for you in a very long time, Sebastian."

Fleet's head pounded. "Devil take it! Clara, have you not understood? I want you to leave me alone!"

His head was swimming, but in the dim light of the carriage lamps he saw that she was looking at him and there was a slight, satisfied smile on her lips. Fleet leaned his head against the seat cushions and closed his eyes in despair. He realized through the clearing fog of his inebriation that he'd declared his love to her. "Dash it, Clara, I am too befuddled to argue." He leant forward, suddenly urgent. "Yes, I love you to distraction but I wish to the devil that I did not! I would go to the ends of the earth for you but I can hardly bear it! The responsibility of it terrifies me."

"It is perfectly simple," Clara said briskly. "I care for you and in return you care for me." She put one small hand against his chest and pushed gently. "Go to sleep, now."

He wanted to argue but he did not have the strength. To sleep seemed easier. So he did.

HE WAS AWOKEN by the white light of a snowy morning illuminating his bedroom. For a brief, blissful moment he could not remember anything, then he flung one arm across his eyes and let out a long groan.

"I have prepared a nice posset for you," Clara's voice said. "I thought perhaps you might need something restorative for your head."

Sebastian opened his eyes. He might have known

Clara would still be here. No doubt she sat up all night at his bedside to make sure he was quite safe. He felt exasperated and deeply grateful at the same time. She looked as fresh as though she were stepping out to a ball. Her dress was uncreased and her eyes bright. He looked at her and felt a hopeless feeling swamp him.

"Your concern is most touching," he said, sitting up in bed to take the steaming cup of sweet liquid. "I have sunk more drink than last night, however. I shall survive."

"You told me that you loved me last night," Clara said. "Do you remember?"

He looked at her. It was too late now for denials and lies. Much too late.

"I remember," he said. "Oh, Clara, darling, of course I remember."

She took his hand. "There is no need to look so terrified, Sebastian. Love is not an illness. It will not kill you."

But to him it felt exactly as though he had contracted an unfamiliar and frightening disease. He had not tested love's boundaries yet. He did not know how far he could trust himself with it. Nevertheless, the need to tell Clara everything now was so acute he could not resist.

"When you fell through the ice yesterday I was so frightened," he said. His voice shook a little. "I thought that I was losing you, there in front of my eyes. It reminded me of when Oliver died." It had actually been worse than losing Oliver. Ten, twenty times more dreadful.

"Oliver was your brother," Clara said.

"Yes. He was four years younger than I was. I always protected him. Until the day I failed him."

The words came out in a torrent. He could not stop now if he tried.

"It was this time of year right before Christmas. We were supposed to be at our lessons but our tutor fell asleep and we crept out. It was too fine a day to stay indoors. We took our skates and went down to the old mill race." He swallowed painfully. "I can still see Oliver now. He skated out into the middle—the ice was hard, we did not realize the danger—and he was spinning around, his arms outstretched… And then he was simply not there." He stopped. Clara did not speak.

"I moved as fast as I could. The ice was cracking all around me. I shouted for help until I was hoarse but no one came. I could see him, under the ice, but I could not reach him. Every time I got close enough to grab him the ice would break beneath me and we would drift apart."

"What happened?" Clara whispered.

"Someone finally saw us. I do not know how long it took. The water was so cold. They brought ropes and ladders but I knew it was too late for Oliver. I was big and strong but he was only small. He was only eight years old! And I could not save him."

He half expected Clara to tell him that it had not been his fault. People had been saying that to him for years until they tired of reassuring him or thought that he was over the tragedy. But Clara did not say that. She held his hand and waited for him to continue.

"It was my fault," he said starkly. "I was the one who suggested we go skating that day. He always followed me. Then I could not help him when he needed me."

He gripped Clara's hand fast. "They rescued me first, you know. I was the heir." His mouth twisted bitterly. "The spare was sacrificed."

He was crying. He could not help it. He dashed the tears away with his hand and found they fell all the quicker for it. He spoke in gasps.

"I have never told anyone this before. I thought I could lock it away but you have unmanned me. You made me feel again. You made me love you. Oh, Clara—"

Clara moved from her chair to the edge of his bed. She caught him and pulled him to her, drawing him down so that his cheek rested against hers. Her arms were tight about him and it felt protected and safe. For a second he hesitated, but it was out of nothing more than habit. Then he let go and felt himself fall, mind and body, to a warm safe place, where he was her strength and she was his.

He did not know how long they lay there, but when he opened his eyes, Clara's face was about an inch away from his, so he kissed her with love and gentleness. Her lashes lifted and she looked at him. He could see from her eyes that she was smiling.

"You need a shave," she said, running her fingers experimentally over the stubble that darkened his chin.

"And a wash. I fear I am most unwholesome."

"You are delightful." Clara rubbed her cheek against his rough one. "I love you, Sebastian."

He savored the words, tasted them. His entire body felt relaxed, released from a terrible torment. His eyes were heavy. He felt so tired. He did not want to resist and after a few moments, to his intense surprise, the sleep took him again.

CLARA DID NOT FALL ASLEEP. She lay looking at Sebastian with a small smile still on her lips. How ruffled and dishevelled he looked. If this was how he appeared when in a state of undress, how much more magnificent would he be when he was totally naked. And at least she might have a fighting chance of seeing that now. It had taken her a long time to realize that in permitting him to dictate her happiness she was helping neither of them.

She wriggled closer to the warmth of his body. He felt solid and strong. She ran a hand experimentally over his chest and he murmured something in his sleep and drew her deeper into the crook of his arm. He smelled faintly of leather and tobacco and lime cologne. Clara buried her nose in the curve of his neck and inhaled deeply. She felt almost light-headed with the warmth and the scent of him. It was a good job that he was asleep for she felt exceedingly wide-awake. Her body tingled. She remembered the way Sebastian had kissed her, the way he had used his tongue and his teeth on her bare breast, and she was shot through with a pleasure that pooled deep within her and made her body tense and wanting.

Then he opened his eyes.

For a long moment she stared into that deep, slumberous blue and saw his gaze darken with desire as he rolled over to pin her beneath his weight.

There was a very sharp rap on the front door followed by the sound of raised voices in the hall.

For a moment Sebastian was still, his body poised above hers, then he sighed and eased himself off the bed.

"What sort of hour is this for visitors to call?"

Clara squinted at the clock on the mantelpiece. "It is past one, Sebastian. You have slept the clock around."

Sebastian stretched. Clara stared. She could not help it. He was still in his breeches and shirt and she was riveted by the deliciously tight fit of the buckskins over his thighs.

"You could avert your eyes," Sebastian said mildly.

"I could," Clara agreed, "but I am not going to."

He smiled. "Hussy."

"I know. But I have waited a long time—"

His eyes darkened again. "No more waiting, I promise you." He bent over and touched his lips to hers and Clara's senses leapt in response to the light caress. She grabbed his shirt and pulled him down to her, kissing him fervently.

The sound of voices was coming nearer. Through the pounding of the blood in her ears, Clara could hear Perch's tones, soothing and respectful, and in response a voice she recognized all too well—Martin, sounding dangerously angry, along with Lady Juliana, high and anxious.

"We know she is here, Perch. She left a note."

Sebastian eased his lips from Clara's. *"You left a note?"*

Clara hung her head, blushing a little. "I thought it was the right thing to do. I did not want anyone to worry about me."

"Whereas now that they know you have been all night at my bedside they will be delighted," Sebastian said dryly. "Your brother is about to call me to account for being a scoundrel and for the first time in my life I am entirely innocent of all wrongdoing."

The door flew open and Martin Davencourt erupted into the room, Juliana at his heels. Clara's heart sank as she saw in their wake her sister Kitty, Kitty's husband Edward, Juliana's brother Joss, his wife Amy, Edward's brother Adam and Adam's wife Annis all jostling behind them on the landing.

"Why is everybody here?" she wailed.

A cacophony of noise broke over them and Clara put her hands over her ears.

"He is half-undressed!"

"She is fully dressed!"

"She is in his bed!"

"The place smells like a taproom!"

"Oh, Clara!" said Kitty, sounding both awed and disapproving.

"Scoundrel! Rogue!" Martin was not mincing his words. "To think I ever called you friend! To seduce my sister—" Before Clara could jump up, Martin had lunged at Sebastian and grabbed him by the remnants of his neck cloth, pulling tight. There was mindless fury in her brother's eyes. Clara heard Seb's breathing catch and saw his eyes start to bulge as, caught off balance, he tripped over backward onto the bed.

"I did no such thing, I swear!" he choked out, breaking off painfully as Martin pulled viciously on the cravat and brought tears to his eyes.

"Martin!" Clara leapt to her feet and hung on to Martin's arm. "Let him go! Nothing happened. I am the one to blame!"

Martin cast her one dark, angry look. "Oh, you need not think that I hold you blameless, Clara. I will settle with you when I have settled with him!"

Seb gave a despairing croak as the tourniquet tightened about his throat. Clara felt genuine alarm now. "Juliana!" She spun round to address her sister-in-law. "Do something! I promise nothing happened between us. Sebastian was too drunk—"

She realized this was not the most helpful defense, when Martin's breath hissed between his teeth with fury and he hauled Fleet to his feet, only to lay him flat out with one well-placed blow.

There was a silence.

"That was very unfair!" Clara said indignantly, scrambling to prop him up. "You have given Sebastian no opportunity to explain himself."

"It was the least I deserved," Sebastian said, fingering his jaw. "Would have done the same thing myself if I had a sister." He looked up at his angry friend and said, "Davencourt, my apologies. I have behaved abominably, even though it is true that your sister is quite unscathed."

"Because you were too drunk to seduce her," Martin said through shut teeth.

"Absolutely. And because I respect her and wish to make her my wife at the earliest possible opportunity."

There was a concerted gasp from the assembled company. Clara thought she saw a slight smile of satisfaction cross Perch's otherwise impassive expression.

"May I be the first to offer my congratulations, your grace," he said.

"Congratulations?" Martin's expression was like boiling milk. "Congratulations? I will *not* permit my sister to marry such a rogue."

"Martin, darling," Juliana said, putting a gentle

hand on her husband's arm, "I completely understand your misgivings but I do think we should consider the matter calmly."

"Calmly!" Martin spun around. "I am not calm!"

"I think we all realize that, dearest," Juliana said. "Now, Clara, you will accompany us home. Sebastian, you will join us for dinner tonight, if you please. Great-Aunt Eleanor is staying and if you pass muster with her then I doubt anyone else will object to your suit."

She took Clara's arm and propelled her forcibly toward the door.

"Ladies and gentlemen," Sebastian said, raising his voice. "Might I beg one moment in private with my affianced wife?" He caught Clara's hand as Juliana escorted her past.

Martin, who had started to look vaguely placated, started frowning again. "Affianced? You try my patience too far, Fleet. You assume too much."

"One minute," Sebastian said. "Please." He kept tight hold of Clara's hand.

Everyone backed from the room with good-humored grumbling and Juliana dragged Martin out.

"One minute only," she warned.

As soon as the door closed behind them Sebastian pulled Clara into his arms.

"I asked you last night but you did not answer," he said. "Will you marry me?"

"Yes!" Clara said. "I am so glad that you asked. I

had quite decided against putting my fate to the touch for a second time. A lady does not wish to appear too desperate."

Seb caressed her hair. "And the special license? Do you wish me to procure one?"

"Yes, please." Clara snuggled against his stroking hand. The latent sensuality of her behavior was doing terrible things to both his self-control and his clarity of thought.

"I am still a bit worried about your brother," he began, knowing there was another matter to be settled.

"We will persuade him," Clara said. She tilted her chin up. "Kiss me, please."

They were still engrossed when the door opened and Perch came back in.

"Mr. Davencourt requests his sister's presence at once," he said, straight-faced, "or he will go to fetch his duelling pistols."

SEB FLEET STOOD in the snow outside the house in Collett Square. It was late; the sky was black and cold, and the stars very bright. In all material terms the evening had been a vast success. Lady Eleanor Tallant, matriarch of the extended family, had given her seal of approval to the match between himself and Clara, and had dismissed Martin's objections in a few pungent words.

"Fleet is solvent, young enough to have his own hair and not require a corset, and influential enough to help your political career," she had said sharply. "You must have windmills in your head to object to such an offer." Then her face had softened. "He also dotes upon your sister, should that have more influence with you."

Martin had then reluctantly offered his hand, and Seb seized it gratefully.

"I do love her, you know, Davencourt," he said. "I would not wish to live without her."

He had seen the effort Martin had made to set aside the doubts and fears Seb knew were only for Clara's happiness. Things were *almost* back to normal.

Now he was supposed to go home and see his betrothed formally and respectably the next day, when arrangements would be made for him to join the family at Davencourt for Christmas, and for he and Clara to be married on Twelfth Night.

But there was one thing he had not done, one thing that required privacy rather than the benevolent observation of the family, one thing he wanted to give to Clara when they were alone.

He watched the lights go out in the house one by one and felt his feet freeze in the hard-packed snow.

Clara's room was at the back of the house and he let himself in through the small iron gate that led into the gardens. His footprints in the snow would give him away to anyone who spotted them, but this was too important not to take the risk. He suspected that for all their newfound harmony, Martin would allow him very little time alone with Clara until they were wed. Which was as it should be, of course. But he wanted her all to himself for a little.

He set his foot to the base of the ivy that climbed up the back of the house. It shivered under his weight but its branches were sturdy. At least the snow would break his fall if he misjudged the venture.

The ivy shook and trembled, sending showers of powdery snow to the ground, but he clung on as his fingers froze to the branches and he hauled himself up painfully to the first floor. The sharp twigs pricked at his hands and ankles.

He gained the ledge that ran around the first floor, then edged sideways past two windows until he came to Clara's chamber, at the end of the house. There was a faint light from behind the drapes. He hoped her maid was not still with her. He hoped she had not fallen asleep. He hoped he had not miscalculated and was outside Lady Eleanor Tallant's chamber instead.

He was wet and cold and scratched. The price of love. He smiled faintly and knocked at the windowpane.

Nothing happened. He knocked again, slightly more loudly. The vine creaked beneath his feet.

Clara's face appeared at the window, wide-eyed and astonished. In another moment she had thrown up the sash and was leaning out.

"Sebastian!" The whisper carried on the cold clear air. "What are you doing? You will fall!"

She grabbed his hand and pulled with all her might. Various parts of him caught on the latch or were squeezed in the aperture. Eventually he made a mammoth effort and half stumbled, half fell into the room and into Clara's arms.

"I came to tell you that I love you," he said, burying his face in her hair and holding her warm body against the coldness of his.

She eased back from him a little. The smile in her blue eyes was delicious. "You have told me that already today, Sebastian."

"I could not wait until tomorrow to tell you again. Besides," Sebastian said, gesturing towards the ivy, which would probably never recover from his onslaught, "I wanted to prove that I would do anything for you, even risk life and limb, flora and fauna, hauling my weight up to your balcony."

He released her and stood regarding her intently. In her flimsy peignoir and similarly transparent nightdress she looked luscious.

She gave a little giggle. "Dearest Sebastian, you have no need to prove anything to me. I know how much you love me."

He felt humbled by her generosity. "Clara, you do not understand. I will always think of you as too good for me." He slid his hand into his pocket. "I brought you this. It is a betrothal gift. I wanted to give it to you in private. I hope that you understand."

Earlier that evening, in full, approving view of the

family, he had given her the Fleet betrothal ruby ring, which he had retrieved from the bank that very day. Now she was looking puzzled.

"A gift? But I thought—"

He held the box out to her. "Take it. Please."

Clara took it slowly, ran her fingers over the smooth, leather case, then opened the box.

"Oh!"

The huge ruby star pendant was nestling in the palm of Clara's hand now, its surface striking sparks from the candlelight. She looked up and her eyes were misty with tears.

"It is the most beautiful thing…"

She laid it reverentially in its box on the window seat, then came and took his hand and drew him down to sit on the bed beside her. She rested her head against his shoulder. "You know that there are things I need from you, Sebastian." She nestled closer. "You always claim that I am too good for you, but you are strong and courageous and loyal, and I admire those things."

Her nightgown slipped a little, the virginal white linen sliding from one rounded shoulder. Beneath it Sebastian knew that she would be soft and smooth, curved in all the most perfect places, warmly inviting.

He averted his eyes.

Her hair brushed his cheek—soft, confiding, innocent. She was tilting up her lips so that he could kiss her. His throat closed with nervousness. He gave her a tiny peck on the lips and withdrew hastily. Clara sat back, looking at his with a suddenly arrested expression.

"You do not intend to stay with me tonight?"

Sebastian stared at her in consternation. "Stay? Of course I will not stay." He knew that he sounded like a dowager. "That would be most inappropriate."

"So says the greatest scoundrel in London," Clara said.

"Clara, you are to be my *wife.* We must do these things properly." Seb wiped his brow. It was an excuse, of course. He wanted nothing more than to take her in the most improper ways imaginable, but he knew he could not do it.

Clara's lower lip quivered. "I am not certain I wish to marry you if you have become stuffy and proper all of a sudden. I do not want a reformed rake as a husband. I want a rake who will devote his attentions to me!"

Sebastian spread his hands helplessly. "You know I am yours, body and soul."

"And it is the physical side of you that intrigues me at present, I confess." She peeped at him. "No doubt I am shameless, but since you are to be my husband..."

She was tracing one finger down the line of his sleeve and when she touched the back of his hand, light as a breath of wind, he flinched as though scalded.

"No."

He could sense the uncertainty in her. She wanted him; she had courage, but in the face of his blank refusal she was too inexperienced to push for what she wanted. His heart twisted. He was hurting her again with a different sort of rejection now. He knew he had to explain to her. It was only fair. The difficulty was finding the words.

Clara covered her face with her hands. "Oh, dear! I was relying on you, Sebastian! I thought that one of us at least would know what to do."

"I do know the theory," Sebastian said. "Clara, I love you! I have never felt like this about anybody before—" He stopped.

Clara's eyes widened. She stared at him for a long moment. "Sebastian, you are afraid!"

He gave her a lopsided grin. "I confess it."

"When you said that I had unmanned you I did not think you meant..." Clara said, beginning to comprehend.

Sebastian looked down. He remained obstinately limp. He sighed.

"I am sorry."

"But what will happen on our wedding night?" Clara wailed.

Sebastian imagined that the longer their betrothal lasted, the more nervous he would become. Sebastian Fleet, the greatest rake in London, reduced to a quivering wreck by a slip of a girl.

Clara was looking at him, her blue eyes wide with apprehension. He felt a wave of hopelessness swamp him. Hell and damnation! The fact that he felt like ravishing her, the fact that he wanted to tear her clothes off and make mad, passionate love to her and yet he was somehow incapable of doing so was the last word in frustration. Theirs had been the most provocative courtship.

Then he saw a spark of amusement in Clara's eyes. The corner of her mouth lifted in a tiny smile. She traced a pattern on the edge of the sheet with her fingers and did not look at him as she spoke.

"Would you be prepared at least to try?" she asked demurely. "My governess always said that when one did not wish to do something it was better to grit one's teeth and take courage than to put off the moment."

Grit his teeth and summon all his courage. Seb drove his hands into his pockets in a gesture of contained fury. That was not how making love to Clara Davencourt should be.

"It is not that I do not *want* to, Clara," he said. "I want to kiss you and take you to bed and make love to you until dawn, but—" He broke off as he saw the rosy color suffuse her face.

"Do you really?" she said.

"Yes!" Seb almost shouted.

Clara looked around hastily. "Quiet! I do not wish Martin to find you here and have to explain that once again nothing has happened between us."

Seb gave an infuriated groan and sank down onto the bed. "This is humiliating."

He felt her wriggle across to sit beside him. Her

breast pressed softly against his arm. She was warm and smelled faintly of jasmine and clean linen.

"Dear Sebastian." She was holding his hand in hers now and he let it rest there because it felt so comforting. "You must not worry about it. I shall not press you for my marital rights."

He looked up. She was so close that he could see the individual black eyelashes and the sweep of the shadow they cast on her cheek in the candlelight. Her cheek was round and smooth and he put up a hand to caress it. He smiled reluctantly.

"I suppose it is a little bit amusing...."

"Yes." She was nibbling at his fingers now, that full lower lip lush against the pad of his thumb. He felt a sudden fierce urge to kiss her that made him freeze on the spot. She withdrew slightly.

"I promise," she said solemnly, "to ask nothing of you that you are not prepared to give."

"Thank you." He started to relax. She gave him a little push and he lay back on the pillows, closing his eyes. When she lay down beside him he did not stir. Convention dictated that he should leave, but for once he was feeling completely at peace.

"Please hold me," Clara said, and he realized that in his selfish fears he had drawn so much on her strength and not given enough of himself back to her. He put his arms about her and drew her close so that her head rested beneath his chin and their hearts beat together.

After a moment he eased away a little and scattered little kisses across the soft skin of her face, paying special attention to those stubborn freckles that had always tempted him. He was trying not to think about what he was doing, trusting to instinct rather than past skill.

She turned her head slightly and her lips met his, then he felt the tip of her tongue touch the corner of his mouth. It set the blood hammering through his body and he opened his lips to hers, hesitantly at first, unprepared for the flash of desire that almost consumed him as their tongues touched, tangled.

Beneath the desire lay acute anxiety. He recognized it with incredulity. It almost paralyzed him. Clara was pressing closer, gently running her hands over his arms and shoulders, sliding the damp jacket from him so that he could feel the warmth of her touch through the linen of his shirt. She was resting her cheek against his chest now and he knew she would be able to hear the racing of his heart.

"I am sorry," he said, kissing her hair. "I do not wish to hurt you."

There was laughter in her voice. "I am no saint on a pedestal. You need not treat me like glass, Sebastian. I shall not break."

"No, but I am very afraid that I might."

She wriggled up until she was looking him in the eyes. "Then we shall break and mend together."

She saw the way his eyes darkened with sudden

heat and felt a rush of the same excitement through her body with an undertow of fear. Now, at last, she sensed she was close to overcoming that last barrier that lay between them.

With one forceful movement he rolled her beneath him, his mouth crashing down on hers, scattering her own doubts and anxieties. Her senses reeled beneath the onslaught, her body arching, pleading for the fulfilment of pleasure. If he should hesitate now…

She felt his fingers rough on the fastenings of her chemise. He was trembling. She refused to give him time to think. She cast the chemise aside, caught his hand and placed it over her breast.

He groaned, but she knew with a flash of pure feminine triumph that she had won. His mouth was at her breast, hot and wet, and she ripped the shirt from his back so that she could touch his nakedness, skin to skin.

When he tore off his breeches and she felt the whole hard length of him against her for the first time, the shock splintered her. It was so strange but so exquisitely pleasurable. She arched again into his hands, and then his mouth was on hers as he came down over her, caressing her, parting her thighs to find that aching softness at the center of her.

He drew back a little.

"I will hurt you now…."

She sensed his reluctance and once again she was ruthless, straining for his touch.

"Then do so. Please..." Her voice broke on a ragged gasp. "Sebastian..."

The pause seemed agonizingly long, but then he was moving with one sure, hard thrust to claim her, and the pleasure and the pain raked her with fire and she gasped, but his mouth on hers silenced her cries. She clutched him to her, feeling her world shatter and reform as he took her with such thorough tenderness that her body melted into bliss. All she could be certain of was that she had his love and would never lose it.

"I LOVE YOU." Sebastian's face was turned into the damp curve of her shoulder. His breath tickled her skin. She could hear the profound relaxation and happiness in his voice and to her surprise it made the tears well up in her throat. Such a painful journey for a man who had rejected his feelings for so many years. She gave him a brief, fierce hug.

"I love you, too, Sebastian."

"I may not always be as good at showing my feelings as you are, my love. It was your sweetness and honesty that shamed me into such admiration for you. If I falter it will not be because I do not care for you."

She understood what he was trying to say. It would take time for him to unlock all the bitterness and unhappiness from the past. That did not matter for she would be there with him.

"As long as you can promise to love and be faithful to me alone," she said solemnly, "then there is nothing to fear."

She felt him smile against her skin. "I can promise that without a shadow of a doubt."

"Good." Clara turned to look at him. "This business between us, then—" she gave a little voluptuous wiggle "—this rather pleasant business of making love… Is it all settled now?"

His lips quirked into a smile. "I think it may well be."

She caressed his chest, feeling his muscles tense in sudden response to her touch. "Do you think that we should do it again, to make certain?" she whispered.

In reply he pulled her down on top of him, tangling a hand in her hair, bringing her mouth down to his.

"Yes," he whispered against her lips. "Yes, I do."

CLARA KNELT on the window seat, the ruby star in its box beside her. In the faint light before dawn it seemed to have a radiance of its own. She looked from her own particular star to the one she had seen that night a few weeks ago as it paled in the dawn sky over the roofs of London.

Have hope.

Have faith.

She smiled a little.

Sebastian stirred and she went across to the bed, slipping into the space beside him.

"How strange," she said, as she cuddled close to his warmth. "I never thought this would be the season in which I found a suitor."

He smiled, drawing her closer into his arms. "I never thought it would be the season in which I found a *wife.* Clara Davencourt, my love, my life."

Dear Reader,

Shortly after I wrote *Christmas Charade*, I had the opportunity to visit London and stroll through Hyde Park, visit the museums and all the other famous sights about town. Comparing my old nineteenth-century maps of the city with the new ones proved to be an eye opener. So much has changed, yet so much has stayed the same! I didn't even have to close my eyes to imagine carriages crowding the streets or high-collared dandies tipping their hats to the ladies.

My husband and I had afternoon tea in a small shop in the Cotswolds and there discovered a route to some beautiful villages that were off the tourist-beaten path. This is definitely one of my favourite areas in England, so I have included it in my story.

With a flutter of my fan and a deep curtsy, I wish you the happiest of holidays!

Lyn Stone

Christmas Charade

by

Lyn Stone

This story is for my good friends
Charlotte and Robert Ballard, in honour of those fine
Christmases we celebrated once upon a time.

Chapter One

London, 1815

"SO WHICH do you think is the new earl?"

Bethany Goodson disguised her interest by plying her fan and pretending to scan the entire ballroom before glancing idly toward the entrance two gentlemen were making. She returned her gaze to her cousin, Euphemia, who was jittery with excitement. "The one in evening dress, I would think. A fellow so come up in the world would not don regimentals even if he is fresh from the wars."

"Well, both are as handsome as sin on a jam tart!" Phemie declared. "You may have the one in the uniform," she said, giving Beth's shoulder a nudge with her own. "I shall have the other."

"I have no use for either, as you very well know." But the Keiths, even at this distance, certainly were handsome enough to make Beth bemoan her need to remain unattached. She took a sip of her ratafia and set aside her glass. "If you'd known them as lads, you would be thinking twice about it yourself."

"Never say it," Phemie said. "Why is that?"

"Jack and Colin were double trouble. I heard that their poor aunt who reared them took to her bed when they were in shortcoats and never left it until they were safely away at school. I trust it was so. They were hellions when they came home on holiday."

"You knew them before I came to live with you?"

"Yes. Earl Whitworth's estate is near ours. The countess was related to our vicar. There were a number of entertainments we, as children, were allowed to attend. Wakes, picnics and the like."

"Wakes for entertainment? I so love the country life." Phemie laughed merrily, still staring impudently at the two dark-haired brothers. "They bear a remarkable likeness, though I must say the one in regimentals looks a bit older."

Beth frowned as she tried to recall. "No one ever remarked on their ages within my hearing, really, though I believe they are some four or five years older than I. Surely the one in evening clothes is the elder. Why else would he dress the part of an earl and the other remain a mere soldier?"

She turned aside for a moment to speak to someone in passing and felt Phemie's pinch just above her glove. "Ouch! Whatever is wrong with you?"

Phemie was fidgeting, causing her white-gold curls to bounce, not to mention her half-exposed bosom that men found even more fetching. "They are coming this way, Beth!" she whispered. "Do smile, won't you? Perhaps they will beg an introduction!"

"Beg?" she scoffed. "I shouldn't hold my breath if I were you. And do stop behaving like a child eyeing treats!"

Beth turned away again, wishing she could disavow any kinship with Phemie at the moment.

But Phemie's fingers bit into Beth's elbow, yanking her back around. She looked squarely into a dark blue-coated chest. Her gaze traveled up a double row of gold buttons, past a jet-black neckcloth framed by wide buff lapels and high collar. Impossibly wide shoulders supported gold-fringed epaulettes.

Slowly her gaze crept upward. His strong chin bore the trace of a cleft and his sensuous mouth stretched into a gentle smile. His brown eyes flashed with merriment.

She immediately lowered her eyes. A mistake to be sure. He wore immaculate breeches, fitted to his lower limbs like a layer of whitewash, leaving little to the imagination and much to stir forbidden thoughts.

Beth rapidly jerked her attention up again where it landed on his mouth. Sweet heaven, where shouldn't she look next?

The mouth moved. "Miss Goodson, I would know

you anywhere. Please forgive my forwardness, but since we were once well acquainted..."

Beth felt her face heat and knew it to be red as fox-fire. "Sir, I believe you have me at a disadvantage."

She did remember which was which, but an introduction would certainly be the proper thing after so many years. She had not seen either of them since she was thirteen, but there was no mistaking they were the Keiths, dark hair, dimples and all.

"Please offer me your hand, sweet friend," he whispered, "else one of these formidable dowager watchdogs will toss me out on my ear. It's Jack. Jack Keith."

She stuck out her hand. He took it and bowed over it, raising it nearly to his lips. So long he held it, Beth had to pull it from his grasp. "Do not presume! Lieutenant, is it?"

"Correct, and no presumption intended, my dear. I do know you well enough to owe you a hair ornament if I'm not mistaken. Some years overdue, I admit, but restitution is certain, never fear."

He smiled so charmingly, she had to return it. "Welcome home, sir."

She noticed Phemie was already engaged in spirited conversation with the other Keith, Colin. The earl. Apparently someone had provided her the requisite introduction and given her permission to gush. Or perhaps that brother was simply as audacious as this one.

Beth could hardly blame her cousin for pursuing

the man. Phemie hadn't a farthing to her name and lived entirely upon the charity of Beth's father. Since looks were Phemie's only fortune, she obviously meant to spend them well. No one knew better than Beth how her cousin dreaded returning to a life of genteel poverty, which she eventually would do if she did not marry wealth. Phemie had a good and kind heart, even if she did allow desperation to guide the affairs of it.

Jack took Beth's arm and gained his brother's attention. "Look whom I have discovered, Colin! Remember the Jollit's lawn party when we were lads? The jam cakes we appropriated? Here is our lookout."

"Ah, yes! And you never peached on us, did you?"

Beth curtsied. "It is true I never told, my lord. Mainly because I was enlisted to aid you in the crime and shared the spoils." She inclined her head toward Jack, then Phemie. "Lieutenant Lord Keith, I do not believe you have met my cousin, Miss Euphemia Meadows."

"Miss Meadows." Jack reached out, took Phemie's hand and did the pretty.

Beth shot Colin a look of censure. "I see that you have already met her, my lord."

He smiled without a trace of guilt for the social infraction and turned the subject altogether. "Now, now, a fellow conspirator must dispense with lordings and call me Colin."

"I must offer you my congratulations, Earl Whitworth. *Colin*," she added reluctantly. "Though I must say I was grieved to hear of your uncle's recent death. Oh, and your cousin passed on recently, as well, did he not? How awful for you both."

"How kind of you to say so," he replied, obviously not terribly grieved himself.

The musicians began to play and distracted him. "If you would excuse us, I should very much like to dance with Miss Meadows. Later, we must catch up on the happenings Jack and I have missed being away all these years."

"If you wish it, my lord," she said, not feeling the slightest inclination to renew her acquaintance with the new earl, but unwilling to be impolite.

"Would you care to dance?" Jack asked her.

Not for an instant did she think she could do so without stumbling all over his shiny black shoes. He made her feel shaky, ill-at-ease. "No, thank you. It's too warm in here for any sort of exercise."

She popped open her fan and put it in motion without any thought to the blasted language of it. Did that mean *go away* or *come hither*? Uncertain, she held it still again.

"Fresh air is what you need," he told her. "Come to the terrace with me."

"Unchaperoned?" she asked, hoping to avoid going without hurting his feelings. She hated feeling so unsettled.

He smiled reassuringly. "Oh, there are enough people out there we shouldn't cause a stir. It is a beautiful night for November. Quite warm. Colin and I must have brought the weather with us from the Continent."

Beth relented. "So you came here directly from the war?"

"Not precisely. Colin and I fought with the Thirteenth Light Dragoons at Waterloo, but since Napoleon surrendered, we have been billeted near Paris. When finally notified of our cousin's death, we took leave to come home, of course."

She strolled out with him, drawing her thin cashmere shawl over her shoulders, looking up at the stars and asking the occasional question about his service under Wellington. He answered, making light of his adventures there. Beneath his jollity, however, Beth detected a note of strain in speaking of his time at war and suspected he had suffered to some extent.

"Obviously, your brother's duties are set in stone, but will you retain your commission?" she inquired.

"No, I plan to take up civilian life again now that the war is at an end. Try my hand at something else."

"And what will that be?" she asked conversationally, well aware that gentlemen adored talking about themselves. Lesson number one in how to get on with the opposite gender.

He surprised her. "Enough of my dreary existence.

What of you, Beth? I may call you so, mayn't I? We've known one another for decades, after all."

"Decades?" she asked, pretending to be highly put out with him. "Sir, I've scarcely lived more than two of them. And I only met you once or twice in passing."

"More than twice," he argued. "And last time we *passed,* I snagged your pretty satin bow and tied it 'round the neck of Uncle's favorite hound. That's a solid background for intimate friendship if you ask me!"

Beth laughed with him. While she did not wish to wed, she saw no harm in enjoying his company for a short while. "Beth, it is, then, Jack. If you promise to replace my bow."

"It was blue, as I remember. I should have kept it as a token." His large, white-gloved hand reached up and brushed one of her black curls off her forehead. He did it so quickly, she hadn't time to recoil from the too familiar gesture. "May I see you again?" he asked. "Perhaps tomorrow?"

Now he *was* presuming, she thought, and decided she must squelch his interest before it took hold. She wasn't deluding herself that his interest grew out of any real attraction. She *did* have a decent dowry that he would be aware of, and he *was* soon to be unemployed. "Lieutenant—"

"Jack," he reminded her.

"Jack. You had best know from the outset that I

have no inclination to accept the suit of any gentleman, no matter how dedicated he might prove or how well I know him. I have decided never to marry, you see, and my decision is quite firm."

He shrugged. "I don't recall proposing, but your refusal is duly noted. Few ladies would run grasping at a man of my poor circumstance anyway."

"Wait and see," Beth advised with a wry smile. If Jack Keith believed none of the young women here would throw themselves at his feet now that he was available, then he must never look in his mirror to shave. "However, your circumstance has nothing to do with my decision. Please do not think so."

"Then could we perhaps renew our friendship if I promise not to deluge you with flowers out of season or write odes to your eyebrows? All I'd like is to drive you through the park tomorrow afternoon. Can't you spare me an hour or so?" He winked to encourage her and set her at ease. It did in a way.

"I suppose I might. So long as you realize this is *only* a rekindling of friendship, nothing more." She granted him a smile of thanks for his understanding.

"I'll contain my disappointment." He took her hand in his and held it. "Now that's settled, tell me why you are so determined to languish on the vine. Some foolish fellow break your heart?"

Relaxed and satisfied she had made her point, Beth answered readily. "I will not marry a titled gentleman and my father would never allow me to wed anyone not so encumbered."

"Encumbered?" he asked with a curious chuckle.

"That is how I view it. Look around you, Jack. Everyone is so caught up in their own importance, they have no thought for others less fortunate. The men strut about in Lords, making policy that benefits only themselves and their kind. Their wives are so committed to attending and providing entertainments, they scarcely have time to serve their primary function as broodmares. That sort of life is not for me."

"You were born to it. How differently would you live?" he asked, seeming keenly interested in her answer.

"I would try to make a difference in the world instead of wasting a fortune on the latest fashions, pouring tea and exclaiming over the latest *on dit*."

He considered her declaration for a moment, as if he truly cared about it, then asked, "And what does the estimable Baron Goodson think of this ambition of yours? Not much, I'd wager."

Beth sighed. "You would win, too. Father grows more adamant each day that I marry. Small wonder after financing four seasons for me. He always threatens to drag me bodily to London if I won't come willingly, so I do come to keep peace between us. This time, he has even chosen a man for me."

"Oh? Whom did he choose, if I may ask?"

"Arthur Harnell, third baron of that name. Do you know him?"

Jack's brows drew together in a frown. "I do. He attended school with Colin and me. A dreadful bully. You'd do well to stick to your resolve with regard to him, Beth. I doubt he would make a good husband for anyone. Shall I rid you of him?" Looking half serious, he ran a hand over the pommel of his gleaming dress sword.

She beamed up at him, thoroughly charmed by his concern. Jack would be a great friend. "Thank you for the offer, but I can dissuade him myself."

"You'll need funding to assume the life you plan, Beth. A wealthy husband could provide that."

"But *would* he?" she asked with a sad smile. "If I marry, not only will my husband's wealth be his alone, my own money will become his, too. If I remain a spinster, at least I may spend my inheritance from my grandmother as I see fit."

"You are naive if you believe you can cure the ills of the world, Beth. There will always be the extremely rich and the very poor. That is the way of things."

"I know that. But suppose everyone who possessed the means willingly took it upon themselves to make a difference in the lives of as many unfortunates as they could comfortably afford. Do you not think everyone's lot would improve?"

"Possibly, but sadly that will never happen."

"Certainly not if I wed some fine lord who would trap me where I cannot make my own small effort."

Jack looked thoughtful. "Do you include Whitworth in your low estimation of these fine lords? If so, I think you unfair."

"Look at him," Beth said, gesturing to the glass doors of the ballroom. "Already he is reveling in all the attention. Do not think he will escape his role, Jack. You will soon see a change in how he treats you if you have not already done so."

"I disagree, but I see your mind is made up. So how many poor souls have you chosen to improve in your fantastical project?"

"Four, I think. Perhaps more, depending upon the amount due me when I receive my inheritance. If," she added, "I can evade Father's plan for me until then." She had grown almost desperate to do so.

"Then we must do something to remedy your situation. At least divert your father's intentions." He suddenly grinned and exclaimed, "You could wed me, you know. I would be happy to let you spend your inheritance, and your dowry, as you will."

She laughed. "I applaud your sense of humor, Jack, and appreciate your attempt to lighten my mood."

"I am quite serious, Beth. I have money. In fact, I should confess that I—"

Beth interrupted. "Thank you for the gesture, but I shall inherit from my grandmother when I reach twenty-five. That should be enough if I go carefully. I am thoroughly resolved now not to wed, and am well content with my lot as spinster. If only I can put off Father's plans until my birthday."

"When is that?" he asked, frowning.

"The fifteenth of January."

Beth could see by his expression that he truly wished to help and was pondering some way to do it. How troubled he looked.

Suddenly a plan dawned on her that might benefit them both. "Tell me, Jack, are you set on courting anyone in particular over the holidays?"

"I had thought that I would court *you*, but you've quite disabused me of that notion. What do you have in mind?" he asked.

"Those plays you and Colin used to get up for our entertainment, do you recall them?"

"Of course I do. We took turnabout at villain and hero. I'm hardly surprised those raucous spectacles stand out in your mind. You took part in one or two yourself, didn't you?" He shook one finger at her. "Yes, you played the faerie queen and Tim Bartholomew captured you from beside the wading pool to hold you hostage. You screamed bloody murder and almost got him whipped before we explained the farce. Brilliant bit of acting."

"Would you like us to arrange another? As in crying off a betrothal?"

"Whose betrothal would that be?" he asked, with a definite glimmer of interest.

"Ours!" she declared with a laugh. "You'll be free of females grasping the coattails of the earl's handsome brother and I shall shed the dreadful Arthur Harnell. At least until Christmas or perhaps the Twelfth Night revel when we shall end it all with high drama for all to hear and see."

"How scandalous!"

Beth grew even more certain it would serve. "Surely by that time, Harnell will have turned his interest elsewhere. I shall inherit Grandmama's money a few days later, which will solve my problem, and you will be free to go your merry way!"

Jack worried his chin, his sensuous lips working as Beth watched him play the notion through his mind.

Beth held her breath, afraid he would find some flaw in the plan. "Well?"

He abruptly dropped to one knee right there on the terrace, grasped her hand and raised his voice. "My darling Miss Goodson."

Conversations ceased and eyes turned their way. A few of the couples strolling about quickly drew nearer to see what was happening. Beth placed a palm to her throat and answered, "Sir?"

"I am agonized with love for you. Take pity!"

"How so?" she asked loudly, quelling her embarrassment, reminding herself that, as the great Shakespeare once said, *the play was the thing.*

"You *must* agree to marry me. Else I shall return to war a broken man, uncaring of a life without you."

"Jack, the war is over," she whispered through unmoving lips.

"Surely the thought counts," he whispered back.

She covered her mouth with her free hand to catch her laughter, knowing that, to others, she appeared to be aghast at the fervor of his avowal.

"Well, answer me!" he rasped under his breath.

Beth sighed theatrically. "Oh, sir, you do me such honor. How on earth could I *ever* refuse?"

He kissed her gloved hand with passion, then rose abruptly to his feet and pressed another kiss upon her brow.

"Lips would be better," she murmured.

"That would thoroughly put you beyond the pale. Now or never, what do you say?"

"Lips," she hissed, "and hurry while we have the audience."

His mouth claimed hers with a zeal that put any thoughts of play-acting right out of her dizzied head.

A scant hour later Jack climbed into the crested carriage behind his brother and collapsed against the soft leather of the button-tufted seats. It was a grand conveyance, he thought, for transporting two scapegraces who probably didn't deserve it. But then, neither had their uncle and cousin, and someone had to ride in the damned thing.

He flicked a finger over the base of the gilded lantern attached to the wall, Beth's opinion of lords and their self-serving ways preying on his mind. "Think we'll get used to all this?"

"Undoubtedly. I'm rather attached already, if you want the truth. You might play hell reclaiming it," Colin informed him, wearing the haughty earl face he had donned for the occasion.

Jack smiled. "I appreciate your coming to my aid this way. You do it so well. Better than I could have done." He immediately fell serious at the thought. "Colin, do you want the title? I'm certain we could devise a way—"

"Good God, no! Tonight was quite enough, thank you very much. I confess I had nightmares our pretense might stretch out for weeks before you found someone suitable to marry." He tugged off his gloves and tossed them aside. "Now you're as good as shackled, I can lay down this cursed role and let you have it."

"Not yet," Jack said. "The betrothal's a ruse." At Colin's look of stunned disbelief, he explained the plan Beth had devised. "She doesn't know it is I who has inherited. She swears she won't take a noble husband. Or any husband at all, for that matter. This may take time, but I can maneuver best if you keep up the charade a while longer."

"The devil you say! You're mad not to tell her the truth. Surely she wouldn't refuse *you?*"

"Actually, I did propose, but she thought it was a jest. Beth only wants a friend at this stage of the game. She made that very clear," Jack said, recalling her words about marriage. "She intends to remain unwed. I intend to change her mind. I need to make her love me."

"Maybe I will accept your offer to make the switch permanent," Colin said with a grimace. "I don't believe you have the wits to hold your hat, much less the damned title."

Jack ignored the censure and slapped Colin on the knee. "I cannot believe my luck. Found her on our first night out."

"Well, don't expect me to keep this going forever. I only promised to free you up until you located exactly the right woman to wed, one not after your wealth and a coronet. You were right to fear interference in a search. Those ambitious mamas were all over me, not to mention that little pudding-pated Euphemia. What unabashed gall, that girl!"

Jack wiggled his brows. "Methinks thou doth protest too much, old son. You showed quite an interest."

Colin shrugged and sighed. "Yes, but she's forward

as any lightskirt." The fact seemed to bother him, but he soon brightened. "Could be she's worth a tup or two, now that I think of it. Perhaps I will give her a go."

"As if that thought just occurred. But you can't follow through," Jack warned. "She's to be one of the family if I play my hand correctly."

"And she will promptly deal Bethany out in favor of herself if she gets wind of our trick. I'm sorely tempted to spill the beans just to watch the fun."

Jack sat up straight and frowned at him. "You gave me your word. Just until I'm gazetted as earl. Six weeks, no more. Then the news will out. By that time, matters will be settled for good. Beth will be mine."

Colin rolled his eyes. "All right, all right. But I want the hunting box in Scotland if I go through with this. And," he added perversely, shaking a finger, "that set of pistols Uncle Martin left."

"Done. But not a word of this until I've won her."

"You selected her rather quickly, Jack," Colin said, a note of worry in his voice. "Almost the moment we walked into the place, she caught your eye and you barely spoke to anyone else. It is so unlike you to purchase the first hat you try on."

"Only if it proves to be a perfect fit and is precisely what I want," Jack argued. "And what is this with you and hats tonight?"

Colin waved that away and continued to bait him. "She's not even the height of fashion, y'know. Blondes such as her cousin are considered the ideal of beauty these days."

"Though I find her lovely, I did not select Bethany for her looks alone. She's strong and strong-minded, that one. Loyal. Trained to perfection, I'll wager. Countess material. A good head on her shoulders."

"Nice shoulders they are, I must admit," Colin commented. "But I still say you might have looked further just to be sure. This is for life, Jack, not a night at the theater."

"She is the one," Jack insisted. Colin would never understand the force that dragged Jack across the ballroom with but one thought in mind. He wasn't certain he understood it himself. But when he had seen Bethany Goodson, he had known immediately she was the right choice. The only choice.

"Well, so long as you don't commence prating on about love," Colin warned. "We both know you better than that."

"So we do, but love can come later. It will, I believe. I like her enormously." More so than he would admit to Colin at the moment. More, even, than he wished to admit to himself. But somehow Jack felt obliged to ease his brother's mind. He was a part of this, after all.

"If I had not been acquainted with Bethany beforehand, I might have taken things more slowly. But I do know her. You know her, too." He hesitated to ask, but knew he must. "Do you have any valid objection to Beth?"

Colin shrugged and grinned. "None comes to mind, except that you won't allow me to tup her cousin."

Jack laughed with him, now eager to expound on his choice. "Beth will help me whip the estate into its former shape. See if she won't. She's passionate about things. Compassionate, too. Though she is a bit idealistic, even that quality speaks well for her. She isn't like many ladies of her class. Beth's very caring."

Colin hummed, glancing out the window of the carriage, acting bored. "Caring, and she kisses well. I see."

Jack ignored the tease and leaned forward to make his point. "That caring attitude of hers actually settled the decision for me, Colin."

"And the kiss. Don't forget the kiss," Colin said.

"That, too. Don't discount the ability to show affection when it comes to a wife. And think what a mother she'd make!" Jack discovered he liked thinking about that. He imagined Beth's rounded body, Beth holding a tiny babe, the two of them gamboling on the lawn with a child. "Yes, I should like my children to have a mother's affection, not just the bare tolerance you and I endured from ours. And from Aunt Florence. Do you ever recall being hugged when you were frightened? Tucked into bed and wished sweet dreams? I *want* that."

"For your little 'uns or yourself?" Colin asked,

laughing. "As I recall, we hugged each other when something scared us. As for the tucking in, I much doubt either of us would have stood for it. We always fell asleep where we ran out of mischief and not always in a proper bed. Speaking for myself, I had a boisterous good time growing up, thank you very much. I wouldn't change a moment of it."

"Knowing how you avoid the sentimental, I'll forgive you the lie," Jack said. "Though I will tell you I doubt you'll find much true affection or sentimentality in *Cousin* Euphemia."

"Ah, but she does have such beautiful...*qualities,*" Colin remarked, while his hands made a graphic gesture to describe her bosom. "And I daresay she's sentimental over some things. Don't imagine that I'm struck to the heart by her, however. She'll abandon me like a boat with a hole in it once I turn from prince to toad, so let's not delay that transformation any longer than necessary, agreed?"

Privately, Jack did begin to worry. For all Colin's savoir faire, he was no more immune to cupid's dart than any other soul. It would be a shame if he came to care for that cousin of Beth's.

Even on very short acquaintance, anyone not totally blinded by Euphemia's appearance could see at a glance there was nothing but avarice in those pretty blue eyes. Her interest in Colin was all too obvious. She had set her cap for the brother she thought was the earl.

"I'm trusting you'll watch out for yourself in this," Jack said.

"Don't I always?" Colin replied.

No, never, Jack thought with a weary exhalation. Even knowing Euphemia's intent and its certain outcome, Colin had not avoided her tonight. Of course, he truly might have something a bit less honorable than marriage in mind. That would never do, given she was Beth's cousin.

It could prove devilishly awkward if Jack's own brother were responsible for deflowering one of the family. But it would almost be worse if Colin were seriously smitten with her, then lost her because he was the younger brother.

"Keep in mind what she's after. She'll learn the truth eventually, and you'll be devastated if you allow yourself to become attached," Jack warned. "She'll be furious with you."

As if Bethany won't be, too. Jack dismissed the voice of conscience. When all was revealed, Beth would understand. By that time she would love him. He was sure of it.

Almost.

Chapter Two

JACK knew there would be no rumors to leak the identity of the new Earl Whitworth, not for weeks anyway. Eventually the news sheets would get hold of it, but that would take a while. He had yet to be gazetted by his peers. Birth records must be confirmed and those—which were in York—must be searched out and verified.

Though he now wished he had not concocted this harebrained scheme, he was saddled with it. At least until he convinced Beth he was not like the men she had refused thus far.

He and Colin were a scant eleven months apart and no one of their acquaintance here in London knew their exact ages. With little effort at disguise, they looked enough alike to be taken for twins. Strictly for amusement, they had played upon it many times while growing up.

They had gone off to school at the same time, entered the military together and were seldom seen apart from one another. Orphaned at four and five, they had come all the way from York to the Cotswolds to live under their uncle's negligent supervision. Jack doubted his uncle and aunt ever noticed which boy was the elder. Or even cared which. They'd had their heir.

Aunt Florence had died long ago. Cousin Hubert, seven years older than Jack, had been in line to inherit the title. But he had died of apoplexy only a month after Uncle Martin succumbed to brain fever. Hubert's death left Jack the unexpected heir.

Colonel Doherty had arrived at Abreville near Paris to assume command and had informed them of the news. Since the war was over and the duties of occupation boring after all the excitement, he and Colin had been glad to come home.

For months the earldom had stood vacant and waiting. According to the solicitors, the estate, Whitfield in the Cotswolds, was a neglected shambles. Only the London town house, where both Uncle Martin and Hubert had died, remained in anything like livable condition. The fortune was still intact, thank heavens, but obviously no one had made use of the wealth when it came to maintenance.

The Whitworth solicitors were made aware that Jack was the eldest, of course, but he had ordered them to keep the entire business of the succession private. So there was no one to contradict Colin and him if they played at this pretense. And they would do so, he decided, until his betrothal to Bethany became real. Until she grew to love him.

"No one else will do," he muttered, half to himself. "She is the one."

"Peculiar of you to be so adamant about a particular woman, no matter how charming," Colin observed with a superior sniff. "Always before, you stood apart, played the prize and simply waited for women to approach *you*. And you acted as if you never much cared whether they did so or not."

Jack admitted that was true. The tactic had worked most of the time. "There is too much riding on this, Colin. I mean to have her and I dare not leave anything to whim or fancy."

It was also true, he reflected, that Colin had always been the one to pursue a woman, to form the serious attachment, and to require a great deal of brandy and commiseration to get over it when things went awry. Again Jack thought of the entrancing Euphemia and her pert little bosom that had heaved so charmingly under his brother's admiring gaze tonight.

Perhaps a word or two of further warning might be in order. "Look, Colin, don't go making a cake of yourself this time, will you? I won't have the time to console you."

Colin laughed too heartily. "Get stuffed, Jack. The Goodson chit has a fork in you already, so don't be shaking a finger at me and talking of cakes."

Beth had spent two days and nights listening to Phemie extol the virtues of Lord Colin. If her cousin was not besotted, she gave a good impression. However, they both knew better.

"You are making my head ache with all this chatter," Beth mumbled. She sniffed impatiently as she evened the loops of the satin bow just beneath her half-exposed bosom. "I swear, dressed as we are, we shall both come down with colds in the chest."

Euphemia edged Beth from in front of the mirror and promptly tugged her own neckline even lower. "Well, you needn't be so eager to display your wares as I must. *You* have a betrothed now."

Beth glared at her cousin. "I told you, Phemie, it was all for show. I cannot marry Jack. Primary reasons aside, he's no more interested in a wife than I am a husband. We might as well not have bothered with it all. Father's withholding approval. He is ignoring the scene Jack and I constructed on Lord Randolph's terrace. He even refused to admit Jack when he called yesterday."

Beth felt badly about that. Word might be out by tonight that Baron Goodson thought Jack beneath consideration. No man greeted that sort of slight with equanimity. She only hoped Jack wouldn't cry off their agreement of mutual protection.

"All the same, you've done your part on the parade field, haven't you?" Phemie said. "Whitworth will be inspecting the troops again tonight and I mean to rise to his expectations!" She preened, lifting one arm in parody of a salute while she inhaled to enhance the thrust of her breasts.

She should measure up, Beth thought with a smile. With that gown of ivory shot-silk flowing over her curves and her blond tresses caught up with faux pearls, she might have been the inspiration for a Grecian statue. If Jack's brother didn't fall over his own feet and eventually land on his knees, it wasn't for lack of planning on Phemie's part.

"It wouldn't hurt you to use a bit of padding, you know," Phemie said with a sage appraisal of Beth's comparatively modest endowments.

Then she squinted at Beth's face, a true concession since she swore squinting caused lines about the eyes. Phemie's one flaw was her farsightedness, an affliction of the eyes that apparently did not extend to her thought processes. "Try a touch of rouge, at least," she advised.

"Pale is all the rage," Beth told her, laughing. Modesty aside, Beth knew she looked well enough. She wore soft blue China crepe accented with a darker blue satin ribbon that matched the slender ones wound within her hair. Her filigree necklace and ear bobs with sapphire chips complemented her ensemble nicely, she thought. For all that she was no great beauty like Phemie, Beth did feel rather pretty for a spinster.

She pinched her cheeks and raked her teeth over her lips to redden them. "There. I am ready."

Phemie rolled her subtly kohl-enhanced eyes in resignation and tugged on her gloves as she left the room. "I swear, you will not even *try* to improve yourself."

"And you overly do." Beth scooped up her reticule and followed Phemie down the hall to the wide staircase.

"Lord Harnell is bound to be there tonight. Do you anticipate trouble over the betrothal?" Phemie asked.

"My hope is that he will immediately find another to plague," Beth said. "I am counting on it."

She could not help but remember Jack's reaction when she had told him of her father's choice of suitor for her. She would see him tonight if he attended the Duke of Cranstonbury's affair. Beth hoped he would so that she could apologize for her father.

Also, it would be comforting if she need not come face-to-face with Harnell alone. But what if matters turned ugly despite Jack's presence by her side? Or because of it?

"Phemie, you don't believe Lord Harnell will cause a scene, do you?"

Phemie laughed. "Just see that he doesn't corner

you anywhere. He might be handsome, but Harnell *is* a lecher. I've thought more than once I might have to slap his face."

Beth looped her arm through her cousin's as they reached the foyer to wait for her parents. "Has he done something to offend you, cousin?"

"Indeed! He *leers,*" Phemie confessed, dragging out the word and leaning close.

"I shouldn't wonder. You usually invite it." She nudged Phemie, cutting off their conversation to welcome her father and mother.

Mother was perfectly beautiful as always, and as inscrutable as she was lovely. She never criticized or admonished Beth. That had been left to the nurses and later governesses. And now to Father, who took the task to heart. Though he was not unkind, he was firm and uncompromising.

Baron Goodson put much store by appearance and was agreeably generous with his praise when the females under his roof lived up to his standards. However, he also liked to believe he made law as to behavior within the family circle. For the most part, he did. The primary exception being Beth's refusal to capitulate on the issue of choosing a husband.

Accordingly he now issued the expected warning. "Bethany, should you make a spectacle of yourself again, you'll not attend another soiree until next summer, do you understand me?"

"Yes, Father," she said. "You will banish me to the country and I shall never have a moment's fun until next season."

Pray, let him do so, she thought, attempting to look dismayed by the prospect. Going home to the country was her dearest wish. She was needed there.

She happened to notice that Phemie was not pretending dismay, but actually hated the thought of leaving London. Beth felt guilty that her cousin's attempt to catch herself an earl might be dashed out of hand before she got it under way.

"Just so!" her father affirmed. "I shall pack you off in an instant!" He concluded his threat with a sharp nod. "Now let us go. I have never held with this *fashionably late* conceit. Promptness is a virtue. Remember that, my girls." He turned and gestured for Stokes to open the door for them.

Beth and Phemie pulled a face at one another while Mother steadfastly ignored the byplay.

Jack had pondered all afternoon on how he could win the favor of Beth's father without revealing the truth about himself. He could hardly court and convince Beth to make their betrothal real if the old man never allowed them together.

"Do you see her?" Colin asked, peering almost desperately over the heads of those already in attendance.

"Eager, are we?" Jack asked as he straightened his

cravat and adjusted his left lapel. Tonight was his last time in uniform. He figured this second public appearance would set in everyone's mind which brother had inherited without actually having to lie other than by inference.

Both Colin and he had been careful to introduce themselves using only the family surname of Keith. Neither was yet used to being addressed as *lord*, though it was quite appropriate for both, even given the ruse they played. Colin was heir until Jack fathered a son.

"There!" Colin exclaimed. "I see them. Hurry." Without a pause, he headed directly for the opposite corner of the room. Jack followed, though he would have wished to wait, meander a bit and see how many swains might be buzzing about his quarry. He liked to reconnoiter, size up the opposition, while Colin was prone to charge indiscriminately. Jack couldn't count the times he'd had to drag him back and out of danger. This might very well prove to be one of those times.

"Good evening, Lieutenant," Beth said to him when he approached her. She wore a wary expression. Her mother stood not two yards away, but her back was turned to them. Why did Beth seem so apprehensive?

"Must we begin all over again? I do declare I thought we were past all this formality." He lifted her hand and kissed it soundly through her glove, not bothering to keep the gap betwixt fabric and lips as was proper.

She snatched it out of his grip, looking right and left to see whether they were observed. "Jack, behave!" she said under her breath.

"What's wrong? Our plans haven't changed, have they?"

"No, but Father is unhappy with me," she confessed, wearing a false smile for the benefit of anyone watching. "He threatened to simply send me out of town—which I would prefer, actually—but at the moment I worry he might proceed with Harnell, encourage his suit even more intensely. They're speaking together at this very moment." She cut her gaze in their direction.

Jack smiled, too. "I see now that I must get this fellow out of the picture once and for all. Leave Harnell to me."

"Nothing rash, Jack," she warned, risking censure by placing her hand on his forearm. "Please."

"What, no duel? I promise to dispatch him neatly. Perhaps even allow him to live, though he won't thank me for it when I'm through with him."

"Jack!" she groaned, the smile gone.

"But that's not a chore for tonight, is it? Come, dance with me, dear heart."

"I dislike bringing it to your attention, *dear heart*, but there's not yet any music."

"Then hurry away with me to the gardens. Soothe my savage breast with the sound of your dulcet tones against my ear. Sweet music enough, I do swear, to set me dancing to your tune forever."

"Stand away from me before you get yourself tossed out!" she hissed. "You are impossible!"

"Quite possible, I promise."

"Possible that you shall be tossed!" she returned.

"Absolutely, but not before they feed us. Where lies the food?" He took her hand without awaiting answer and ushered her toward the next room where the buffet should be. On the way, he caught Colin's eye and gestured for him to follow. As he had feared, the eager Euphemia was in tow.

That mattered little in the immediate scheme of things. At the moment Jack only wanted to remove Bethany from the proximity of her parents and ply his suit for a while.

A half hour to an hour of that endeavor, and then he would corner Baron Goodson to see what might be done to establish an accord with the man.

Unless, of course, Beth proved right and he was thrown out on his ear for an infraction of manners before he accomplished his goals. It was proving devilishly hard to keep his hands off of her. She was delightfully saucy, his Beth.

They appropriated one of the white-clothed tables and sat with Euphemia and Colin. Those two immediately retreated into a small world of their own, making sheep's eyes at one another while Jack tried to ease Beth's anxiety. After a second glass of punch and a sampling of the buffet, she had calmed to the point of discussing their betrothal.

"Father certainly will not announce it in writing," she warned, keeping her voice low so that no one around them could hear. "He doesn't even recognize it. How will we go on with this if he gives the betrothal no credence?"

This seemed a perfect opportunity to leave so he could amend the situation. "I shall try to get him alone and speak with him."

Her beautiful mouth rounded as she frowned. "Oh, Jack, I don't know..."

"Keep these two company while I attempt it," he said as he rose. "And save me a dance when the music begins. Three of them. That should send the flags up."

"I daresay," she agreed. "We shouldn't need a public announcement after that."

Jack left her there and made his way back to the ballroom. No sooner had he stepped inside than he felt a strong grip on his arm. He turned to see Harnell scowling at him. "Come outside," the man ordered.

"Unhand me if you want those fingers to remain intact," Jack said pleasantly. At his meaningful look of warning, Harnell let go.

Jack calmly brushed at his sleeve and proceeded

toward the doors opening out to the gardens. It was rather chilly out tonight so they were virtually alone. Only two couples strolled the paths some distance away, fully occupied and oblivious of anyone else.

He faced Harnell. "Speak your piece, then I shall speak mine."

"Leave Bethany Goodson alone." Harnell spat the words.

"Warning me off my own fiancée? How positively gauche of you, but then you always were lacking in good sense when it came to—"

Harnell's fist almost reached its mark when Jack caught it, squeezed sharply and felt a bone pop.

He smiled at his opponent's cry of pain and observed him grasping his damaged thumb. "Bit of advice, old man. Keep the thumb on the outside of the fist. It's only out of joint. Next time you could get it broken if you aren't careful."

"I'll kill you, Keith!" Harnell rasped through gritted teeth.

"Not unless your aim improves." Jack dropped the casual tone and got serious. "Abandon your suit of Miss Goodson and this stops here. Do not and you may expect considerably more than a dislocated digit. Now get the hell out of here and do not let me see you again. My patience is gone."

Sweat stood out on Harnell's brow, he was breathing in gasps and his eyes were narrowed to mere slits.

Jack gave him credit for prudence when he said nothing more. Yet he didn't leave.

"This conversation is finished, I believe," Jack told him. "You may go now."

He waited until the seething Harnell had rejoined the assembly within, then followed. The man was nowhere to be seen. Prudent, indeed.

Jack searched the ballroom for Baron Goodson, and saw him exiting alone, ostensibly to find a game of cards in the adjoining chamber set up for such.

"My lord, a word with you?" he said as he caught up to him.

"I have nothing to say to you, Keith." The baron continued across the room.

"Whitworth has a definite interest in your daughter," Jack confided. And that did the trick. Baron Goodson stopped in his tracks and gave him full attention.

"The *earl*, you say?" Curiosity animated his features, then suspicion. "But it was *you* who—"

"Could we find someplace private, sir?" Jack asked politely.

Having a baron such as Harnell sue for the precious Bethany's hand was one thing, but catching an earl's regard was quite another. It must be every father's dream, marrying a daughter up in society. How strange to be the *up*, Jack thought.

Personally, he felt it was ridiculous, allowing so much importance in a man's societal rank, but he knew it counted heavily with a man such as Goodson, especially one seeing to his daughter's future.

Jack had known he might have to use the title, though he wasn't quite prepared to reveal that he was the earl. Bethany was not ready for the truth yet. She mistrusted any man with a title and power. The poor little dear seemed convinced that the loftier a man was, the more he would be set against her philanthropic plans. And she could not afford to wed a man without means, such as she believed him to be.

Jack admitted he probably didn't deserve her. But he would have her anyway. With that objective in mind, he followed where Goodson led and they soon entered a small parlor or morning room just off the conservatory.

The baron promptly drew out a cigar and began fiddling with one end of it. Patiently, Jack waited as the baron trimmed, lit and was puffing away on it. Finally the man spoke. "So the earl has an interest, does he?"

"Most assuredly."

His lordship cocked his head to one side and blew out a blue-gray stream of smoke. "Then how is it *you* were the one kissing her and proposing on the terrace at Randolph's place? And don't believe for an instant I haven't noted your brother's salivating over my niece!"

Jack was ready for that. "Well, sir, it is well known about town that your daughter has refused every titled gentleman who has offered for her. How is one to get to know her if she won't let them near? Colin and I figured that if she were attached to me and he pretended a tendre for her cousin, the four of us would naturally go about together and come to know one another quite well."

The baron frowned as he sorted through this. Then he asked, "Are you saying that you are actually keen on Euphemia?"

Jack put on his best imitation of a love-struck expression. "I will say she *is* quite remarkable, sir."

"Humph. Well, I guess she could do worse. Do you have anything to recommend you if Euphemia returns your feelings?"

Zounds, he was getting in deeper by the moment. "This is not a suit for Miss Euphemia's hand, sir. Not yet, and perhaps not at all." Definitely not at all. The thought of it made Jack shudder.

The baron cocked his head, drew on his cigar and nodded. "I understand that, but I won't allow anyone to court my niece if I know he has no prospects at all. There's the off chance something might come of it."

Jack sighed. "I have my back pay, sir, will have the price of my commission shortly, and my brother will share the Whitworth wealth. We plan to manage the estate together, he and I."

"For you are, neither of you, worth much apart, are you? Not trained in managing anything larger than a curricle, I'd wager. Well, I suppose it couldn't hurt to let you squire my girls about for a time. See if you take with 'em." He mused for a few minutes. "Might be a problem. Harnell has pestered me for some time for Bethany's hand. I did vow I'd encourage her to think on it."

"No, sir, you won't want to pursue that. I know the man well and I assure you he would never suit for a daughter of yours. If he presents any protest, I will see to him."

"No, no, let's not be hasty. Suppose Whitworth decides Bethany's not for him? She must have someone to wed who's appropriate, and I swear she's gone through most everyone else who is remotely eligible."

"Suppose I swear to you on my honor that if Miss Bethany can be brought to the altar at all, she will have the title of countess?"

The baron's eyes went wide. "How can you promise such a thing? Whitworth's his own man, surely."

"I speak for him."

"Why does he not speak for himself?"

This was not going quite as smoothly as Jack envisioned. "Well, sir, I am the man of business. I give you my solemn word Whitworth will wed her if she agrees. She is the one for him, but she must be allowed to know him to know this for herself."

The baron waved his cigar around. "All this talk of *knowing*...I trust you don't mean in the biblical sense."

"Good God, no! Sir, I regret if you mistook my

meaning. I—Whitworth has nothing but the utmost respect for Miss Bethany."

Goodson grunted in what passed for a laugh. "Bit of a jest to see what you'd say." He shot Jack a crafty look. "But you be warned, boy. I remember you well from times past when you and that brother of yours made havoc amongst us there in the county. See you don't make a jest of my girls. I am an excellent shot."

"We shall draw up the contracts if you like. Whitworth's offer only wants the full agreement of the lady in question and it's as good as done." Jack stuck out his hand to shake on it.

The baron was slow to respond, but eventually did. "Very well. I shall see to the papers. Shall we agree on terms?"

"Anything you wish in the way of dowry will suit. Our estate is healthy. Your daughter will never want for anything."

"Very well. But if I see any indication either you or your brother has betrayed my trust, I shall have your heads on a plate, Keith, regardless of Whitworth's rank." He stubbed out his cigar, signaling that the interview was over.

Jack accompanied Goodson back to the gathering in the ballroom, then went his own way to find Bethany.

Now he had arranged a way to court her, but regretted the deception necessary to gain the opportunity. If the baron didn't shoot him, Bethany well might once the truth came out.

Jack counted on the supposition that Goodson would willingly accept *any* earl for a son-in-law and forgive the ruse once explained.

His one hope for Bethany's forgiveness would be to make her fall madly in love with him before he had to confess. So much in love that she would accept him title and all.

Sadly, to effect that, he must allow his brother's infatuation with the mercenary Euphemia to continue. That particular attachment was bound to end in disaster, but the die was cast and there was little to be done about it now.

He would simply have to stock up on brandy and prepare Colin as best he could.

Chapter Three

THEY were hardly settled in the barouche and on their way to Hyde Park the next afternoon when the trouble began. Colin took the seat beside Beth while Jack sat with Phemie. It would appear to anyone observing the outing that the brothers had switched the objects of their pursuit. Phemie protested, and Beth was not certain she liked the idea, either. Had they changed their minds?

"I spoke with Baron Goodson last evening," Jack said with a smile. "He is of the opinion the four of us should remain equal friends and not form any particular attachment as yet."

Phemie scoffed and glared at Colin. "Of course, he would suggest that. He wants you for Beth!" Her bottom lip protruded in a pretty pout.

"No, no, I'm sure that is not the case," Colin argued. He looked adoringly at Phemie. "I think, rather, that he would like to place some distance between Jack and Miss Bethany." He turned to smile apologetically at Beth. "Your father can't be all that delighted that you have tossed aside a baron for a soldier, now can he? No doubt he hopes—"

"That she shall have an earl instead! *You!*" Phemie insisted, firmly drawing Colin's attention back to her.

He reached forward, clasped her hand and patted it. "Now, now, take heart. At the first stop, we shall change places, Jack and I. Will that suit you?"

Beth exhaled sharply, impatient with all of them. "I think I shall sit up front with the driver. This deception is altogether too convoluted for my taste."

Jack laughed as if he thought she were joking. "Mine, too, but it was a condition agreed to so that we would be allowed to escort the two of you." He looked quite pointedly at Colin and Phemie, then back at her.

Beth realized that he was doing this as a favor to his brother who was obviously enamored of her cousin. If she refused to play along, Colin would not be able to court Phemie. And worse, Beth admitted to herself, she would appear available again to the likes of Arthur Harnell.

"Uncle doesn't even credit your betrothal to Jack," Phemie declared. "That should tell you something."

"Ah, but the word is out since the evening at Lord Randolph's," Colin assured them. "Even if it is not in print, everyone is talking."

"Then why must we pretend?" Phemie demanded. A perfectly good question, Beth thought. She smiled and cocked her head at Jack, awaiting the answer.

"All we must do is share our dances equally at whatever functions we attend and go about together as a group rather than as two couples. If we do not, Lord Goodson will not allow us to call. Then Bethany most likely will be subjected to more pressure from Harnell and her father."

"And Whitworth will not be allowed to court me, the poor cousin," Phemie surmised.

No one said anything to that. So, in mutual and silent agreement, they proceeded with their ride.

In the fortnight that followed, Beth discovered she rarely minded the arrangement. Lord Colin, with his ready sense of humor, kept them laughing with his constant gibes at his brother. And Jack, a bit more clever and reserved, proved devilishly quick with ideas for entertainment.

They rode together almost every morning, stoicly parading down Rotten Row as if it were summer and they were showing off their latest equine acquisitions. Then they would burst into a gallop, racing across the green and through the trees, reveling in the freedom not possible in warmer weather when there actually were crowds. Even the little season had ended now and attendance in Town had dwindled sharply.

If nothing else, enforced togetherness with Phemie

and Lord Colin prevented Beth's attraction to Jack from getting out of hand. Even so, she often caught herself anticipating his slightest touch. The mere brush of his hand against her back or at her waist sent a thrill of warmth throughout her body.

She had taken to wearing a corset, trying to prevent it, but it was of little help. At least, that was the excuse she used to abandon the stiff, whalebone garment. Most slender women had cast them aside as unnecessary with the French empire fashions. Filmy flowing fabrics and raised waistlines only called for a light chemise that was fitted beneath the bosom and lifted one's chest higher by the straps at the shoulders.

Beth shivered, merely recalling how Jack had once trailed an ungloved finger along the low neckline of her newest Worth creation of delicately embroidered gauze. Though she had brushed his hand away and feigned exasperation, she had been none too swift about doing so. His suggestive smile had her in a tizzy the rest of that night. She seemed to grow more shameless by the day.

At present they were alone again in Lady Raythorn's conservatory and Beth feared Jack had something similar in mind the way those dark eyes of his all but devoured her.

"We should return to the card room," she said, sounding reluctant even to her own ears.

"Not yet," he whispered, his lips very near her ear.

"I went to too much trouble to get you here." His hands slipped 'round her waist and cradled her against him.

"Jack, behave yourself!" she gasped, closing her eyes, relishing the feel of his hands on her. "Where are Phemie and Colin?"

"Heavily into a game of whist, I expect," he said distractedly as he nuzzled her neck with his chin. "Do you care?"

Not really. At the moment she seemed not to have a care in the world save that someone might arrive in this deserted place full of dead plants and interrupt them. "You should not…" She breathed the words only out of convention. *He should. He really should,* she thought as one of his hands cradled her breast and the other slid slowly down the front of her gown. Her very thin, supple gown that molded itself to her body and allowed her to feel every flex of those strong, elegant fingers.

Her blood sang in her veins. Pinwheel lights whirled behind her eyes. She felt certain she could hear her heartbeat in her ears, an irregular rushing sound, growing more and more rapid until something, some foreign noise, intruded.

The door rattled, then squeaked as someone attempted to force it open. Immediately Jack's hands left her. "Hurry. This way," he rasped.

Beth allowed him to push her through a nearby door she had not noticed being there. It opened into the garden and was obviously for the gardener's access and not meant for guests. There stood a small toolshed nearby, almost totally concealed from the rest of the garden by a giant trellis overgrown with ivy. "In here," he said, keeping his voice low as they ducked inside the small building.

"Can we not get to the terrace?" she murmured, terribly afraid someone had noticed their absence at the party and come looking for them.

"Not without being seen if someone is still in the conservatory," he admitted. "We'll wait a bit, then make our way around and come into the ballroom as if we've been strolling through the gardens."

"How long must we wait?" she asked, her question barely audible.

"Long enough for this," he whispered. He turned her in his arms and his mouth met hers with an urgency that surprised her.

He had stolen kisses before. With the exception of the first one the night he proposed, they had been playful, brief, and not meant to incite. This one, Beth thought as she surrendered with lips parted and seeking, definitely had that intent.

Knowing she might never have another chance to explore a kiss this fully, she poured her very soul into it. She met his questing tongue, returned the query with her own and tasted the absolute fullness of desire. Hot rich spiced wine he was, drugging to the mind and dangerous to a spinster's resolve. Beth breathed in his subtle scent. Too subtle, teasing her to identify it, to fill herself with it. With him. She could not get enough.

She buried her fingers in his hair, holding him as if she feared he would abandon her. Smooth as silk, his dark waves closed over and around her hands, a gentle, warm caress.

The brocade of his waistcoat abraded her bosom through the thin pleated gauze of her gown and the silk of her chemise. She felt the tips of her breasts tingle as they pressed tightly to the hardness of his chest. Another hardness moved sinuously against her lower body. She knew instinctively where it belonged, where she wanted it, though no one had ever told her precisely how man and woman came together. Why had no one ever told her that? Or how powerful the need would be?

His mouth left hers and pressed against her ear. "I cannot take you here," he whispered, his voice rife with longing. "I dare not, but I want you, Beth. I want you more than life."

Her breath shuddered out as his heat continued to sear her everywhere they touched. She knew she should speak. She should shove him away and run. But even if she wanted to, which she did not, Beth knew her legs would fold beneath her. She pictured herself a puddle at his feet. This was madness.

"I need you," he rasped, then his tongue traced the shell of her ear and near the opening. Wet heat flooded her entire being and she groaned. "Come to me," he murmured. "Late in the night, come to me." His palms molded the roundness of her hips and pressed her hard against him. "Please." Fire shot through her.

"How…where?" she demanded, her eager words halting, breathless.

For a long time he said nothing. He remained perfectly still, though she knew what the effort cost him by the way his body tensed, the way he deliberately forced air into and out of his lungs.

When he finally spoke she could hear his frustration. She could feel it, hate it, wish it away. "Forgive me," he said, his voice almost normal, though very sad. "We cannot."

"Why?" she demanded before she thought how it would sound. He must think her the veriest wanton in London. Or anywhere else.

In the moonlight through the window she could just detect his smile, a sad smile, as he pulled away enough to look down at her. "Because it would be mad," he said. "Because it would be wrong. Because there is no way to do this and not ruin you forever."

"Yes, there is," she told him, again without any thought past the desire that urged her on. "Not tonight. Tomorrow," she told him, her words all but tripping over her tongue. "At half past eleven in the morning, wait outside Chez Arnaud milliner's shop in your carriage. I shall be alone and wearing a plain gray cloak and a bonnet that conceals my face. Where we are to go from there, you must arrange. And you must have me home by three."

He appeared reluctant as he expelled a harsh sigh.

"It will be all right," she assured him.

"Only if you agree tonight that you will marry me. Otherwise…"

"No!" she said with a short laugh. "You know my views on marriage, Jack. But even if I am to spend my entire future as a spinster, I need not do so as an old maid! I will meet you."

He brushed a curl off her brow and gently kissed where it had lain. "Suppose you like the physical aspect of marriage, will it change those views of yours perhaps?"

"I cannot let it," she told him frankly. "There are too many other considerations. However, I do admit you have made me curious…about things. And we *are* the best of friends." She brushed against him on purpose.

He made a pained sound in his throat and closed his eyes. Then he moved away from her so that they were no longer touching except for the hand that clutched hers. "Until tomorrow," he agreed, somewhat grudgingly. "For now, I had better return you to the ballroom or neither of us might survive your father's wrath past this evening."

They set out for the terrace, but he turned when they were halfway through the dark garden. "Beth, I should apologize."

"Do not dare," she whispered. "Remember, half past eleven."

The next morning Colin was still arguing for the liaison while Jack kept voicing second thoughts. All night Jack had worried about it, so much so that his brother had guessed the cause of his turmoil. They had few, if any secrets, living in each other's pockets since Colin's birth. He provided a good ear if not always sound advice. Jack often accused him of being a conscience whittler. Perhaps that had been what Jack sought in admitting his quandary in the first place, and that troubled him even more.

"I shall have to tell her beforehand," Jack insisted.

"About the title?"

"Yes, and also that I fully intend to change her mind about marrying and that I wish her to marry *me*. And why."

Colin scoffed. "You've already asked her. That's enough, I should think. She will only dig in those pretty heels of hers and become even more adamant about remaining unwed." He smiled slyly and nudged Jack's shoulder with a fist. "Persuade her, man! Make her want it. Make her think it's her idea. You can do it!" He paused a second, then added, "Besides…if there is the possibility of a child…"

Jack frowned. "I swear I can see horns growing out of your head. I do have a bit of honor left, y'know."

Colin laughed. "But you'd toss up her skirts all the same."

"No. No, I shall either tell her the truth—"

"And lose her completely," Colin warned with a firm nod.

"Or I will refuse to compromise her today. Yes, that would be best in any event. What man wants a woman to succumb to him only to satisfy her curiosity?" He threw up a hand for emphasis.

"You want her any way you can have her," Colin said with a barely suppressed laugh. "Admit it."

"I *will* have her, too, but not today. You're right about one thing. It's too soon to tell her about the title. Perhaps in a week or so she'll be ready. I do think she's beginning to more than simply *like* me."

"I should jolly well hope so considering what she suggests you do this morning!" Colin exclaimed as he checked the folds of his cravat in the mirror and smiled at himself. "You can bring her here to the house. I'm going to run up some debts for you about town. Won't be back till late this evening."

Jack shook his head. "No need to stay away. I'm not taking her anywhere but for a long ride in the carriage."

"Dashed inconvenient, tupping an untried maid in a bouncing conveyance." Colin shrugged. "However, do what you must."

"As if you would know anything about tupping in carriages," Jack muttered, "or untried maids, for that matter." He left Colin still grinning at his reflection.

Snow started to fall as he began his outing. The pale gray clouds spat large, lazy flakes that melted as they touched the cobblestones. The weather seemed too warm for any great accumulation, though there would be plenty of mud on the unpaved roads and byways. Jack needed to complete his task of acquiring a wife and return to the estate before winter truly set in. There were people there who would be depending upon him and who must be wondering how they would fare with the new master.

All too swiftly his carriage arrived at the appointed place. Chez Arnaud's appeared to be a modest shop, one of many located on Elvin Street and frequented mostly by the merchant class. Sprigs of ivy and holly with red berries festooned most of the windows. Among the greenery were strewn various items to be sold—tins of tobacco, gaily painted toys, woolen scarves, gloves, and, of course, hats. The places of business looked rather cheerful when compared to the more exclusive shops along Pall Mall with their understated displays.

He sat in the carriage peering out the window for

some time before he saw her emerge from the milliner's carrying a small striped hatbox. Immediately, he opened the door and stepped down to assist her inside.

Only when they were comfortably settled with the shades covering the windows did she throw off the hood of her cloak and smile up at him. "How did you know it was I instead of some shop girl?" she asked with a laugh.

How had he known? There must be hundreds of such women wearing gray cloaks in this part of London. "I know your gait," he explained as he reasoned it out for himself. "The set of your shoulders, the tilt of your head, the way you move. I never even thought to question whether it was you."

"Hmm. Next you'll declare my every motion fascinates you," she said, pretending amusement, though he could feel her quiver of apprehension.

"Just so. But I might have welcomed anyone who marched up to me since I've been waiting so long," he said, teasing her. "Did you have trouble getting here?"

"Not at all," she assured him. "I only thought a bit of a delay would make you more eager to see me. Did it?"

Jack laughed and kissed her hand through the ostrich-skin glove she wore. "Did I not seem eager enough last evening?"

A pretty frown wrinkled her brow. "In a way, but

then you thought better of it, I think. I almost feared you would not meet me." She drew in a deep breath and let it out slowly. "Well then, where are we to go for our tryst?"

He had instructed his driver to seek out streets with little traffic until notified otherwise. Jack slid one arm around her and drew her close. He kissed her forehead. "We must talk about that, Beth."

"Ah, I hear a sharp reluctance in that tone of yours. Have you decided not to, um, enlighten me?"

"Not unless you would make an honest man of me in the near future. You must say you love me," he dared.

"I love you," she replied in a very matter-of-fact tone of voice. "But there's no need to marry."

Jack sighed. This seemed a losing battle, but he was far from surrender. "How can you say you love me and in the same breath deny my proposal?"

All frivolity disappeared from her expression. "Oh, Jack, you are the dearest man I know. But I have told you I cannot marry. There are too many reasons to list."

"Fear of connubial duty is not among those, I take it?"

She shrugged. "No. Actually, that is the only benefit that I can imagine. I have money, which I intend to manage myself. Now tell the truth. If we wed, you would be the master of it all, would you not?"

"Legally," he admitted, "though I would not touch a pence of it. You would be free to do as you like with what you bring to the union."

"There will *be* no union," she stressed. "Suppose I decided to toss my entire fortune away to poor orphans or such, would you consider it good business to allow that?"

"*All* of it?" he asked, certain she was making a jest. Until now, he'd rarely had enough to meet his own needs, much less that of strangers.

Her curt nod told him he had made the wrong answer.

"You see?" she asked, snatching her hand away from his. "You would object. You would believe it your duty to advise and if I did not choose to honor that advice, you'd feel compelled to save me from myself, am I correct?"

Jack knew he was on shaky ground here. He dared not lie about that in the event her example became a reality one day. It would be so like Beth to beggar herself—and perhaps him, too—by giving with open hands until there was nothing left to give. With that kind heart of hers, she would try to save the entire population of poor. But he wanted her, kind heart and all. Most especially her kind heart.

"Beth," he said carefully. "Do you truly believe I would marry you for your money?"

"Heavens no!"

"What if I were wealthy and titled and vowed you could dispense of your funds in any way you chose?"

She shrugged. "But you are not. And if you were,

that would only reinforce my resolve. A wealthy man would be even more circumspect than you when it comes to managing me. And a titled one would require too much in the way of social niceties. All my plans would fall by the wayside while I catered to duties as his wife. Meaningless entertainments," she said in a dull voice. "You know what those are like. Even as daughter to a baron, they test my patience and hamper my life. Trust me, if I ever did stoop to marriage, it would not be to a title."

So there it was. Making the admission would make no difference except for the worse, and he might lose her forever on the spot if he confessed. He could not help but wonder about those plans she spoke of that were so dreadfully important to her. "Why not simply tell me what it is you wish to do with your inheritance? I might well agree it needs doing."

"It is no concern of yours. I do not need your advice, or permission or your blessing. If I married you, then I *would* need all of these things," she declared. "So I never will."

"Never is a very long time," he warned as he took her hand again and pressed it to his heart. "You say you love me."

She smiled again, almost sadly this time, and caressed his chest affectionately. "I do, Jack. I have no better friend than you."

He gazed into her eyes meaningfully. "I do not wish to be a mere friend, Beth."

"Then be my lover, too," she whispered, and offered him her lips. "It is what I want, as well."

He took her, abandoning himself to the delicious feel of his mouth on hers. The swift current of desire enveloped them and carried them away. She felt it as keenly as he, Jack knew, for her breathing quickened and the sound she made was one of want. She meant what she said. She wanted this.

But Colin's last taunt kept him sane. A carriage was no place to make love to the woman he wanted as his wife. And yet, he knew he had to do something greater than he had done thus far to bind her to him.

Need and practicality almost won out over honor, and might have done had the carriage wheel not hit a particularly deep hole in the street that jounced them apart.

Beth laughed, rubbing her nose. It had bumped against his cheekbone. Her bonnet hung askew, its stiff velvet brim badly dented. She had never looked lovelier or more desirable. He was so tempted to knock on the roof of the carriage with his cane and order the driver to take them to the town house. Once there, Jack was certain he could convince her she could not live without their lovemaking.

But suppose she decided she could? Beth knew nothing of intimacy, and the first time for a woman was not entirely pleasant, so he had heard. In this respect, he was as uninitiated as she. He'd had a variety of women, but none who had been new to the experience.

In the end it was this worry, not Jack's dratted honor, that had him persuade her they must abstain. First, he had to convince Beth to marry him. Once he had her word she would, then he could risk it.

"I never thought you were a prude, Jack," she said, teasing him as he tried to repair the bend in her bonnet. "However, perhaps it is just as well."

"What do you mean?" he asked, pretending only slight interest, his gaze firmly fixed on the brim of the hat he was coaxing back into shape.

"I would probably have missed you even more when we part. Father has said we must return to the country tomorrow before the weather worsens and the roads become impassable. That is why I must return by three so I may see to packing."

Jack's hands stilled at their task. She was leaving? Why had she not said so? How could she have thought to give herself to him this afternoon, then simply leave town in the morning as though nothing had happened? Damned if she would!

He hurriedly listed in his mind what was left to be done in London. Not much, but at least another week's worth of errands before he could follow her. There was more paperwork concerning the inheritance, the town house to close, items to order for the people at the manor so they would have enough for the winter.

"Colin and I should leave Friday next," he declared, stating the fact as if he'd made the decision earlier. "We shall call on you and Euphemia a week from Saturday if that is acceptable."

"No!" she exclaimed, then seemed to think better of her too violent protest. "Sunday. Come for supper on Sunday. That would be better. Saturdays are...too busy." Her voice softened as did her expression. "I am happy you won't be far away."

"Are you?" he asked, his tone more clipped than he meant for it to sound. They were nearing her house now and he did not want to leave her on such a curt note. "You'll be glad to see me?" he added.

"Yes, of course," she said, tying the bonnet's ribbons beneath her chin. "Even if you do find me quite resistible, there's no reason we cannot remain friends and neighbors."

Her very calm stirred a fury in Jack he could not suppress. He grasped her face and kissed her as assiduously as he knew how. He drew deeply from her sweetness and stole that complacency of hers straight away. His hand molded her breasts, first one, then the other, caressing them with feverish intent as he aligned her body with his so that she would know what the nearness of her did to him.

Only when she was gasping for breath and shuddering with need for him did he release her and set her away. *There, see if you can find where your serenity went, young lady,* he thought as he struggled to contain the renewed fervor of his own desire.

The carriage stopped. He forced a placid smile, opened the door, got out and offered her his hand to alight.

"Have a lovely trip," he said as if his knees weren't fit to buckle beneath him. As if his arms did not ache from the loss of her in them. As if his trousers fit him as perfectly as they had when he'd donned them this morning.

The sound of her response might have been a word of farewell. He might have understood it if the blood had not been thundering in his ears like a herd of wild horses.

But her eyes were wide, shocked, the pupils dilated with arousal. Two could play at this game and, for more reasons than one, he was infinitely glad he'd had more practice.

Chapter Four

"I WISH Father had not insisted we go to the Marstons' this evening," Beth said. She tugged down the skirt of Phemie's hastily pressed gown so that it hung straight. "I had hoped we could leave in the morning as planned." The snowfall had grown heavier during the evening hours and her father had decided to postpone their journey another day.

She did not want to see Jack so soon after their parting this afternoon.

"Well, I am glad to be going," Phemie declared. "Colin hasn't come up to scratch yet, but I almost have him there."

"He and Jack aren't likely to attend," Beth told her. "Any party will be sparsely attended this late in the year. Almost everyone that isn't in permanent residence here will have left for the country for Christmas. And there is the weather to consider."

"Oh, they'll be there," Phemie assured her. "I sent word to Colin that we'll be attending."

"You did not!" Beth exclaimed in shock. "Oh, Phemie, that simply is not done! What will he think of you?"

"That I am hoping to see him tonight. I do swear you will lose Jack if you insist on playing by society's rules, Beth."

If Phemie only knew the rules Beth had been so eager to discard, she would be horrified. "For your information, I do not mind *losing Jack,* as you put it. You know very well I am not in the market for a husband. And you will wreck your own chance at Colin if you continue to chase the poor fellow like a hound after a hare."

Phemie grinned. "Ah, but the hare's slowing these past few days. Methinks he wants to be caught."

"And the hound is salivating," Beth muttered to herself. But who was *she* to throw stones at Phemie after last evening and this afternoon? Beth had done considerably worse than send 'round a note announcing her intention to attend a party.

So Jack would be there tonight after all. What on earth could she say to him after that passionate parting kiss he had given her? Why was she so powerfully drawn to the man? Her good sense flew right out the window every time he so much as looked at her.

Beth admitted her one real fear was that she would begin to entertain hopes that Jack would suit her as a husband after all. When she was apart from him, she could reason well enough and know that it would never work. But when he kissed her, held her and looked into her eyes, Beth's resolve wavered.

Papa was waiting when they descended. He wore a special, tender expression when he looked at her tonight. She wondered why. Had he been maneuvering behind her back again with Lord Harnell? She hoped there would be no more harsh words between them about such things. She loved her father, hard head and all. But he said nothing, only escorted Beth, her mother and Phemie to their waiting conveyance.

The trip took less than a quarter hour since Marston House was very near their own. They were fashionably late, despite her father's penchant for promptness, because of having to unpack their gowns to wear and have them pressed.

"He's not here," Phemie whispered, her dismay evident after a quick survey of Lord Marston's large drawing room.

It proved to be a rather small gathering, just as Beth had predicted. There were only thirty or forty people, all milling about now while a group of musicians played softly so as not to drown out conversation. There would be no dancing. The weather was too cold to open the huge ballroom required for that.

"We shall likely have games later," Phemie said dully. "I do so hate games."

"So do I," Beth agreed. "I expect the library and the morning room will be open and warm for those who do not wish to participate." She glanced back toward the door leading from the main hall. "I believe I shall go and see. Wait here."

Her main objective was to find a place to sit out the party. The noise within the room had already begun to make her head ache. She did not want to admit her disappointment that Jack had not and probably would not arrive since the party was already well under way.

The library was all but deserted. Only a few people had taken refuge there. Beth was about to return and tell Phemie when one of the servants appeared holding a folded note. "Miss Bethany Goodson?" he queried.

"Yes?"

"A gentleman instructed me to give this to you as soon as you arrived." Once the footman had handed her the note, he left.

The note was written on plain ivory paper. *Crucial that we meet. Hurry upstairs, three doors down from the room set aside for the ladies. Do make haste.* The signature was a large, bold *J*.

Beth refolded the note and stuck it into her reticule. The note had to be from Jack. She knew no one else with that initial, at least not well enough to be the recipient of such a message. Had something terrible happened?

She left the library, but not so hurriedly as to draw

attention to herself. The wide staircase led off the end of the hall and curved to the upper floor. The doorway to the first bedroom stood open and Beth could see no ladies inside. She hurried down the hallway to the third door as instructed. It was open only a crack. She slipped inside and quickly closed it.

No matter how dire the reason, she knew she would have no excuse if caught in a bedchamber alone with a man. Too late, she wondered if that was his intention all along. Before she could turn to leave, strong arms grabbed her from behind and a hand closed firmly over her mouth.

"Now try and refuse me," a deep voice growled.

The arm around her middle lifted her off her feet and propelled her straight toward the huge tester bed. Beth kicked at his legs, knowing her slippers would do little damage. Her arms flailed, unable to connect with any part of his body or head. Fury at her helplessness blocked out most of her fear.

She bit the flesh of his hand, gaining herself one good breath and a half scream, soon muffled. He cut off all sound then when his hand also covered her nose.

Beth had realized immediately that the man was not Jack. Arthur Harnell pinned her to the bed with his weight. Her head swam dangerously from lack of breath. She continued to struggle, calling soundlessly to the one man who could save her. Then her mind shut down completely and she fell limp.

* * *

Jack felt an unaccountable sensation of urgency as he and Colin approached Euphemia. Her expression of glee annoyed him, but he was used to that. Beth's face kept flitting through his mind, but it was nowhere to be seen in actuality as he scanned the chamber.

"In the library, I believe," Euphemia told him without being asked. Her titter of a laugh grated on his nerves. But that was not the source of uneasiness. Something was wrong; he felt it.

"Excuse me," he mumbled as he stalked back to the hall, ignoring the greetings that came his way. He entered the large comfortable room lined with ornate shelves laden with leather-lined tomes. She was not here. Where the devil was she?

He turned too abruptly and ran headlong into Aurelia Sapps, a friend of Beth's whom he had met several times. "Pardon me," he grunted, then set her gangly body aside to proceed in his search.

"If you are looking for Bethany, she went upstairs," the woman told him with a sly grin that revealed a mouthful of protruding teeth.

"Thank you," he snapped, and went out the door, on his way to the stairs.

"Wait, Mr. Keith," she called as she rushed to catch up. "I can go in the retiring room and see if she's there if you like."

Jack slowed, realizing how ridiculous he must look

dashing about the way he was doing. He turned to her and offered his arm as they reached the staircase. "Thank you, Miss Sapps. I would appreciate it. How did you know I was seeking Miss Bethany?"

She laughed, a sort of honking sound that put him in mind of a happy duck. Her beaklike nose and bright yellow gown with its feathery ruffles did nothing to detract from that impression. "Who else? You're so obviously smitten with her," she said. "I saw you kiss her and propose on the Randolph's balcony that night. Verr-rry romantic, sir, I must say." She honked again, more softly this time. Her long, strong fingers bit into his arm in a squeeze of emphasis.

"Yes, well, I'm in love with her, you see." Never hurt to make that abundantly clear when this woman had such a firm grip on him.

"Good for you!" she said merrily. "And her, too. I must say I envy you. Not likely I shall find a man myself, not with my looks. Even the dowry's not enough, Pa says."

Aurelia Sapps was the daughter of a poor baronet married by necessity to an incredibly wealthy heiress. The mother's fortune came directly from trade in whisky, an industry publicly frowned upon by the ton. She hadn't a prayer of making a noble marriage even if she were a great beauty, which she definitely was not.

"I'll just pop in there and find her for you," Aurelia said companionably. Her wide, toothy grin flashed.

Jack smiled back, thinking how he might learn to

like the woman for her straightforward ways and friendliness if he had the time. Her eyes were nice, a bottle green that looked well with the color if not the style of her bright red curls. "Thank you, Miss Sapps. I would be eternally grateful."

Jack stood outside in the corridor, arms crossed over his chest, rocking heel to toe impatiently. Then he heard a sound from down the hall, a muted, throaty sound of distress.

His anxiety increased. With no concern for the propriety of what he was doing, Jack threw open the first door, then the next, and yet another. Behind the third, there on the huge bed, he saw Harnell, Bethany trapped beneath him, rucking up the hem of her lavender gown.

Jack flew across the room and dragged Harnell off her by the scruff of his neck. He whirled him away from Beth and landed a solid blow to the man's mid-section, then an uppercut to the chin. Harnell dropped to the floor unconscious.

"Beth!" Jack rushed to her and turned her over on her back, coaxing her to come around.

"Oh, my heavens!" came a throaty voice from the doorway.

"Get me a cold cloth!" Jack ordered Aurelia Sapps. "She's fainted."

"That bastard!" Aurelia snapped as she quickly closed the door and hurried to the table where sat a porcelain ewer and basin. She dampened a cloth and brought it to Jack. "Did he hurt her?"

Beth was reviving. Jack sat beside her, holding her close and brushing the hair back from her brow with the cloth. "Are you all right, Beth?" he demanded.

She nodded and grasped his hand. "I'm fine. I think. He…he tricked me up here. I thought the message was from you." Jack felt a shudder run through her as her worried gaze sought his. "He did not…?"

"No, no, he didn't. Take a deep breath now." Harnell had not actually succeeded in his primary intent, but Beth was obviously shaken. Jack cradled her head against his shoulder. "Be calm. Everything's all right now."

Aurelia kicked at the unconscious Harnell. "He needs a lesson, that one. Is he dead?"

"Not yet," Jack admitted. "Killing him here would be in poor taste. I decided to wait until he leaves the house."

"I've a better idea," she announced, one red eyebrow raised and her lips stretched to one side. "My mama's pa can deal with this one. He can toss him overboard when he sails again."

"Never mind. I'll rather enjoy taking care of him myself."

Aurelia shook her head. "Then you'd have to explain it. It will ruin Bethany if this gets out."

Beth was fully alert now and sat up. "Aurelia? What are you doing here?"

"Getting myself a lord to marry," the redhead announced. "If you're quite recovered, you two help me undress him. Well, half undress him. Then we'll put him on the bed."

"What do you have in mind?" Jack asked. He had figured it out, but wondered if the woman was quite sane.

"Obvious, isn't it? Come, get busy! I'm fairly strong. The three of us should be able to lift him, don't you think?"

Jack frowned. "You don't want Harnell. He's cruel, as you can see, up to his neck in debt, and not worth having."

"You're absolutely right, Mr. Keith, and I don't plan to keep him, just wed him. He'll be shipping out soon after the ceremony, and will be glad to go. I only want the freedom a wedding ring will provide. Let's get to this before he wakes."

Jack and Beth helped strip Harnell of his coat and waistcoat while Aurelia squatted and tugged off his shoes and tight white pantaloons. The three of them lifted him onto the bed.

"You two hide in the dressing room if you want to see this," she advised with a quirky grin.

Jack took Beth's arm and guided her to the small room set between the bedchambers and left the door ajar. They watched in awe as the tall, gawky Aurelia Sapps ripped her yellow gown down the front, mussed her tangle of red curls and kicked off her shoes. She clambered up beside the unwitting Harnell, settled herself with a couple of wiggles, drew his limp arms around her and screamed the house down.

Beth laughed nervously and Jack shushed her. It was a small matter to sneak out through the fourth bedroom that also adjoined the dressing room in which they hid. The crowd that rushed upstairs and into the chamber with Aurelia and Harnell had no thoughts for anything other than the totally shocking compromise that had just occurred.

"Are you steady now?" Jack asked her once they were headed back down the corridor.

"Not really, but Aurelia's not the only one who can act. Do I look as disheveled as I feel?"

He stopped in front of the retiring room, tucked an errant curl behind her ear and allowed his gaze to travel the length of her. "You look lovely, but you might want to duck in here and compose yourself. Shall I wait for you?"

"No. Go back and make certain Aurelia is all right. Her father looked apoplectic. You might be needed to help manage Harnell."

Jack glanced back down the hallway where people were beginning to exit the room in question. "I don't like to leave you," he admitted.

She looked up at him, her eyes swimming with tears and a grateful and adoring smile on her face. "Thank you, Jack. Thank you for saving me."

"My pleasure," he said, returning her smile. "I would do anything for you, Beth. You must know that."

"What an excellent friend you are," she whispered.

He almost told her then that he loved her. But he realized the news might shock her as much as it did him.

When he had seen another man trying to take by force what Beth had so generously offered him, Jack had fully understood the sheer depth of his feelings for her. What he felt went well beyond his conviction that Beth would be the best choice for a wife, a countess who would help him rebuild and reorder.

Even if she were as silly as Euphemia, as homely as Aurelia or as vapid as her mother, Jack knew he would still love her. Maybe he had loved her all along, even as a child. He had never forgotten her, that was for certain, and admitted now that he had been infinitely glad to find her unwed and available that night at the Randolphs'. He had gone straight for her and never thought to look further afield.

What a tangle he had made of things. The truth would unravel soon now and he had to work quickly to ensure that she loved him, too, at least enough to marry him.

She patted his arm and turned to go into the room where he could not follow. "I shall see you later, downstairs," she said.

Jack hesitated. What he wanted most was to toss her over his shoulder immediately and spirit her away, perhaps to Gretna Green on the border of Scotland and marry her there. But that would make him no better than Harnell who would impose his will on her without a care for her feelings. No. Jack knew he had to make her love him. Somehow.

Beth avoided Jack for the rest of the evening, even though it made her feel guilty to do so. He cast her long looks across the room, which she pretended she did not notice. When he made to approach her, she immersed herself in conversation within groups he dared not interrupt. He would be hurt by her avoidance, she knew, but Beth feared what she would say next if they spoke privately again.

There were the children to think of, her promise to them and to herself. While she thought Jack would be sympathetic to her plans for the future, she could be mistaken. As mistress or wife, he would demand most of her time and she would be prone to provide it. How could she be a proper mother to four children who weren't even his, and still give him his due?

Phemie took her arm and led her to the morning room that stood deserted now that the crowd had begun to engage in games. Her father was deep into a card game at the moment and would not be budged to leave early.

"Tell me what has you so overset, Beth," Phemie demanded as soon as they were alone.

Beth sank onto the settee and blurted out what had happened abovestairs. Then she confessed her feelings. "I am afraid that I have grown to love him, Phemie, and I cannot afford to do that."

Phemie remained quiet until all was revealed, then asked, "What will you do?"

"I won't see him tomorrow if we remain in London. And if he follows to the country next week and calls as promised, I shall plead the headache and remain in my room. It will only take a few instances of such pretense and he will give up and find someone else."

"Why won't you simply tell him your real reason for refusing to wed? Surely you owe him that much after all he did tonight," Phemie suggested.

"To what purpose? He would agree to accept my terms. I know that. It's the sort of man he is. But I do not believe I could endure it if he began to resent me for what I am bound to do," she added, confirming her own worst fear.

"For love I would endure anything," Phemie declared, her face set with a determination Beth had seldom seen in her. "Even poverty."

"Well, you certainly needn't worry about that," Beth said, sounding acerbic and regretting it immediately. "I am sorry to be blunt, but if Colin weds you, you shall have it all. Dispense with this posturing about the title and living in grandeur before he stops trying to win your regard. Let him know that you want him for himself."

"I truly do," Phemie admitted. "If he were penniless and without prospect, I would throw myself at his feet even more assiduously than I have already done. However, a drastic change in me at this late date would seem suspect, would it not? He would merely believe it another ploy. Besides, he does not love me as I love him and obviously never will. He finds me amusing, is all. I should abandon the cause as lost, though it breaks my heart even to think of it while there is the least chance."

Beth embraced her. "Ah, Phemie, what can we do but go on as best we may? Do you think this will be the saddest Christmas we have yet spent?"

"I do," Phemie said with a weary sigh. "When Jack gives you up and finds another, Colin will not hang about after me. It is just as well we face spinsterhood together. I shall devote myself to your cause, I suppose. My meager stipend might help a bit. You are welcome to it."

"No!" Beth said, aghast at this new and unexpected side of her cousin. "You must not give up on Colin! Not if you love him!"

"As you love Jack," Phemie reminded her with a wry smile. "Perhaps things will not seem so dark once we return to the country. You will resume your responsibility to your children and I shall help you.

They must miss you as terribly as you do them, especially the baby, poor little dear."

Jack offered a hasty, over-the-shoulder apology to Lord Marsten as Colin all but dragged him away from a discussion about parliament.

"That was rude. What's so urgent?" he demanded. "Has something happened?"

"God, yes!" Colin tugged him toward the entrance hall and motioned a servant to bring their capes and hats. "Let's get out of here."

"No, I want to see Beth before I leave."

"Trust me, Jack. It is imperative you hear what I must tell you before you see her again."

Intrigued, Jack followed suit as Colin donned his cape and left without even a farewell to their hosts.

"Now what's amiss?" Jack demanded once they were settled in the carriage.

"Brace yourself, Jack," Colin warned. "For once, my eavesdropping has proved the adage that says it's unwise."

Jack almost smirked. "Heard ill of yourself, have you?"

Colin sighed and looked away, propping one arm against the window and his chin on his fist. "Actually, no. I was rather heartened in that respect, though the rest of the conversation I could gladly have done without."

"Well, give over. Was it about me?"

"About Bethany." He met Jack's eyes, his own glinting in the carriage light with something akin to outrage. "She has children, Jack."

"That's absurd! Beth's never been married."

"I hope that was a lie. If not, she has bastards, one but a babe in arms! I heard her and Phemie discussing them in the morning room. This is why she's refused you, and probably every other man who had plied a suit for her hand. If she weds, her husband must learn what she has done."

Jack's mouth had dropped open. He clicked it shut and ground his teeth. "I do not believe it," he said finally. "You simply misunderstood."

"No, Jack," Colin declared, shaking his head. "There is no possibility of that."

It would explain everything. Her refusal to wed, as Colin had stated, and also her willingness to make love without benefit of marriage. She had obviously done that before. More than once.

His heart felt like lead in his chest. Broken pieces of lead that weighed so heavily, he could scarcely breathe around them.

"I am so sorry," Colin said as he leaned forward and laid a hand on Jack's shoulder.

"Not half as sorry as I am," Jack muttered as visions of Beth darted through his mind. Beth laughing as she flew along the path in the park on her little brown mare while he gave chase. Beth licking the chocolate from her upper lip in Gaston's Coffeehouse. Beth looking up at him adoringly not an hour ago with unshed tears glazing her eyes.

He wanted to weep himself for what might have been. "I wish I didn't know," he said out loud, more to himself than to Colin. "God, I wish I'd never found out."

"I had no choice but to tell you. What will you do now?" Colin asked, his voice laced with sympathy and regret.

"I don't know." Jack covered his face with one hand and shook his head. "I truly do not know."

Chapter Five

JACK stared down at the invitation Colin had handed him. He almost crushed it in his fist. He had spent a terrible week in London after the Goodsons left, and now had been at Whitfield Manor for an entire fortnight. To say the least, the city had not been the same without her. These past two weeks had proved hell on earth, especially knowing she was but five miles away. And now, to tempt him further, came this stiff bit of vellum requesting the honor of his and his brother's presence at Christmas dinner tomorrow with the baron and his family.

It was already Christmas Eve, a bleak day at Whitfield and they had not even gotten through breakfast yet. The coffee tasted like yesterday's dregs and the food was damned near inedible.

"I am going," Colin announced, grimacing as he set down his cup. "Of course, I shall make your regrets for you."

"Will you answer as Earl Whitworth or shall we dispense with the sham? I doubt Euphemia will welcome you with open arms when we do." Jack tossed the invitation in his direction.

Colin picked it up off the table and placed it beside his plate. "You might want to peruse the London *Gazette* before you wipe that scowl off your face. No use wasting a bad mood." He pushed the folded newspaper within Jack's reach, tapped idly at a boxed item on the outer fold that he had been reading, then doggedly resumed drinking his coffee.

"God in heaven!" Jack exclaimed when his gaze landed on the article. The Baron and Baroness Goodson announce the betrothal of their daughter, Miss Bethany Goodson, to Lord John Macklin Keith, lately lieutenant of His Majesties Thirteenth Hussars... "Goodson announced the engagement! And it names me, not you! But why now? He's given up hope of the title."

Colin shrugged and sighed. "So he has. You're stuck, old fellow, unless Bethany honors her original agreement with you to cry off publicly. You might want to speak with her about it."

Jack's stomach roiled. His breakfast seemed bent on making a return path up his throat. The very idea of seeing Beth again troubled him. Could he remain cool and detached? Could he go through with the farce they had planned when he wanted her so much he thought he would die of it?

Forcing himself to stay away from her was one thing. Reuniting, then ending it all with the pretense of a squabble might be more than he could handle. His anger was too real. His feelings for her as scrambled as the eggs he'd just eaten.

How could she have lied so abominably?

You lied to her, his conscience reminded him.

That lie of omission hurt no one, he argued.

It will wreck your brother's hopes when the truth comes out, his inner voice declared.

"Do you love Euphemia?" Jack asked Colin.

His brother sat back in his chair and crossed his arms over his chest. "What a foolish question! Do you take me for an idiot?"

"Damn me, you do love her," Jack said in a near whisper. He saw the answer in Colin's eyes. "I feared as much. I should never have allowed this charade to continue past that first night."

Colin got up and paced over to the window, looking out toward the neighboring estate. Jack knew he could see nothing of Goodson House, of course, for it was well beyond the large copse of trees that lay in between. "Save your worry for your own predicament, brother. I will have Euphemia Meadows." He turned to Jack. "I regret any embarrassment it may cause you in the future, but I plan to marry Phemie. We shall live elsewhere, of course."

"No!" Jack protested. "You will live here, Colin! This is your home now as much as mine. We agreed to share everything! We have always shared."

Colin smiled. "Not this, Jack. Every time you look at Phemie, you will think of Beth and what might have been. I cannot—will not—do that to you."

Jack was still trying to summon up an argument that might work when Colin walked out of the dining room.

The estate was in virtual ruin. Almost all of the household staff had left by the time he and Colin arrived. They had probably gone even before his uncle and cousin had died. As far as he could tell from the books, no one had paid them their wages for some time now. The only ones left were a deaf, half-blind cook and the frail, doddering butler, both far too old to seek employment elsewhere.

Those working the land and living in the cottages feared him as they had the former earl. Jack seemed unable to convince them he meant to improve their lot and that he had sufficient funds to do so. They cowered whenever he came near and refused to answer even the simplest questions.

The accounts were a shambles. The house was unkempt. He was not trained to take charge of an estate. He might have bulled his way through it and succeeded despite that, but his heart was not in the effort. He needed someone.

He needed Beth. As much as he might try to persuade himself he merely required a helpmeet to put the old homeplace to rights, Jack knew he needed her more for himself. Much more.

But Beth had said quite clearly she would not have him. And, knowing what he knew about her, he shouldn't want her anyway.

Why not? that small voice inside his head asked him. Why not, indeed? So she had children. What of it? He could scarcely damn her for taking a lover when he'd had more than he could count over the years. But was there more than one? How many children were there? he wondered for the hundredth time. At least two. Speculation on the matter had deviled him constantly these past three weeks. Whose were they? Had she loved and been left in the lurch by some cad? Or more than one cad?

Strong, sensible Beth. Who else had seen that vulnerability she kept so well hidden? Who else had preyed upon her passion as he had almost done? Small wonder she insisted on remaining single. She must be incredibly wary of the entire male gender.

God help him, it suddenly ceased to matter how she had come to motherhood. He still loved her. He still wanted her. Her soft sweetness, her wit, her laughter and her desire for him could not have been feigned. She had been afraid to tell him of her past, that was all.

Perhaps if he told her he knew of her mistakes and that they made no difference in how he felt about her, it might change her mind about marriage. Surely in her desperation to avoid future scandal should she be found out, she would jump at his offer. The baron certainly would once Jack told him about the title.

He passed Colin on the stairs as he hurried up to change into his riding gear. "I'm going to see her."

"Now?" Colin called, turning to follow him up.

"I mean to marry that woman one way or another."

At the top of the stairs Colin caught his arm and whirled him around. "Jack, consider this carefully. Are you certain you—"

Jack shook off his grip and proceeded to the master chamber, not bothering to answer.

"Wait! Let's talk about this!" Colin persisted even as the door slammed in his face.

Hurriedly, Jack pulled on his riding boots and exchanged his morning coat for a tweed jacket. He ran a hand through his hair and slapped on his hat. Best do this before he lost his fervor.

He rushed out to the stables, saddled the gelding, mounted and rode hell-bent for Goodson House.

When he arrived, he was welcomed by the housekeeper, a pleasantly plump woman who greeted him with a questioning smile.

"I—I've come to call on Miss Goodson," he declared.

"She is not here," the woman told him. "I believe she is with the children today. She always spends her Saturdays—"

"Where?" he demanded, ignoring the frown his curt words caused. "Where are they if they aren't here?"

She pressed her fingertips to her lips for so long he thought she would refuse to answer him. Then she looked past him down the road to the village and said, "At the cottage, sir."

"Which cottage?" he snapped, following her line of vision.

"The second after you pass the bridge, sir," she directed. "You will see her blue pony cart there, I expect."

Jack turned swiftly, leaped down the steps and remounted.

He could not countenance why the baron would relegate his grandchildren to a cottage at the edge of the village instead of housing them properly within the manor house. Damn the man for his haughty ways and fear of scandal! Those poor little mites were not to blame for their existence. He would see they never felt themselves in the way of things at Whitfield. Not in the manner Colin and he had believed they were. Children needed acceptance and welcome from those around them. And love. Beth would love them, he knew, but that was not enough.

He spied the blue cart drawn to the side of a quaint

little thatch-roofed dwelling. The large gray pony had been unhitched and was tethered nearby, grazing idly. Jack dismounted and wrapped his reins around a small tree.

Now that he was here, his sense of urgency began to abate. Actually, it disappeared altogether. Frantic wailing emanated from inside the closed door while high-pitched voices clamored for attention. "Mama, Mama! Me, me!" he heard. "Mama!" one of the little ones screeched. Good Lord, how many were in there?

He approached the door and barged in, certain she must need assistance. No point in knocking. Thunder could not be heard in such a melee. "Beth?" he called over the cacophony.

She was crouched beside a cradle where little arms and legs protruded, kicking and flailing above a fat little body. He could hardly see the face of the child with its mouth open that wide.

"Jack!" she exclaimed, barely audible over the noise.

Three other children were assailing her, screaming for attention. The largest looked to be about four years old, the baby in the cradle not more than one, if that. He knew little of children, save for remembering his and Colin's own early years.

But they were people, after all, and he was usually good with people. He scooped up the smallest one that stood outside the cradle and rested the child against his shoulder while he tugged the eldest away from her.

Beth stared at him transfixed, or perhaps worried, even as she slid one arm around the remaining child and patted the screaming one in the cradle.

"What are you doing here?" she asked. He more or less had to read her lips.

"I wanted to tell you that I know about—ouch!" The little wretch he had shouldered bit him right through his shirt collar. Jack shifted it so that it lost purchase with its teeth. "It's of no consequence," he told Beth loudly. "Everyone makes errors in judgment."

The curly topped girl whose hand he was grasping kicked his shin. The solid-soled shoe she wore bounced off his boot. "Stop that!" he ordered, and immediately her faced screwed up and her ear-piercing howl joined that of her cradle mates. "Are all these...."

"Mine, yes!" she confessed. "All *four.*"

"Damn!" he muttered.

"You mind your tongue in front of my children!" she shouted, her harried expression turning to one of outrage.

"As if they could hear me over this caterwauling!" he replied, jouncing the one in his arms, hoping the motion would startle the wee bugger into silence. No such luck.

"Let's get them quiet," he shouted to Beth. "I need to talk to you."

"Be my guest!" she shouted as she flung up her

hand. "Pour Mary some milk. It's over there." She gestured toward the shelf on the far wall.

He wondered which one Mary was, the kicker or the biter. Well, something had to be done. He plunked the biter on the well-scrubbed flagstone floor beside its sobbing older sister and located two cups. Just as he picked up the jug to pour, two sturdy little arms grasped him around his knees. Milk flew everywhere, most of it landing squarely on top of the younger of his two charges, the rest on his boots.

The sobbing stopped. The biter sat quivering in a puddle of white, looking up at him with wide blue eyes, lashes dotted with white droplets.

Beth laughed. She grasped her sides and laughed so hard all the children turned to stare at her, their former concerns apparently forgotten.

"Beth, are you quite well?" he asked, his voice entirely too loud in the relative silence that followed the spill. If the poor girl was not mad, it was a flaming wonder.

She managed to contain her mirth long enough to nod. "Wipe off Martha if you will. I'll change her in a moment. Mary, come here, dear."

The kicker trotted over obediently and flung her chubby arms around Beth's neck. The serene maternal smile Beth wore held Jack spellbound for a moment before he remembered his task.

He found a rag hanging on a nail beside the shelf and squatted to mop off the baby's head. It smiled up at him, showing small white evenly spaced teeth as its tongue lapped the milk from around its mouth. Dimpled hands patted at the puddle surrounding it. "So you'd be Martha," he said, apropos of nothing. "Hello, ducky."

Martha giggled, seemingly thrilled to be soaked through and being daubed at by a total stranger. He cleaned off her head and shoulders as best he could and left her sitting there, smacking her palms and swirling her tiny fingers in the milk.

Beth somehow detached herself from the others and came over to lift the child off the floor. Jack watched, enthralled, as she quickly stripped the baby of its clothing and dunked it into a small wooden tub half filled with water. "Second bath within the hour," she explained. "Our nurse has gone for a bit of rest at her sister's house."

"Much-needed respite, I would think," Jack observed with a wince. "But what of you? Will you manage without her help?"

"I manage very well, thank you, but Darcy will be back within the hour. You need not stay on that account."

The baby in the cradle was silent now except for sucking sounds. Jack glanced across the room where Mary the Kicker and the other one were standing on the bed pointing out the window. "Should they be up there? Might they fall?"

"They have the agility of goats, believe me," she told him without even bothering to look. "Now why are you here?" Her hands seemed to fly, drying the child—Martha, he recalled—and pulling a small, checked garment over the baby's head.

Jack exhaled. He wished he had her full attention for this, but realized that, under the circumstances, he could hardly expect that. "I have known for some time about your children. Colin overheard you and Euphemia discussing them at the Marston party. I have come to the conclusion that you need a husband as badly as I need a wife. Perhaps even more so. The announcement of our betrothal is in the papers, as you must know."

"Yes, I was shocked. Obviously he is more desperate than I thought."

"I believe we should carry through."

"Oh, you do, do you?" she asked. "We did have a clear understanding, Jack. A plan. We shall hold to that. Come tomorrow night and live up to your word."

"Beth, be reasonable. You have four children! How can you deny they need a father? What happened to him, by the way? Is he still about?"

"I have no idea what has become of him, nor do I care. He abandoned them and has no right to call himself a father!"

Jack felt an urge to kill the bastard who had hurt Beth so. He also had to admit a part of that desire was jealous rage.

Just then a soft thump sounded and a scream ensued. Jack tore across the room and swept the child up in his arms, patting its heaving back and holding it close. "There, there, you're fine. The rug cushioned you. Hush, hush, sweeting. Did you strike your head on something?" He ran his palm over the soft dark locks and felt for a bump. "No, no, see? You had a fright, is all."

To his great amazement, the child quieted and nestled against him, its small legs wrapping halfway 'round him as it clung like a monkey.

His heart settled back in his chest where it belonged, but felt full now. He was good at this. He could be a father. He *would* be, he realized. If Beth married him, he would be responsible for her children. Mary, blue eyes widened, sat on the bed with her fingers in her pretty bow-shaped mouth. Milky little Martha who liked puddles, clung to Beth's skirts. And this one, whatever its name, embraced him with such trust. He let his eyes stray to the cradle where lay another, barely of an age to stand upright. It slept now, obviously worn out by its struggles.

Beth stood near him, her head cocked to one side and her eyes narrowed as she watched him sway back and forth. After a moment she picked up Martha and plunked her down on the bed beside Mary. Then she reached for the one he was holding. "You had better go now," she said softly. "It is past time for their naps."

"Who is this one?" he asked, unable to help running his hand over the child's head once more.

"Diana," she said. "Why?"

Jack shrugged and smiled. "I wanted to know. She has hair like yours."

Beth's expression was unreadable. "And the others? Are they like me, do you think?"

Jack looked at Mary. "She has your mouth. And Martha, your laugh. Her eyes are the same color, too. Yes, they are very like you. Lovely, all of them."

She continued to hold his gaze with hers and still he could not fathom what she was thinking. "Go home, Jack," she said softly. "Leave now. I shall see you tomorrow evening. You and Colin will attend, won't you?"

"Of course." He nodded and backed toward the door. "Until tomorrow then."

"Do not forget our arrangement," she told him.

When he would have argued, she held up a hand. "We can be friends afterward. Close friends, if you like." Her meaning was clear as crystal, but he would not settle for being a mere lover. Taking a lover was precisely how she had acquired four children she had to keep secret. That wicked determination not to marry had served her ill. Well, he would remedy that in short order!

"There is something else I must confess to you," he said, hoping that telling her of his title might make some difference. It certainly couldn't hurt since she was already dead set against marrying him. At least they would have no more lies between them.

The baby stirred and began to fret again. She glanced toward it, then back at him. "Tomorrow, Jack. Please go now."

Yes, tomorrow would do well. "Goodbye, then." He directed a small wave at Mary and Martha who sat perfectly still on the bed, watching him. Mary wriggled her fingers at him, then quickly stuck them back in her mouth. Jack played his last card of the day. "I love you," he said to Beth, and kissed her quickly.

He heard her swift gasp, but she said nothing. In fact, he could swear she had begun holding her breath.

Jack exited the cottage and left her there with her children. Soon to be *their* children if he had any say in it.

Beth clenched her eyes shut and exhaled sharply the moment the door closed. Lord, she could not believe what had just happened. The emotions warring within her exhausted her more than the children's collective tantrum.

She was so angry she could spit. Jack actually believed she had taken a man to her bed and borne his bastards, one after another! Damn Jack Keith and his condescending concern!

But you would willingly have gone to his bed.

"Yes, but I *love* him!" she argued with herself.

However, Jack had not known that. She had not known it herself at the time. How could he think other than what he did, given her eagerness to allow him such liberties?

There, all tangled with the anger, was relief. She had never thought to see him again. He had not called as he'd promised. She'd had no need to feign the headache to avoid him. Small wonder after his finding out about the children. But he had come, after all. He had come, offering to make good their bogus betrothal to protect her good name. Did he believe she could have birthed four children in succession and kept it secret hereabouts? La, but he was naive if he thought that possible.

And dear. He was so dear to say he loved her. She knew he did not, of course. Perhaps he loved her as a friend, but if he loved her as a woman, he would surely have taken her when she offered herself in London. But he had not. No, Jack was simply a dear, sweet man who would go well out of his way to save her.

Had he not done so when he rid her of Harnell? Now he felt obliged to save her again, a needless sacrifice on his part.

Everyone in the county knew Beth had taken responsibility for the children of poor Lily Nesmith whose worthless husband had abandoned her during the last pregnancy. Lily had pleaded on her deathbed after birthing little Deborah. Beth was already so attached to the children, she could never have said no.

If Beth believed for a moment that Jack loved her half as much as she loved him, she might consider relenting. She might turn over her entire fortune when she inherited next week and trust that he would do right by the girls she claimed as hers.

He had seemed quite taken with them, despite their crankiness today. What a tender way he had with little ones. Who would have thought it of a former soldier?

Phemie burst into the cottage. "I saw Jack ride past the house on the way from the village. Has he been here?"

"Yes, he was here," Beth admitted, unwilling to relate what had happened or her feelings about it at the moment. She distracted Phemie with a question. "Have you seen Colin?"

"No," Phemie admitted, wringing her hands. "They've been in residence at Whitfield House for two whole weeks, Beth. I cannot understand why he has not called. I know I said I would give him up, but I miss him so dreadfully! Haven't you missed Jack?"

Beth sighed. "Of course, but that's neither here nor there. Well, you shall see Colin when he comes for Christmas dinner tomorrow."

"They are coming?" Phemie fairly danced with excitement. "Jack has promised they will be there?"

"He said they would. So run home and decide what to wear. I shall be along shortly."

Beth needed time alone to plan how she was to break her betrothal to Jack and sound convincing. Would the vicar, the mayor, the squire and their wives find it entertaining? And would she ever be able to make her father understand?

He had recently taken to the notion of having Jack as a son-in-law, despite Jack's lack of consequence. Papa had sent the announcement to the London papers before she knew he had written it. She supposed he had grown truly desperate on her behalf after Lord Harnell's betrothal to Aurelia Sapps had been announced.

Beth had no heart for the chore of devising a confrontation. It appeared Jack had stolen that heart while she wasn't looking.

Chapter Six

CHRISTMAS DAY had dawned with a cold drizzle of rain, reflecting Beth's mood precisely. She wanted to weep with frustration. All through a sleepless night, she had tried to imagine a dialogue that would serve to end her betrothal to Jack. Yet each attempt proved fruitless, ending only with him taking her in his arms and forgiving her supposed transgressions that, by anyone's lights, should be unforgivable.

Preparation for the Christmas dinner had not served to distract her. Even the children's excitement over being brought to the manor house had not done so. Her father's insistence that they occupy the unused nursery had come closest to taking her mind from her most immediate problem. At last, after a full half year, he had accepted that her attachment to them was no passing fancy. Even her mother had bestirred herself to welcome them.

The other guests had been here nearly an hour now and had spent the time exclaiming over the warmth and welcome of Goodson House dressed in its Christmas finery. Holly, ivy and various other greenery festooned the mantels, wound around the stair rail and graced the clutches of candles spaced about the parlor. A huge yule log burned within the fireplace and the scents of cinnamon and nutmeg filled the rooms. It was almost time to eat and still the Keiths had not arrived.

"Finally! They are here!" Phemie exclaimed as she peered out the window at the circular drive. She nudged Beth's shoulder with her elbow. "I feared they had decided not to come, they are so late. Should we wait here or go and greet them at the door?"

"Wait," Beth declared, not about to move from her seat at the pianoforte. She fixed her fingers on the keys and began playing a carol softly as she looked up at her cousin. "You mustn't seem so eager, Phemie. And for goodness' sake, exhale, would you? You look fit to burst right out of that dress."

"Says she who rarely fills one out," Phemie sniped playfully. "Shoulders back, here they come."

The men entered, barely taking time to acknowledge the other guests as they made their way through the room. Colin approached first, nodded in greeting to Beth, and then turned his full attention to Phemie. The two moved far enough away to speak privately, leaving her to deal with Jack.

"You play beautifully," he said, lounging comfortably with one elbow on the instrument. "Do you sing?"

"Not well," Beth admitted. "Do you?"

"Like the finest frog in your pond. Shall I?"

Beth laughed and stopped playing at the end of the first verse. "No thank you. We've precious few guests as it is. I would hate to drive them back out into this weather before we've fortified them with food."

As if on cue, dinner was announced.

She stood and he reached for her hand. Bowing low over it, he actually touched it with his lips. No one would think a thing of it, she realized. Everyone believed them betrothed. In fact, they were. It was up to her to break the contract.

"How are the children?" he asked as they strolled toward the dining room. "Are they here?"

Beth looked away. "They are upstairs with Darcy. Father decided the cottage is scarcely warm enough since the weather's turning off quite cold."

"I'm glad to know he's that compassionate, especially since they *are* his grandchildren. Is the nurse to bring them down into company this afternoon?"

What a strange question for him to ask. "No, of course not. Whyever would she do that?"

"Whyever not? I for one should like to wish them happy Christmas. I've brought trinkets and sweets."

What was he up to? "Kind of you, I'm sure, but

young as they are, they will be more comfortable in the nursery."

"Especially when these neighbors you've invited might object. I suppose they know nothing of the children." He glanced around at the other guests, Vicar Dunn, Squire McFaddin, Sheriff Tanner and their respective wives.

Beth granted Jack patience since he did not know the full truth concerning the births of her daughters. "Of course they do. Everyone knows of them."

"Then why not show them off? They are handsome children." It sounded like a dare.

"And so well behaved," Beth said with a quirk of her brow.

He did not laugh as she expected, but looked quite serious. "Bring them down, Beth. I recall how Colin and I were hidden away like pesky rodents when Uncle and Aunt had guests. You saw how we turned out."

She frowned up at him, realizing suddenly just how unhappy his childhood must have been. The best Beth could recall, old Whitworth had not been a pleasant fellow and his lady had done nothing but whine.

"Please do not worry, Jack. They are far too young to be affected by exclusion."

He said nothing, but his sensuous lips firmed into a straight line and he refused to look at her.

"Oh, very well," she conceded. "I shall send word to have Darcy dress them and bring them in for a few moments after dessert. But only if they are still awake, mind you. You have seen for yourself how need of a nap can wreak havoc." She stopped long enough to give the order to one of the footmen and watched him hurry away to relay her message to Darcy.

Jack squeezed her hand and the look on his face was reward enough for any inconvenience this might cause. Despite the oddity of his request, it caused a warm and giddy sensation that felt as cozy as Christmas itself.

What a fine father Jack would make. If only he truly did love her. Could he have meant it? Was it possible?

Dinner was pleasant enough though Beth barely tasted any of it. No one intruded on the conversation Jack kept up with her during the meal. Not until dessert was served, when her father tapped his glass with a fork to gain everyone's attention.

"A toast!" he announced as he stood. "To my daughter, Bethany, and her intended, Lord John of Whitfield. Happy life!"

"Here, here!" everyone commented as they stood and raised their glasses high.

Bethany cast a meaningful look at Jack, leaned close and whispered, "Our denouement must be put into effect very soon. Are you prepared?" He merely smiled at her.

Her father continued. "If there is no objection, we shall join you ladies in the withdrawing room shortly."

Her mother murmured her assent and led the way. There would be time for the women to refresh themselves upstairs and for the gentlemen to smoke or do whatever they must. Then the play she and Jack had planned to end their betrothal must commence.

Lord, how she dreaded it. Could she feign a temper and give him a setdown? Would he reciprocate or bow out gracefully? What excuse would she use? She could not think of a single reason why she should not marry him. Except that he did not really love her and she could hardly use that. She much doubted there was a couple within this company who had wed for love. She and Jack should have discussed this in more detail, Beth thought as a galloping case of nerves assailed her.

She rushed upstairs, tried to calm herself, checked her appearance and hurried back down. Long before she was ready, the men filed in, obviously having foregone their cigars for the pleasure of feminine company.

Jack joined her immediately. "Your father mentioned he would like us to have a Christmas wedding," he said, appearing amused by the suggestion.

"Ah, a year-long engagement," she said with relief, knowing that would give them plenty of time to stage their breaking of the betrothal.

He chuckled softly and brushed her ear with his lips. "No. I believe he would like the vicar to perform it *today.*"

She drew back and looked up at him in horror. "Today? But...but that's not possible, even if we wished it so. There are banns—"

"Already called. We should have attended church."

"I was afraid you would be..." Beth clamped her mouth shut, but saw that he understood her despite the fact that she didn't finish. She had not gone to church in the village because she feared she would see him there.

"Your father is quite efficient. Announcement in the papers, banns called in our home county. He has thought of everything, even having a houseful of guests to witness the event."

"There's no license," she argued.

"Easily obtained since he *is* the local magistrate, Beth."

"Oh."

Jack trailed his fingers up the underside of her arm, the backs of them grazed the side of her breast. No one could see the gesture, but Beth's breathing grew rapid and her face heated.

"Stop!" she whispered. "What are you doing? Do you wish me to slap you and end it here and now?"

"That's up to you, of course. I would as soon you didn't. Marry me, Beth. Today."

She huffed impatiently. "You are only offering because you think I need saving, and I assure you I do not! Leave off this teasing!"

He slid his arm around her and squeezed her waist. She jumped away. "Sir! You forget yourself!" The words came out more loudly than she'd intended. Conversation halted.

It was now or never. "I shall not wed a man who has so little regard for my wishes!" she announced, not altogether certain what she would follow that announcement with. Everyone was watching them now.

"Beth, my darling," he replied, also raising his voice so that all could hear. "You know your slightest wish is my command. You have but to name it."

"B-but I..." She stuttered for a moment, then grasped words at random. "I have no desire to live in London, I have *told* you! I detest the city and I shall *not* reside there no matter what you say! If that is what you require, then we must call off our agreement!"

He inclined his head and his smile grew wider as he replied, "It was but a suggestion, my dear. We shall live wherever you choose. In fact, I prefer the country myself. Here, it is, then."

She cast about for something, anything, to counter his concession. "You...you...you will not want the...the children to live with us and I shall not give them up!"

He laughed. "Whatever gave you such a notion! Of course they shall live with us. Where else would they live?"

Beth saw Darcy and the children standing in the

doorway to the withdrawing room, as entranced as everyone else by the one-sided argument between herself and Jack. Little Mary pulled away from the young maid and darted across the room.

Jack scooped her up and chucked her under the chin. He beckoned Darcy and the tweenie assigned to assist her with the little ones.

He looked at Beth. "You fear I won't claim these darlings? Why, look at Mary's brows. How could I deny her? She is the image of me, don't you think? And, Martha," he added, brushing his free hand over the child's head. "I see both of us in her."

"Jack," Beth said, hardly able to contain her laughter. Mouths were hanging open all over the room. He was actually attempting to make everyone believe they were *his!* Borne of *her!* God love him, she should make matters clear. "You do not understand..."

He brushed aside her protest. "It is time you let go this aversion to marriage, Beth, and grant me the opportunity to get acquainted with my children. If for no other reason, you must honor our engagement and marry me as soon as possible. Please."

She decided it would serve him right if she agreed. "Very well," she said with a curt nod of her head. "If the vicar is prepared."

A gasp went up from those assembled, and then whispers and chuckles abounded as the excitement spread. Her father beamed. Her mother rolled her eyes. Phemie slid onto the stool of the pianoforte and began playing a gay little tune totally inappropriate for the occasion. Colin began to sing off-key.

Mary clapped her hands and chimed in, making up her own lyrics while the other little ones noisily vied for their part of the attention.

It was not a solemn ceremony. The vicar had to shout to be heard. Jack laughed out loud when Beth purposely omitted the word *obey* from her vows. His *I will* resounded like a shout when an unexpected lull occurred.

Beth might have thought the entire ceremony a mockery had Jack's kiss not been the one brazenly serious act of the afternoon. Her own sigh blended with that of numerous other ladies present. A shameless romantic, her Jack.

And suddenly as that, Beth felt married in truth. She belonged to Jack Keith and he belonged to her. For better or worse, the deed was done. There was no undoing it.

Hours later Phemie locked her arm through Colin's as they headed for the stairs. Everyone was leaving now that the bride and groom had departed. The wedding festivities had lasted well into the evening.

How good it was to have Colin under the same roof. He had remained so that Beth and Jack would have more privacy for their wedding night at Whitfield Manor.

"I'll just show you where you are to sleep," she told him.

"How kind you are to trouble yourself," he replied, his smile as devilish as could be.

"Well, our scheme worked well, did it not?" she asked, supremely proud of herself. "Beth never suspected a thing."

"A tribute to your talents and mine, my dear. Neither did Jack. All that was needed really was for him to be without her for a while. He was so miserable!"

Phemie offered him her most adoring gaze. "I am so happy you came to me that next day for an explanation of Beth's children instead of asking Beth herself. If you had not confessed how much Jack loved her, I should never have confided in you. You must take full credit for their happiness."

"You had as great a hand in it. If you had not informed your uncle that Jack was the true heir after I confessed it, he might never have gone along with the plan to cook up this hasty wedding."

"Oh, he knew all along," Phemie told him. "At least after that first week. He always made it a point to investigate each of our suitors quite thoroughly." She shrugged and dimpled. "He had only put forth that dastardly Arthur Harnell to encourage Beth to choose another. You must admit it worked."

Colin's look of surprise tickled her. "So you knew from the start I wasn't the heir?" he asked. "And still you allowed—"

"Uncle is not the only one with a need for all the facts," she admitted. "He investigates. I snoop."

Phemie watched as he shook his head in wonder as if unable to think of a comment. Men needed prodding at times to speak their mind. And if their minds were not yet made up, prodding was even more essential.

"So, is your proposal forthcoming or shall I be forced to persuade you?" she asked prettily.

He blew out a breath of frustration. "At the moment, sweetheart, I fear I have little to offer you."

"You have yourself," she argued, "and that is *all* I require." And it was, of course, but he also would inherit a tidy sum from his maternal grandmother, according to Uncle's findings. No point in her giving away the surprise now, however.

His gaze softened as he stopped on the stairs and cradled her face in his hands. "How could I ever have thought you a fortune seeker? Why did you pretend?"

"Perhaps I feared exposing my heart?" She blinked up at him, letting her eyes fill with unshed tears.

"Oh, love, we play too many games to conceal what we feel," he said. "That serves no purpose, does it?"

"None at all that I can see!" she said with a brightness to rival all the candles in Auntie's huge chandelier. "Come, let's celebrate with a tot of Uncle's

Christmas cheer. I had a decanter delivered to your chamber when I ordered the room prepared."

He frowned. "Are you certain that's prudent, Phemie? We could be discovered. Remember what happened to Harnell and Aurelia Sapps."

"Yes, I remember," she said with a shrug and a daring smile.

He smiled back, looking as wicked as he ever had. "You're about to *persuade* me, aren't you, Phemie?"

On the way home to Whitfield, Jack struggled to keep his desire banked. Beth went out of her way to tempt him just as she had all afternoon and evening. He had been hard put to keep his hands off her even in company.

The moment they entered the drafty old manor, he regretted not whisking her away to somewhere grander, more in keeping with a honeymoon. But had he done so, it would necessitate traveling, and the five miles they had come provided quite enough of that.

He lifted her in his arms the moment old Carnes opened the door. "Meet my wife, Carnes," Jack shouted to the butler.

"I'm too old to beat anyone, milord," the deaf old fellow assured him in a crackled monotone.

Beth giggled as Jack carried her all the way upstairs, her arms around his neck, toying with his hair, sending flames licking through his veins.

"You are a troublemaker," he said as he tossed her onto his bed. "And a horrible tease!"

She laughed gaily and kicked off her slippers as she peeled off her gloves. "Who's teasing?"

"You might have waited until we were home to begin the seduction," he said in mock accusation as he sat beside her. He tossed off one boot and then looked at her. "I sincerely hope you won't regret this."

"So do I," she agreed, suddenly serious. "Were we too impulsive, Jack? Will you be sorry?"

He leaned back and embraced her. "Never in a million years." To prove it, he kissed her slowly and thoroughly, tasting her passion, her joy and her fears, as well. "Don't be afraid," he whispered against her ear. "Living without you is the worst fate I could imagine. Living with you is all I want in life."

She snuggled closer, returning his kisses, hampering his efforts to undress them both. Somehow, together they managed and soon lay as God had made them.

"You steal my breath, you are so beautiful," he told her as he feasted his eyes on her loveliness. "You smell so sweet, of jasmine and woman." His lips trailed down her throat to the ripe, small breasts already peaked and awaiting his kisses.

"And you, of spices and adventures in faraway places," she replied breathlessly.

"You are my grandest adventure by far." He fought the need to consume her on the instant, hoping to draw out their lovemaking, to make their first time memorable. He caressed her every curve, her slender waist, the gentle flare of her hip, a firm thigh and the sweet turn of her calf. How glorious was the smooth, warm skin that was his alone to touch. When his hand trailed up her inner thigh, she shuddered. Her sweet moan almost undid him completely.

"The sounds you make incite me," he said, his lips against her ear as his fingers sought her heat. "You want this," he murmured, his mind drugged with need at discovering how ready she was for him. "I want you, Beth. Only you."

She answered with a soft and wordless plea as he covered her and positioned himself to take all she offered. He might not be her first, but he vowed he would be her last.

"I am beyond waiting," he warned as he thrust inside her, claiming her with more aggression than he'd intended.

Her sharp intake of breath occurred the instant he realized his mistake and he stilled, unable to breath for the space of a second. "Oh, Beth," he groaned finally. "You *lied*." But what a marvelous lie it was. He *was* her first. Her first and only.

"You assumed," she murmured, now moving beneath him, urging him with her body to complete what he had begun.

With the greatest effort of his life, Jack gentled his

passion and spent it slowly, allowing her time to adjust to his invasion, drawing each foray out with almost excruciating delays.

"Exquisite," he breathed as he loved her. "Incomparable. Without equal." She proved all that and more.

Her body responded with an eagerness that tested his resolve to its limit. The instant he felt control desert him, she surrendered herself completely, driving him over an edge of pleasure he had never even dreamed existed.

His mind blanked of everything but soaring sensation, a breath-stealing explosion that left him unable to move. Their bodies seemed fused with a oneness he knew would remain in spirit long after they arose from this bed. She was his. Only his.

Her voice dragged him back to reality. "I suppose you must be wondering."

"I suppose. I am beyond guessing at the moment," he confessed, almost wishing she would simply lie there and let him feel. Thinking proved difficult in his present state. Reluctantly he made himself move to her side so that she could breathe comfortably. "Are you all right?" he remembered to ask.

"Mmm," she hummed, and he could hear the smile in it. "Better than that. I knew you would be excellent at this, but I must say you quite exceeded my expectations." She shivered and burrowed even closer.

He wanted to take her again, but figured he should

wait until his heartbeat regained some sort of normalcy. Besides, his curiosity deviled him now that she had brought the matter up. "How did you get the children?" he asked. The question sounded rather lackadaisical considering the importance of it.

"Adopted," she explained. "Do you mind?"

"That must be why they don't resemble us much," he said lazily as he stroked her back.

"Could be."

"What is the little fellow's name, by the way?" he asked. "You never said."

"You never asked. *Her* name is Deborah. They are all girls."

Jack smiled as he buried his nose in the curve of her neck. "They'll need brothers then. And there must be an heir to the title. Shall we?" He slid his hand down to her hip and coaxed her to lie on top. He loved the way her breasts pressed against him and her body seemed to seek his with unerring accuracy.

"An heir?" she questioned, bracing her arms on his chest to look down at him. "Oh, I see. You are heir to Colin now. But surely he will have sons."

The moment of truth. "I am Whitworth, Beth. Not Colin."

Her brows drew together and she tugged a tuft of his chest hair. "You lied, Jack!"

"You assumed," he said, repeating her excuse for their former misunderstanding. "Do you mind?"

She thrust out her chin and looked away, taking a moment to decide whether she should be angry. Then she faced him again. "In the spirit of Christmas, I suppose I must forgive you. But there can be no more secrets, Jack. No more charades. Not ever."

"Then you should admit that last secret you would keep from me." He sighed when she did not reply. "Well, I'm waiting."

"What secret?" she demanded.

"That you love me, you silly widgeon. There's no need to prevaricate about it now. It's clear as day and you'll never convince me otherwise."

She laughed merrily and propped her chin in one hand while she drummed her fingers against his chest with the other. "You'll have to torture that one out of me. Make me confess."

"Before this night is over," he warned as he moved beneath her suggestively. "I shall have you singing the words, see if I don't."

She brushed her fingers over his brow and bestowed the sweetest kiss of peace. "Happy Christmas, Jack."

"A day to remember," he assured her, "and a night to repeat forever."

* * * * *

Dear Reader,

If you are like me, the first word that pops into your mind when someone mentions Christmas is *presents*! From the divine gift of love to the tokens of affection exchanged by lovers, families, friends and co-workers, the season is symbolised by the spirit of giving.

Edwina Denby, the heroine of my story, is called upon to offer a unique kind of gift to Miles Hampden, a young soldier she secretly admires. In exploring her life as a soldier's daughter growing up in India, I came upon the ancient legends every child there would have heard. Although the Ramayana stories are from a different culture a world away, I was struck by how the themes of honour, sacrifice, courage and duty still resonate, as they have since the legends were written over two thousand years ago.

Great and timeless as these virtues are, it is love, selfless and self-sacrificing, that is truly life's greatest gift. I hope you will enjoy watching as Miles and Edwina find and offer this gift to each other.

Julia Justiss

The Three Gifts

by

Julia Justiss

To the men and women of our armed forces who daily go into harm's way all over the world so that we at home may be safe.

Chapter One

Outside Lisbon, Mid-November 1810

LIEUTENANT MILES HAMPDEN squinted into the setting sun at the twinkling of campfires that marked the enemy positions at the far side of the Lines of Torres Vedras. Fewer tonight, he noted. Having apparently accepted that he would not be able to lure Wellington out of his maze of defensive fortifications to do battle, it appeared General Messena was beginning to withdraw his troops.

So the French were leaving Portugal, as he would be shortly, Miles thought, shivering as a gust of November wind swirled over the barricade. With what little emotion remained to him, he could almost pity the half-starved enemy their long winter march through the barren countryside back to Spain.

He would be returning to the warmth and plenty of England, just in time for the beginning of the Christmas season. A prospect that, until the grim news that came last week, he would normally have greeted with gladness.

Instead of finding Hampden Glen decked in a festive array of holly and mistletoe, he would walk into a house wreathed in black. Instead of joining family and servants to haul in a Yule log, he would make a solitary pilgrimage to the family crypt that had held, for nearly a month by the time the letter reached him, the remains of his father and elder brother, killed in a carriage accident on their way home from a county fair.

The first raw blast of grief had faded, leaving him to go numbly through his duties for the few days remaining before he would catch a transport back to England. No longer simply Lieutenant Hampden of the Third Foot, but Viscount Hampden, head of the family and guardian to his widowed sister-in-law and her little daughter.

He would miss his comrades and the often dull, occasionally terrifying business of soldiering. But despite the fact that Wellington's army had not yet managed to drive the French out of the Peninsula, Miles had no choice but to resign his commission.

Not since, in the same cruel twist of fate that had turned a second son into a viscount, the new heir to the Hampden title had become Miles's cousin Reginald—a debauched gamester of such ill repute that even Wellington, generally loathe to release a battle-tested officer, had gruffly observed when he gave Miles his condolences that 'twas nothing for it but for the new viscount to sell out.

Eyes still watching the campfires, Miles's mouth hardened as he thought of Reggie. Already known as a drunkard, a cheat and a bully at Oxford, after being expelled from the university, his cousin had settled in London, where he further tarnished the Hampden name with escapades of vice and high-stakes gaming.

No, Miles could not remain a soldier and risk having the fate of gentle Agnes and her little Beth fall into Reginald's soiled hands. Nor could he tolerate the prospect of his cousin squandering the assets of the estate that generations of Hampdens had carefully tended.

Of course, as Wellington had wryly observed, if Miles were quick enough about the business, he might find a wife from among the Marriage Mart lovelies in town for the season, breed himself an heir to secure the succession and be back in time for next summer's campaign.

His general's dry humor gave his dulled spirits a slight lift. With a soldier's uncertain life stretching before him, he'd never given much thought to the marriage that duty—and the looming threat of Reggie inheriting now made a matter of priority. Beyond the basics of good breeding, competence and compatibility, what sort of woman should he choose?

Hunching his shoulders against the cold, he replayed in memory the short catalog of ladies who'd impressed him. There was the sultry Portuguese contessa with the dark eyes and smoky voice, who would doubtless enliven the marriage bed. The cool blond beauty he'd imagined himself in love with his first year on the town—elegant, perfectly gowned, a charming hostess, but whose conversation concerned solely ton gossip or fashion. Lacy Standish, the neighbor he'd grown up with, practical, easygoing, an accomplished estate manager, but more a friend than a potential lover.

It seemed he'd never met anyone who possessed all the qualities he admired in a lady—which didn't augur well for finding a suitable life's partner on the double-quick.

Sighing, he concluded that he would have to do the best he could with the selection available when the time came. Since, mercifully, now was not that time, he put the matter out of mind.

'Twas nearly full dark, signaling the end of his watch. After exchanging pleasantries with the lieutenant who relieved him, Miles retrieved his horse and rode off, hoping his batman would have some hot tea waiting and perhaps have found a hare for the stew pot.

His ears had barely registered the loud report of a musket when a stunning, red-hot blow slammed into his back. And then he was falling, falling out of the saddle into the inky dusk.

FROM A MURKY HAZE, Miles fought back to consciousness, his eyes drawn to a flicker of light. *Enemy campfires.* Then he realized he was gazing not over the barricade, but at a lantern hung near where he lay propped upon a cot, agonizing pain radiating from his back and chest.

"Thank God, you're awake!"

Through the confusion and discomfort, Miles recognized the voice of his friend and fellow lieutenant, Allen, Lord Sanbrook and cautiously turned his head.

"Steady now!" Sanbrook admonished. "Wilson says you must remain as still as possible."

"What…happened?" Miles asked.

A different voice—another friend, Lieutenant William Wheaten—answered, "The trooper on duty says a sniper hit you just as you were leaving the barricade. And the bastards are supposed to be retreating! A pox on frogs and all things French."

"How…bad is it?" Miles asked.

There was an ominous pause before Sanbrook said, "You took a ball through the back of your shoulder. It appears to be still lodged in your chest, though with this cursed darkness and all the bleeding, Wilson says 'tis difficult to tell. The devil of it is that Dr. MacAndrews is away in Lisbon and not due back until tomorrow."

Miles fought to stay conscious. "Wilson is here?"

"Aye, sir, right here," the surgeon's assistant said.

"Can you…remove the ball?"

"That's the rub of it, sir. That ball mighta come to rest between your heart and your lung—or mayhap it broke into pieces. I'm no physician, you know, and I'm not about to go probing about in there, for seeing as little as I can see and knowing as little as I know, I'd kill you for sure. You'll just have to hang on until the surgeon gets back."

Even through his pain, Miles could discern the note of fear in the assistant's voice.

"Will I…make it…until morning?"

"We'll surely be praying that you do," Wilson replied.

He could be dying, Miles realized. It seemed ironic, after coming unscathed through a fistful of battles, and the bitter retreat to Corunna, that he might be snuffed by a sniper's bullet while practically on his way out of the country. He longed to give in to the throbbing demon biting at his chest and sink back into oblivion, but a nagging sense that there was something important, something vital he must do, made him fight the looming darkness.

Duty came to him in a cold sweat of awareness.

Reginald.

"Can't let…Reggie inherit," he croaked, trying desperately to rally his strength.

"Damn, I'd forgotten the succession!" Sanbrook said.

"Nothing for it, old man," Wheaten said. "You'll just have to hold on until the sawbones can treat you.

"Could he will his estate to a comrade?" Wheaten asked. "Just for peace of mind," he added hastily.

"Probably not," Sanbrook answered. "If he tried to transfer assets to someone not kin by blood or marriage, Reginald would be sure to challenge it, and the courts would likely uphold the legal heir."

"If the matter is important," Wilson broke in,

"he'd best do something about it now, while he's still conscious."

Sanbrook fixed Wilson with a look. "You think it's that critical?"

Wilson nodded. "Regret to say it, but I do."

The surgeon's assistant didn't think he'd see morning, Miles realized. For the first time, fear swept over him. He could accept his own death, but surely heaven would not let his brother's already bereaved family suffer further!

With his last reserves of strength, he clutched Sanbrook's hand. "Must…do something."

His friend regarded him steadily, then nodded and turned to the surgeon's assistant. "Wilson, you know Sergeant Riggins of the Second Regiment? He's a solicitor by trade, I believe. Have him fetched here as quickly as possible. So, Hampden," he said, looking back at Miles, "it appears William and I will have to find you a bride."

Chapter Two

EDWINA CROFTON DENBY was rolling bandages at the small wooden table in her father's billet when her mother looked up from her needlework and frowned. "Such a sad duty for a young woman on a fine fair night!" Mrs. Crofton observed. "You ought to tease Papa into taking you to Lisbon. With Christmas soon upon us, there's bound to parties honoring General Wellington where you could dine and dance and enjoy the company of his handsome officers."

Edwina gave her mama a fond smile. "You know my work with the wounded brings me solace, Mama. And you also know Papa wouldn't dare take me to Lisbon, for he would have to take you, too, and the admirers you always attract would drive him quite distracted with jealousy."

Mrs. Crofton laughed. "Nonsense! I may have been a belle long ago, but 'tis you who would command their attention now." She hesitated, and Edwina braced herself for the advice sure to come.

Her mother continued, "'Tis more than a year since Talavera. I know you've said you have no wish to marry again, but you are still so young! You should pull your heart from the grave and look about you."

Despite her discomfort with her mother's well-meant advice, Edwina had no intention of putting a period to the argument by revealing it wasn't grief over her lost husband that made her disinclined to remarry. "I'm content to be here helping you and Papa."

"Yes, and we do love having you, but you deserve a home of your own. A husband, and children to delight you as you have delighted us."

A pang pierced her heart. If only Daniel could have given her a child, perhaps the disaster that had been her marriage would have been worth the pain. Damping down that old, familiar disappointment, she said, "Please, Mama, I don't wish to talk of it."

Tears brimming in her eyes, Mrs. Crofton came over to pat her daughter's hand. "I'm sorry, my dear, for broaching the matter again. Only you know how much your father and I long for you to find the happiness we have. The happiness you had with your dear Daniel."

Edwina swallowed the lump in her throat and vowed anew never to reveal to her tenderhearted mama how great a lie that was. Nor did she wish to risk bringing on an attack of the vapors by revealing what she really intended to do once she'd seen Papa safely through this war: return to England and use the money she would inherit from grandfather to set up her own establishment.

Thanks to his bequest, the Lord be praised, she need not marry again.

A knock at the door pulled her from her thoughts. With the responsiveness of a combat officer of many years' experience, her papa, who'd been dozing in an armchair by the fire, jolted awoke and paced to the door.

He opened it to reveal two soldiers standing in the shadows, lamplight gleaming on their officer's lacing. "So sorry to disturb you, Major Crofton," one of them said. "We've come to beg an urgent favor."

"Enter, gentlemen, and warm yourselves by the fire," her father replied. "May I offer you both some port?"

"No, thank you, sir," replied the first. As they strode toward the hearth, Edwina recognized Lieutenant Wheaten and Lieutenant Lord Sanbrook from a neighboring regiment, the Third Foot. "We must be off immediately."

"How may I help you, then?" her father asked.

"One of our comrades was gravely wounded by sniper fire a short time ago. As you may know, Dr. MacAndrews is not in camp at present. His assistant, Corporal Wilson, sent us to see if your daughter might come assist him."

Her father gestured to Edwina. "Ask her yourself."

Lord Sanbrook turned pleading eyes toward Edwina. "I know 'tis late, ma'am, but could you please come? Wilson says, except for the doctor himself, you have more experience than anyone in nursing the badly wounded and—" the two lieutenants exchanged an uneasy glance "—I'm afraid our friend's case is desperate."

"Who is the wounded soldier?" Edwina asked.

"Lieutenant Hampden."

Her mother gasped. "Oh, the poor man! Was he not supposed to leave for England in a few days?"

"Yes, ma'am," Wheaten confirmed.

Edwina drew in a shocked breath of her own. Though she didn't know the lieutenant well, she had been intensely aware of him every time he'd chanced to visit Papa's regiment. It was not just his handsome face and tall, commanding figure that drew her eye, but an aura of confidence and enthusiasm that lifted the spirits of everyone he met—even this rather shy widow of no particular beauty.

"Of course I will come," she replied. "Let me get my cloak."

A few minutes later, wrapped in that warm, fur-lined garment, she set off on horseback, her thoughts consumed with worried speculation about the lieutenant's condition. From the looks that passed between his friends and the grim lines into which their faces settled as they rode, she surmised that his condition was indeed perilous.

How sad it would be if such a vital, compelling young man were to lose his life tonight.

After a short ride, they reached the hospital tents. But to her surprise, after helping her down from the saddle, Lord Sanbrook put a restraining hand on her arm.

"Before you go in, I must explain the singular circumstances in which Lieutenant Hampden now finds himself. I beg you will hear the whole before you respond, even if some of it seems a bit...shocking."

Puzzled, Edwina answered, "Of course. Only tell me at once, that I might go assist Wilson."

"The ball that pierced Lieutenant Hampden's shoulder may have lodged in his chest. Wilson dares not probe for it and fears Hampden may not survive until the surgeon returns tomorrow. As I imagine you've heard, Miles recently became Viscount Hampden. As matters now stand, should he die, his cousin, a vice-ridden, debauched gamester, will inherit. He would also become guardian and trustee to the recently widowed Lady Hampden and her young daughter. I assure you, did you know Reginald Hampden as I do, you would realize the Devil himself would be more fit to have charge of such innocents."

"Then we must all hope Lieutenant Hampden confounds Wilson's expectations and survives."

"And so we do. But hindering Hampden's fight to survive is his great distress over what his kinswomen would suffer at his cousin's hands, should he succumb to his wounds. That, ma'am, is the matter with which we most need your assistance."

Edwina nodded. "I shall be happy to help in any way I can."

"The assistance we require is of a rather...personal nature. To state it baldly, ma'am, we propose to have you marry Lieutenant Hampden."

Edwina shook her head, sure she could not have heard him correctly. "You wish me to do what?"

Coloring faintly, Sanbrook cleared his throat. "Marry him," he repeated, more confidently this time. "You see, if Miles is married, he can will the guardianship of the widowed Lady Hampden, as well as all the assets of the estate which are not entailed, to his wife, with his solicitors as trustees, thereby protecting his niece and sister-in-law and at least some of the Hampden estate. The necessary paperwork is being completed as we speak and a chaplain is standing by to perform the ceremony. All we lack is a bride." He smiled at her. "We sincerely hope to persuade you to play that role."

Edwina stared at him for a full minute. "You must be mad," she said flatly, and turned back toward her horse.

Lord Sanbrook caught her shoulder. "Please, ma'am, don't go! I know 'tis an extraordinary request."

"Indeed," she said, shaking off his hand.

"Only consider! You'd be easing the last hours of a valiant soldier and—pray excuse me for putting the matter so crudely—saving the jointure and quite likely the person of a grieving widow from being ravished by a man who would hold her completely in his legal power. I beg you to think it over again before you refuse."

"I should dismiss it outright," Edwina retorted. The very notion that the handsome, titled Lieutenant Hampden would even consider taking to wife a nondescript widow of scant beauty and few family connections was ludicrous. Suddenly suspicious, she turned on Sanbrook. "This was your idea, wasn't it?

Surely Lieutenant Hampden did not send you on such a mad scheme."

"It was indeed his wish, ma'am, which he will shortly confirm. He would, of course, have preferred to explain the whole to you himself, but Wilson and I thought it best for him to conserve what little strength he has left. Please, ma'am. We should not ask this of you were the situation not truly desperate."

Unbelievable as it all seemed, she could tell from his voice and manner that Lord Sanbrook was in deadly earnest. It still seemed outrageous—a clandestine midnight marriage to a dying nobleman—but if the heir to the Hampden title were as dissolute and unprincipled as Sanbrook painted him, the thought of a widow trapped in legal thrall to such a man was equally appalling. Despite her initial resistance, she felt compassion stir.

"I concede the situation appears grave. But what if I agree to your proposal and, by God's mercy, Lieutenant Hampden survives?"

"Then if you both wish it, you may tear up the contract and go your separate ways, with no one the wiser."

"Just like that?" Edwina angled her head to gaze up at him. "I cannot imagine any chaplain agreeing to marry us on such terms."

Sanbrook returned a rueful grin. "Were the circumstances not so extraordinary, I expect you would be correct. However, being well acquainted with the excellence of Hampden's character and realizing the gravity of his condition, Chaplain Darrow agreed to officiate, as long as you pledge that you are entering this…unusual union of your own free will. Should Miles survive, a small gift in appreciation of your efforts could be arranged. Whereas, if our hopes for his recovery are not answered, you would of course receive a generous widow's competence."

Edwina stiffened. "If I agree to this, I will accept no reimbursement of any kind. I shall do it only to safeguard Lady Hampden and ease Lieutenant Hampden's suffering. But I shall not agree to anything until I hear this astounding proposal from Lieutenant Hampden's own lips."

Sanbrook nodded. "Then let us make haste while that is still possible."

Edwina wasn't sure what she expected, but from the sickly sweet odor of blood emanating from Hampden's cot and the panicky expression on Wilson's face, she realized Sanbrook had not overstated the gravity of his friend's condition.

"Thank heaven you be here at last!" Wilson said as he advanced to meet them. With a glance over his shoulder at his patient, he continued in softer tones, "Near half a dozen times, I feared I'd lost him."

Lord Sanbrook addressed a man in the uniform of a sergeant. "Is all the paperwork ready?"

"Aye, sir," the sergeant replied.

"You're sure it will withstand a possible court challenge?"

The sergeant gave Lord Sanbrook a chilly look.

"Before I signed on with Wellington, I was the best solicitor in Liverpool. Try as they might, not the fanciest of London lawyers will be able to find a loophole in these documents."

While the men talked, Edwina found her attention drawn to the man propped on the cot. Pain cut furrowed lines in his forehead as he exhaled shallow, panting breaths. From the fixed gaze of his eyes and the clench of his fists on the cot frame, she sensed that he was holding on to consciousness only by a ferocious effort.

Pity and regret for a life that appeared almost certain to be lost soon swelled in her breast.

Then Lieutenant Hampden saw her. The legal and social ramifications of the dilemma faded from mind as, in his fevered eyes, she read the desperate plea for help of a wounded being to the person he knew could ease his torment.

Without another thought, she walked over and took his hand. "Lieutenant, I was so sorry to hear of your injury."

"Thank you…for entertaining…so outrageous a proposition, Mrs. Denby."

His fingers, damp with sweat, barely returned the pressure of hers. "Hush, now, you must save your strength," she said, her heart contracting once more with pity. "Are you sure you wish to do this?"

"Would do me…utmost honor…if you consent…to become my wife," he said, panting a bit at the end.

Afterward she could not remember ever making a

conscious decision. She simply heard herself saying, "I would be honored to accept your proposal."

"Excellent!" Sanbrook said. "Chaplain Darrow," he called, "The vows, if you please."

Emerging from the shadows at the far side of the tent, the reverend nodded to Sanbrook, then turned to address Edwina. "You are sure you wish to do this?"

For an instant, panic swept through her, but a single glance at Hampden's pain-lined face was sufficient to banish it. "Yes, Father Darrow. I am sure."

"Very well, my child. May God bless you for your compassion." Placing his hand over the limp fingers Edwina still held, the reverend began to read the familiar words of the wedding service.

As the proceedings went forward, Edwina had to suppress a hysterical giggle at the unreality of it all: the flickering red glow of the lantern, the wounded bridegroom gasping out his vows, his friend helping him place the heavy, bloodstained signet ring on her finger. Then it was over and the chaplain proclaimed them man and wife.

"Save the kiss...for later," her bridegroom whispered. His eyes fluttered shut and he sagged back, as if a great burden had been lifted.

For one charged moment, Edwina thought her new husband had expired, until her panicked eyes noted the slight rise and fall of the chest that indicated he remained, for the moment, among the living.

Sinking down on a stool, she numbly accepted the congratulations of the minister and the solicitor, who speedily withdrew. An awkward silence fell between her and the friends of the man on the cot to whom, apparently, she was now legally married.

"He shall be forever in your debt," Sanbrook said softly. "'Twas a truly noble and unselfish act."

"Indeed, ma'am," Wheaten echoed. "But this must be all quite a shock. May we escort you back to your father's billet now?"

Unreal as the wedding appeared, it seemed callous to vow to honor, cherish and obey and then ride back to her father's encampment while her titular husband lay dying. Nor, in truth, did she know yet what she would say to her parents about this night's odd business.

"Corporal Wilson, you did wish my assistance nursing…the lieutenant?" she asked, unable to get her lips around the word *husband*.

"Indeed, Mrs.—Lady Hampden. It would ease my mind."

Edwina shook off the little shiver—part apprehension, part something else she didn't wish to identify—at the sound of her new title on his lips. "Then I shall stay and tend him. You believe the ball may be lodged in his chest, I understand. Then I don't suppose we should move him."

"No, ma'am."

"If I might have some water, to cleanse the wound and cool his brow? And if either of you has some spirits, I can give him a sip to ease his pain, should he wake." She gave Sanbrook and Wheaten a slight smile.

"I shall try my best to make his last hours as comfortable as possible."

Lord Sanbrook bowed. "Allow Wheaten and me to assist. As Darrow said, your compassion does you great credit."

Edwina waved off his praise. "Nonsense, 'tis only fitting. Since it appears that, however briefly, I am now his lordship's wife."

Chapter Three

LORD HAMPDEN'S WIFE. Edwina would have laughed, were the situation not so tragic. Once upon a time, she might have felt like the heroine in one of the gothic tales Mama so enjoyed, to find herself suddenly married to a handsome, titled, agreeable young man. Until Daniel, seemingly the embodiment of every girlish dream, had seared through her life and burned such childish ideas to ash.

Only in a tale as fantastical as the Hindu legends her ayah used to tell her when she was growing up would Viscount Hampden *choose* to marry Edwina Denby, daughter of a baron's younger son and a wealthy merchant's daughter. Not only was she far beneath his touch in the eyes of English society, she had seen him at regimental parties, surrounded by a cooing coterie of local ladies or dancing with the slender, doe-eyed Portuguese beauties he apparently favored. He would hardly pick a tall, plain, brown-haired English girl whose only notable attributes were a fine set of hazel eyes and the promise, several years hence, of inheriting a fortune. Particularly since, if the gossip being whispered about the encampment were accurate, the new viscount had no need of an Indian nabob's riches to refill the family coffers.

She sighed. If she had known when she first met him how badly Daniel *had* needed that wealth, how differently her life might have transpired!

At least she had entered this marriage mercifully free of illusions. And she could repay the trust Hampden had placed in her by capably tending her temporary husband.

At that moment, Lord Sanbrook returned with a basin of water. "Here you are, ma'am. After discussing the matter, Wilson and I thought that once you've done all you can for Hampden, Wheaten could escort you home. We'll stay with him the rest of the night."

They wished to spare her having to watch as Hampden breathed his last, Edwina thought. Not a tragedy she was keen to witness, yet part of her, illogically enough, resisted the idea of abandoning the man whose limp fingers she still retained in a light grasp. "I shall remain until I am fatigued, at which point I will gladly claim the lieutenant's escort. Ah, you found brandy."

After Sanbrook handed over the water and the spirits, Edwina set to work. She had thought Hampden unconscious, but as she gently eased his jacket open to wash his chest, he stirred under her touch. "Thank...you," he murmured.

Heartened to find him still responsive, she said, "Would you like some water? Wilson has propped you high enough that I believe you can drink, if I hold the cup."

The lieutenant returned a barely perceptible nod. A whistled inhale of breath after his first sip told her it must hurt him to swallow, but he persevered. After refusing her offer of spirits, he braced himself, only his gritted teeth revealing the cost of his silence as she finished cleansing his wounds.

Having done all she could to give Dr. MacAndrews a clear field on which to treat his patient if, by God's mercy, the lieutenant survived until his return, she sent Wilson away with a request for more clean water.

A feeble tug at her hand startled her. "Don't...go," Hampden whispered. "Please stay and...talk to me."

He must have overheard his friend's intention to bear her away. Once again, sadness and sympathy swelled in her breast, strengthening her resolve not to leave him. How many dying soldiers had she sat beside simply talking, filling their last hours with a feminine presence that soothed them with memories of home and family? Surely she could do no less for Hampden.

"Of course," she replied. "What shall I say?"

"Tell me...about you."

She supposed it was only natural that he would want to know more about the woman he'd so precipitously married, though her recent past wasn't something she enjoyed recounting. Best to summarize briefly and move on.

"Papa came to India in the army as a young man, where he met Mama, the daughter of a prosperous East India Company merchant. I was born and grew up in Bombay, living there until Papa's regiment was recalled here to the peninsula. Shortly before we were to leave, I met and married a young officer, Daniel Denby. He…he was killed at the battle of Talavera."

Hampden's eyes flickered. "Son of…Lord Alveney?"

Edwina stiffened. What had he heard? "Yes," she replied cautiously.

"Good family," Hampden said, closing his eyes again.

"Yes," Edwina returned drily, relaxing a trifle. Good family indeed. How many times had Daniel reminded her what rare good fortune it had been for one of her humble birth to snare a husband of such exalted lineage?

"After that, I felt I should remain and help Mama care for Papa until the war ends," she continued, hoping to forestall any inquiry he might make about why the widow had not returned to England and the shelter of her husband's family. "Mama has the sweetest of good natures and never complains, no matter how wretched the conditions, but she's not very… practical."

One blue eye opened. "You're…practical?"

"Oh, very," she confirmed. The only talent Daniel had grudgingly come to appreciate was her ability to create an oasis of comfort out of the chaos of an army on the march. "I've become quite an excellent campaigner, able to set up in anything from a hovel to a tent, and capable of coaxing a meal from the most unlikely ingredients. In addition to always having a fire blazing and a hot drink ready when Papa returns from duty."

"Excellent…skills for a wife," Hampden observed, his lips curving in the slightest of smiles.

Edwina felt herself flushing, unsure whether or not he was mocking her. "That's enough about me," she said, determined to turn the subject. "I should like to know more about you, too, but we'll save that for later. What else would you have me speak about?"

"Nursed a friend. Had…high praise…for your stories."

"Stories about India?" she asked, wondering if his comrade had been one of the wounded whom she'd distracted from his pain by recounting tales of valor, wisdom and treachery from the epic poems that had captivated her as a child.

"Yes. India," her husband whispered.

Relieved to escape more personal matters, after coaxing Hampden to take another sip of water, Edwina sat back. A pang of sadness and something else shot through her as his fingers moved on the cot, seeking hers.

Laying her hand on top of his larger one, she took a deep breath and began, "Long ago there lived a handsome prince named Rama. Sent by his father the king to a neighboring land whose ruler sought a strong and valiant prince to marry his daughter, Rama entered the competition for the hand of the beautiful Princess Sita.

Of all the noblemen assembled, only Rama succeeded at every challenge the ruler set before them. Sita soon fell in love with the resourceful prince, and he with her. The young lovers were married with great pomp and ceremony.

After the couple returned to Rama's home, his father announced his intention to turn over the throne to Rama. But the king's second wife objected. Reminding the king that he had once promised to grant her any two wishes, she told him that her first was to have her son rule instead of Rama. Her second was that Rama be banished.

Loyal and honorable as well as brave, Rama accepted that his father must keep his word. He meant to leave his beloved wife behind in the comfort of his father's kingdom, but Sita insisted on accompanying him into the wildness of the forest. 'As shadow is to substance, so a wife is to her husband,' she said, pleading that he let her walk before him and smooth his path...."

As Edwina narrated her story, Lieutenant Lord Sanbrook nodded off and Wheaten began to snore softly. Gradually the tenseness in Hampden's body eased, until finally he fell into a light sleep, his breathing growing fainter and more shallow.

He is slipping away, she thought, tears stinging her eyes. But when she paused, intending to wipe them away, she felt an almost imperceptible tightening on her fingers.

Hampden's blue eyes struggled open. "Don't... stop," he said, his voice the merest breath.

Edwina swallowed past the constriction in her throat. "I won't," she promised.

And so, through the rest of the long night, Edwina continued relating the adventures of Prince Rama and his bride. By the time the darkness outside the tent began to lighten with the approach of dawn, her throat was as hoarse and aching as her heart and she no longer tried to restrain the tears dripping down her cheeks.

This time when she raised a hand to swipe at her eyes, however, she found Lord Sanbrook awake, watching her.

"You've done far more than anyone had a right to expect," he whispered. "Miles is unconscious now. Let Wheaten take you home. I'll stay with him until...the end."

Exhausted, drained—and angry at being forced once again to witness the cost of war, for which the politicians back in England had no appreciation—she nodded. Gently she slipped her fingers from the lax but still warm hand in which they had rested through the night.

"I'll call upon you later," Sanbrook said as she rose.

Edwina turned to walk away, then paused. Though the thought of making such a gesture under the eyes of his friends brought hot color to her cheeks, she nevertheless felt compelled to bend down and brush her lips against Hampden's forehead. "Farewell, husband," she whispered.

"Go get some rest, Lady Hampden," Sanbrook said.

How astonished Mama would be to hear her called

that, the thought struck Edwina as she followed Wheaten out of the tent.

SHE WAS WALTZING in the arms of a strong young man—her bridegroom. Giddy with happiness, she turned to wave at Mama and Papa, who beamed their approval from the head table under the tent erected on the grounds of Papa's quarters in the Bombay cantonment. Men in red-coated dress uniforms glittering with medals swirled past her, women in a butterfly hue of gowns clasped in their arms.

Her new husband pulled her scandalously closer, molding her against his well-muscled length. Her breasts tingled, her belly and thighs flamed as the movements of the dance brushed her against her husband's legs and abdomen…against the hard bulge in his breeches.

Soon enough they would steal away, and with sighs and kisses she would be free to shed his garments and explore every inch of the body that tantalized her, as he explored every inch of hers.

Laughing with the sheer wonder of it, she glanced up. Somehow the tented cantonment had vanished, replaced by the glitter of a Lisbon ballroom. Instead of Daniel's grim visage staring down at her, finely molded lips smiled in a face whose heated, intense blue eyes promised their owner, too, was anticipating the delights of the bedchamber.

Miles Hampden's face.

Edwina woke with a start to find her skin flushed

and her breathing rapid. So vivid was the dream, it took her a moment to separate illusion from reality.

How had her mind gotten so muddled? she wondered, trying to still her pounding heart. She'd noticed Lieutenant Hampden as he came and went about his duties, of course—what woman could not? But from where had such scandalous thoughts about him sprung?

Suddenly she remembered—the midnight tent in a red glow of blood and candlelight, the hastily performed ceremony. Miles Hampden was now her husband.

He'd done nothing more amorous after the ceremony than squeeze her fingers, Edwina reminded herself. Nor, she felt certain, would he have been inclined to proceed further even had he not been gravely wounded. There was absolutely no reason that the memory of his hand holding hers should make her fingers tremble and burn.

As for her dream, she should dismiss it. After all, in the way of dreams, everything else about the images had been distorted. Certainly Daniel had never looked at her with such desire in his eyes. Even as early in their marriage as the morning of the wedding breakfast, she'd had to feign the aura of happiness.

Better that she rise and dress, figure out something to tell Mama and then go tend her new husband.

If he still lived.

She'd just thrown on her clothes and run a brush through her rioting brown curls when a loud pounding on the house's outer door brought her rushing into the main room.

Standing on the threshold, obviously trying to coax Mama's Portuguese maid into allowing him entry, was Lieutenant Lord Sanbrook.

A glance at his ashen, hollow-eyed face sent Edwina's stomach plunging and she brought one hand to her chest. "Is he—" she asked in a voice gone suddenly faint.

Lord Sanbrook's face broke into a grin. "No! He's much improved. Come, you must see!"

Wearing a frilly dressing gown with a matching lace mobcap over her blond curls, Edwina's mother emerged from her bedchamber. "What's all the fuss?" Mrs. Crofton demanded. "Who has improved?"

Before Edwina could decide how best to answer that question, Sanbrook said, "Your daughter's husband."

Chapter Four

WHILE ASTONISHMENT registered on her mama's face, Edwina flashed Sanbrook a warning look before turning to the maid. "Bring coffee, please, Juanita?"

The girl nodded, her dark eyes alight with curiosity. Edwina suppressed an inward groan. Juanita's command of English might be less than perfect, but unless Edwina was much mistaken, whispers of a midnight marriage would begin to circulate within the camp as soon as the maid left to draw water.

Shrugging off that concern, Edwina continued, "Won't you both sit? After I tell Mama what happened, Lord Sanbrook, I will be happy to accompany you."

As they sipped the scalding brew, Edwina sketched for her mother the events of the previous night. "If Lieutenant Hampden is, as I sincerely hope, on the way to recovery," she concluded, "all that transpired will soon be reversed, so I beg you will mention this to no one but Papa. Please, dear Mama?"

"Married!" her mama exclaimed, shaking her head.

"Edwina, how could you—and in such a havey-cavey fashion! Oh, 'tis most upsetting!"

"Do not worry, Mrs. Crofton, everything was quite properly done," Lord Sanbrook assured her. "Regardless of what transpires next, your daughter and her good name will be fully protected."

"Married," Mrs. Crofton repeated. Suddenly her face broke into a smile of pure delight. "And to such an excellent young man!"

"Now Mama, 'twas not a true wedding," Edwina cautioned.

"Well, married is married, to my way of thinking," Mrs. Crofton muttered, a gleam in her eye.

Edwina sighed. "I shall try to do better at explaining it all later, Mama, but now I must see Lieutenant Hampden. Has Dr. MacAndrews returned?" she asked Lord Sanbrook as she rose and fetched her cloak.

"Yes, earlier this morning," Sanbrook replied. "He was able to locate the remaining fragments of the ball just beneath Hampden's shoulder blade, which means—praise God—the injury is less serious than we originally feared. He will require careful tending, but it appears Miles has an excellent chance of making a full recovery."

"That *is* wonderful news," Edwina replied, genuinely happy for the lieutenant. She would much rather their hasty marriage be quietly reversed by its participants than terminated by her unexpected husband's death.

"Shall we go, then, Lady Hampden?" Lord Sanbrook said. "Miles has been asking for you."

"Lady Hampden—ooh, I like the sound of that!" Mrs. Crofton said, smiling again.

"Don't accustom yourself to it, Mama, for 'tis only temporary," Edwina advised, throwing a repressive look at Juanita, who carefully avoided her gaze. Her clandestine marriage and, if God smiled on the lieutenant's recovery, its subsequent cancellation would set tongues wagging, but the embarrassment would hopefully be short-lived.

At least she would not have to conceal the truth of this marriage from her parents, as she'd had to hide the travesty of her first one.

With that encouraging thought, she took the arm Lord Sanbrook offered and walked out of the house.

AS SOON AS THEY EXITED, Edwina said to Lord Sanbrook, "I assure you, despite Mama's...*romantical* notions, I am fully prepared to abide by the conditions of the bargain we made last night. I'm sure Lieutenant Hampden will wish to go about dissolving the union as quickly as possible, and I shall do all in my power to assist him."

Sanbrook gave her an approving nod. "I would imagine he does intend to do so, once his recovery progresses, but he told me this morning that for the present, he wished you to be treated with every courtesy as his wife. He specifically instructed me to insure you were addressed by your proper title. So," he added with a grin, "if I may help you to mount, my lady?"

Surprised, Edwina raised her eyebrows, mild resentment flashing through her as she accepted his assistance. Of course, an aristocrat like Hampden would want to have even a temporary possession marked as his own. He'd doubtless never considered that it might be easier for her if everything about their brief marriage were handled as discreetly as possible. Even under the best of circumstances, she'd have a great deal of unpleasant gossip to face down once he was gone and she returned to her former name and position.

A moment later she chastised herself for a lack of charity. It was most unfair for her to convict the lieutenant, about whose character she knew so little, of blind self-absorption. The concern for the fate of his sister-in-law and her child that had driven Hampden to embrace so drastic a means to protect them certainly spoke well of him.

Of course, those kinswomen were of his own rank. In the unflinching light of day, would he be embarrassed by his hastily acquired bride?

A wave of remembered humiliation washed through her, shaking the calm she'd resolved to display and making her clench her teeth to keep back tears. By the time they reached the hospital tents, her empty stomach was queasy.

Well, she was no longer an infatuated maid with a head full of empty dreams and a heart to be broken, she told herself. If she dealt with Hampden in a sensible, matter-of-fact manner, surely any embarrassment either of them felt would be of short duration and they could go about disentangling their lives with the cool dispatch that would be best for them both.

After they dismounted, Lord Sanbrook put out a hand to stay her advance. "Miles said he would like to speak with you privately, if you would permit."

Edwina damped down another wave of uneasiness. "Since in his current condition, the viscount could hardly overcome me with the force of his ardor, I imagine I shall be safe enough alone with him," she replied, trying for a light tone.

"Then I will leave you to him," Sanbrook replied, clearly relieved to have been given permission to withdraw.

For a few more moments she tarried, watching Lord Sanbrook stride away. *Time to begin bearing the weight of last night's hasty decision,* she told herself. Then, squaring her shoulders and taking a deep breath, Edwina opened the makeshift door to the hospital tent. As she caught sight of her husband, her mouth dried and the words of greeting shriveled on her lips.

The man on the cot this morning, his big-framed body alert rather than slack-limbed, his face smiling rather than creased in pain, appeared to be mastering his injuries rather than succumbing to them. His color only a bit pale, Lieutenant Hampden watched her as she approached, his lips curved in a smile whose potent charm hit her right in the belly while his avid, blue-eyed gaze captured hers. "My lady wife! Please, do come in."

He looked, she thought, swallowing hard, somehow much...larger than he'd appeared last night. Larger and far more virile and commanding than a man who'd taken a shot through the shoulder only last evening had any right to look. It seemed unbelievable that this imposing man with the compelling eyes could truly be her husband.

For an instant, a vision from the dream that had awakened her—Hampden's arms around her, his torso rubbing hers—flashed through her mind, setting her body aflame in all the appropriate places. She felt heat flush her face. Heart pounding, she forced herself to advance. Perhaps she ought to consider marrying again, she thought as she struggled to recapture her calm, if she were going to be prey to such lustful urges.

But not to a man as well-born and attractive as Viscount Hampden.

One such disaster of a marriage had been quite enough.

SO THIS WAS THE LADY he'd married, Miles thought. Of course, he'd known by reputation the woman Sanbrook had suggested to him as a bride, but his personal acquaintance with her had been slight.

Miles studied the tall, slender form and graceful carriage of the young woman walking toward him, taking in the pale oval face around which light brown curls peeped from beneath her bonnet. Her eyes met his appraising gaze squarely, he noted with approval, only a slight flush on her cheeks testifying to whatever chagrin or discomfort she might be feeling.

Those eyes—ah, yes, he remembered her eyes from the first time he'd met her in her father's camp. Her cheeks flushing then as they were now, she'd raised them to him shyly as she'd murmured a greeting. Large, lustrous eyes of a hue between green and blue that reminded him of the sparkling, aquamarine ocean off the Portuguese coast.

They were as mesmerizing as the husky, warm-as-melted-chocolate voice that had flowed over his agonized body through the night and brought him ease. Indeed, he was more than half-convinced that, worn down by pain, exhaustion and worry, he might have yielded his spirit to those demons of the night, had that beguiling voice not kept him tethered to earth.

To his surprise, she curtseyed before taking the stool beside his cot. "Good morning, my lord. I'm delighted to see you looking so much better."

So, she wished to be formal? Since he wasn't sure yet how to proceed, perhaps that was best.

"Thank you, Lady Hampden. I'm equally delighted to be feeling better. Though, given the extraordinary favor you have done me, might you consider calling me Miles?"

She smiled slightly. "I appreciate the honor, but since, the Lord be praised, it appears that last night's—arrangements—are no longer necessary, I would be more comfortable if we address each other as the mere acquaintances we shall shortly once again become. Indeed, if you wish, I am quite amenable to pretending the whole, ah, business never transpired."

A bit disconcerted by her seeming urgency to be quit of him, Miles shook his head. "I'm afraid it will not be so easy. At this distant remove from England, I expect we could probably get by with simply tearing up the wedding contract, but vows uttered before a minister of God, whatever the setting, are rather more binding."

Her green eyes blinked before she lowered her face. Butterfly wings, Miles thought, distracted by the play of the long lashes against her fair skin.

"I see," his wife said in small voice. "So we shall have to apply for an annulment through the church?"

"I'm not sure. Under normal circumstances, an annulment would be almost impossible to obtain. But," he added hastily when she looked back up at him, those lustrous eyes wide with alarm, "the circumstances being far from normal, I had hoped Chaplain Darrow might be persuaded to…disallow the proceedings. When I asked him about it this morning, though sympathizing with our situation, he informed me he did not feel he had the authority to do so and recommended that we consult the bishop's representative in Lisbon. I have every intention of fulfilling the hope that my wound will heal and the soil of Portugal will not, after all, be my final resting place, but until I am completely certain of that outcome, I would like to leave in place the legal protections for my family we were at such pains to construct. You understand my caution?"

She'd lowered her head again, her small even

teeth worrying her lip—a rather lush lip, he noted with masculine appreciation. "How, then, do you wish to proceed?"

"I had intended to keep our compact secret—until the men in my company somehow learned about last night's wedding and came by this morning to either toast my survival or console my widow. I must beg your forgiveness for proceeding without first asking your approval, but I decided at that moment to confirm the news. I wish to show everyone I expect you to be treated with the same deference as if the wedding had taken place in your family's private chapel or at St. George's instead of in a tent."

"So there can be no slurs or innuendo attached to my name," she said after a moment. Again color came and went in her cheeks. "That was kind of you, my lord."

Pleased at her understanding of his motives, he gave her his most charming smile. "You do not think you could try *Miles?*"

She shook her head firmly. "*Lieutenant*, or *Hampden*, if you prefer, is more proper."

"I suppose for the present I must settle for *Hampden*. Until we sort this out, it might be more comfortable for you to avoid the curious or impertinent by spending much of your time here, as a new wife would be expected to tend her wounded husband. While I regain my strength and we become better acquainted, we can consider how best to resolve this matter."

"There is only one resolution that was ever contemplated if you survived, my lord—a complete dissolution of the agreement. Surely you can understand *my* concern about that."

Once again, Miles felt stung. Then, his usual good humor reasserting itself, he said wryly, "And here I was, considering that since I'm already a rather fine fellow, becoming a titled nobleman of means would render me an irresistible matrimonial prize! But now that the news has gotten out, you must realize the considerable harm your reputation might suffer if we disavow the proceedings. I'm not in habit of marrying ladies and then abandoning them."

She met his gaze steadily. "I didn't mean to be disparaging. But 'tis nonsense to consider yourself in any way beholden to me, nor am I in need of assistance. Since I intend to remain here with the army, where I am well-known and where the circumstances that prompted our bargain would be well-appreciated, I doubt my reputation will suffer. I thought I made it quite clear to Lord Sanbrook last night that I would not..." Her flush deepened and she looked away, avoiding his glance. "That is to say," she continued, "there is no question of any, ah, reimbursement, other than your thanks for my assisting you through a time of great anxiety."

"You certainly did that. Even more, you kept me alive when Wilson had all but despaired of my survival."

"Well, he may have been worried last night, but from what I understand Dr. MacAndrews discovered this morning, it appears you were never in peril of succumbing."

"We needn't dispute that now. May I ask you for one more favor—to tend me until I am well enough to proceed to Lisbon? Your excellent nursing shall ensure that I do recover, and we will have time to discuss ending our bargain in the manner you desire."

Again she hesitated. Miles found himself more strongly driven to obtain her agreement than he could have imagined. "I promise not to be too much of a burden," he coaxed. "And besides, I want more of your story."

Mercifully, that brought a smile to her face. "I can't believe you remember any of it."

"Of course I do! 'Twas a fascinating tale, about a valiant prince and his faithful bride and a banishment. You must tell me the rest."

She shook her head. "I can't imagine you are truly interested."

"But I am. The heroic scale of the saga you recounted reminded me of the Greek epics I studied at Oxford."

Looking pleased, she nodded. "The Rama stories are nearly as old. My ayah made each tale so wonderfully vivid, she kindled in me a love of literature I still possess. Being a rather shy child, I naturally gravitated to reading."

"Your brothers or sisters did not bedevil you into more active pursuits?"

"No. 'Tis a harsh climate, as you may know, and Mama's other three children died as babes. Growing up mostly alone, encouraged later by a governess who also loved the classics, I became what the ton would call a veritable bluestocking."

"What better occupation for a bluestocking than to use her erudition to entertain her recuperating husband?"

He was treated to a pointed glance from those sea-green eyes. "Her *temporary* husband."

Miles grinned. "We shall see. I have no intention of making you a widow just yet."

Those exquisite eyes flared wider. "'Twas not what I—oh, you're funning with me!"

He was still smiling at her indignation when Dr. MacAndrews walked in.

"Lieutenant, I'm pleased to find you well enough to converse. And 'tis good you are here, Mrs. Denby. You can assist in my examination."

"Lady Hampden," Miles corrected gently.

Looking at him in surprise, the doctor opened his lips as if to make some light retort. At the hard gaze Miles fixed on him, he seemed to think better of it.

"Excuse me, I meant no offense. It is just that I've worked so long with Edwina—Lady Hampden, and with the circumstances so...odd, 'tis difficult for me to think of her as your... Well, no matter." Turning to Edwina, the doctor said, "Might I ask your aide, ma'am?"

By the time the surgeon had done probing, Miles was more than ready to accept his wife's help in sagging back against his cushions.

"Both wounds look good," the doctor said as he tightened the last bandage, "and I'm reasonably sure

I got all the pieces of the ball that struck you. We'll know by day's end, for if I missed any, your fever will spike. You're bound to have some fever in any event. I understand you and your—" he raised his eyebrows and sent a faintly reproachful glance at Edwina "—wife hope to depart for Lisbon soon, but you'd best count on remaining here most of a week, to be sure that chest means to heal properly."

His head still woozy, Miles made no protest. "I…I am not as keen on departing as I thought I was."

"Are you feeling ill?" Edwina asked, touching her hand to his forehead, concern in her voice. "Let me fetch you some water."

Despite the nausea clamoring for his attention, before she turned to go, Miles caught her hand and brought it to his lips. "That would be most kind," he murmured.

After he released her, Edwina stood for a moment simply staring at her hand before turning on her heel to follow the doctor out of the tent.

With a sigh, Miles closed his eyes, which made the tent stop spinning and helped quell his queasiness. He'd done a good morning's work for a man who'd nearly stuck his spoon in the wall last night, he thought.

He'd convinced his reluctant bride to agree to nurse him. He felt deeply responsible for having led her into a dilemma of his making, and he wanted to be sure they had sufficient time to find a satisfactory way out.

He'd not been speaking lightly when he said he didn't marry a lady only to later abandon her. In full possession of his faculties, he'd made a vow before God, and though he may have thought when he'd pledged his troth that the span of time until death would part them would be measured in hours, still he had made a sacred promise.

His new wife was doubtless only being sensible in resisting the idea of remaining tied any longer than necessary to a man she hardly knew. Wounding as it was to his self-esteem, he was impressed by her independence and lack of concern for worldly consequence, for she surely realized that becoming a viscountess would mean a far easier, more privileged life than the one she now led.

Besides, assuming he survived, last evening's events only underlined the imperative that he marry and beget an heir. Since he'd already managed to acquire a wife, it might be wise to ascertain if they suited well enough for him to try to persuade her into making their temporary alliance permanent.

SO HER HUSBAND was not as recovered as he'd first appeared, Edwina thought as she carried out the water bucket. He must convey that impression of strength through sheer force of personality, since it seemed he was capable of convincing one to do almost anything, whether it be persuading the doctor to let him ride off soon to Lisbon, or talking her into continuing to nurse him. Especially since, given the intensity of the reaction he evoked in her, remaining near him was probably a bad idea.

It wasn't just his physical attractiveness—although that was far too compelling. As a soldier's daughter, she had a natural admiration for an officer whose troopers considered him courageous and resourceful, for who knew better the character of their commander than the men he'd led under fire? In the short time she'd been connected with him, he'd shown himself a caring individual, too. Already he'd disarmed her resentment over his publicizing the wedding by explaining he wished to protect her from gossip.

She shook her head ruefully. 'Twas hard to be offended by such consideration. And this morning, rather than simply making conversation to smooth over the awkwardness of their situation, he'd seemed genuinely interested in her upbringing in India and the colorful stories that one of the regimental surgeons, chancing to overhear her relating them to some of the wounded, had pronounced "heathenish nonsense."

Edwina smiled. In the eyes of his society, she offered him nothing as a wife, but at least she did have an endless supply of legends with which to divert him. The smile faded as she considered how alarmingly engaging Lord Hampden was turning out to be. Given the fact that dissolving their marriage was going to take longer than she'd expected, she'd best take care, lest when he departed for England, she was left with something more painful than idle gossip to overcome.

She looked down at the hand he'd kissed, now clasped around the water bucket. The dratted thing still tingled.

Yes, she concluded with a sigh, spending a week in close proximity with Lieutenant Miles Hampden was probably a very bad idea indeed.

Chapter Five

SEVERAL DAYS LATER, Miles awakened from a nap to find his wife gone and Allen Sanbrook sitting by his bed.

"How about some ale?" Sanbrook asked. "Nothing like a bit of home-brewed to speed you back to health."

Miles accepted a mug and took a long sip. "Ah, now that's the taste of England!"

"Indeed." Sanbrook downed a swallow of his own. "Have you consulted Sergeant Riggins yet? With you making such a fine recovery, I imagine you shall be released to travel soon, and you'll want to have made progress on unsnarling your legal tangles." He took another sip and sighed. "Probably have to wait until you reach Lisbon to sort out the religious ones."

"I don't plan to begin undoing anything just yet."

"Why not? Surely there's no longer any doubt that you'll survive your injuries. And it will be better for the lady to undo the business quickly. I know you've tried to protect her, but the longer the marriage lasts before its dissolution, the more awkward her position is likely to be afterward. And she does mean to remain here. When I spoke with her yesterday, hinting that she might wish to accept a settlement and return to England, she froze me completely."

Miles chuckled. "That I can believe."

Sanbrook shook his head and laughed. "You'd think I'd accused her of entering into this arrangement with the intentions of a grave-robber! She frostily informed me that the matter of remuneration had been settled the night of your injury and she would thank me never to mention it again. Delivered the whole speech in such a top-lofty manner, she put me in mind of your grandmother. Now there was a tartar! But as I said, if she's determined to stay with the army, it's bound to be damned awkward when you leave here without her."

Miles put down his mug. "At the moment, I have no intention of leaving here without her."

Sanbrook's eyes widened in surprise. "You can't intend…that is, I don't mean to disparage Mrs. Denby, but—"

"Lady Hampden, if you please," Miles interrupted, his tone mild but his voice holding an edge of warning.

Sanbrook colored. "Um, yes, Lady Hampden. Ah, I see! You will have her accompany you to Lisbon to make working out the details of the annulment easier. Probably wise."

"You mistake me, Allen. I'm not at all sure I wish to proceed with an annulment."

"Not proceed?" Sanbrook echoed, frowning. "I

know you appreciate her coming to your aid, Miles, but that's carrying gratitude a bit far, don't you think? Her father is naught but the younger son of some obscure baron and I understand her late husband's family doesn't even recognize her. She's a fine, courageous lady, I'll grant you, but she could never be considered a suitable wife for a viscount. Only think what your grandmother would say were you to bring home such a bride for Christmas!"

Miles smiled. "I expect she'd say I should do what I like, and the rest of the family be damned. It is *my* wife we are discussing, not some theoretical lineage out of Debrett's. And if I am to see the same woman over the breakfast table for the rest of my days, I should prefer her to be one I like and respect. Besides, recognized by the Alveneys or not, she's said to a nabob's granddaughter. Nose it about that she has inherited great wealth, and all but the highest of sticklers will accept her."

Sanbrook angled his head, considering, then nodded. "Since there's no taint of the shop about her, that might answer. Luckily for you, the Hampden estate is well-breeched enough that you have no need of her supposed fortune to buttress such a claim."

"Neither encroaching nor a shopkeeper, but a wonderful cook," Miles added, a grin breaking out as he lifted the cover from an iron pot on the table beside them, releasing a mouth-watering aroma. "Only see what an excellent stew she brought me. Savory chicken and vegetables, here on the siege lines outside Lisbon in November! The best my batman has been able to manage of late is a few dried carrots. She told me she was a good campaigner, but I swear, the woman's a wizard."

"I hardly think ferreting out chickens in a war-ravaged countryside is a skill your family will appreciate."

Miles's smile faded. "If they don't, they should. Come now, Allen, you know I wasn't bred to be viscount, nor do I have any inclination to spend my life in London, like some of the macaroni merchants we saw when we came up from Oxford. Indeed, her complete absorption with the trivia of the ton was what convinced me I wasn't in love with the blond chit I met that Season."

"The Magnificent Millicent," Sanbrook said drily. "Still the most exquisite creature I've ever beheld."

Miles shrugged. "I'll wager she couldn't wring a chicken's neck and make her recuperating husband the best stew he'd ever tasted."

Sanbrook broke into a reluctant laugh. "No, I'm quite certain she could not. But once you get back to Hampden Glen, you'll have servants aplenty to cook and forage. Your wife will be expected to occupy herself with very different duties—duties the new Lady Hampden may be ill-prepared to handle."

"I sincerely doubt there's anything she couldn't handle. What's more, I *like* her, Allen. She's the quickest study I've met in a female, understanding my meaning without my having to explain every point. Far from turning missish when her good deed devolved into this cursed coil, she's remained calm and reasonable. And in her own way, she's quite attractive, though she never resorts to feminine wiles to try to win her point. I think we could deal as well together as any couple who've made a marriage of convenience, and better than most."

"You *think,*" Sanbrook echoed. "But you're not sure yet what you mean to do. Remember, then, that you'll shortly be back in London, where you'll have a wealth of more suitable women eager for your attentions. Since the lady in question has indicated from the outset that she is perfectly willing to release you, 'tis not a matter of honor to uphold the agreement. Please, Miles, consider carefully before you make irrevocable an arrangement you may later come to regret."

"Since I know you speak out of genuine concern, I'll take no offense at the advice," Miles replied tightly, surprised by the depth of the anger evoked by his friend's disparagement of Edwina Denby. "But I'm becoming surer by the day that the current arrangement will suit me best. I'm less sure whether she'll agree to keep me."

Sanbrook looked at Miles incredulously, then burst out laughing. "Not keep you? A piece of that ball must have lodged in your brain!" He picked up his mug and stood. "I've got watch, so I must go. Enjoy the ale—and your exemplary stew."

Miles stared thoughtfully at his friend's retreating back. He was reasonably certain that if he did decide he wanted Edwina Denby to remain his wife, persuading her to agree was going to be a challenge.

After nodding to Lieutenant Lord Sanbrook, who bowed as she passed him in the brilliant winter sunlight, Edwina entered the dim hospital tent. As her eyes adjusted, she found her temporary husband lounging on his cot.

"Ah, my lady wife! Let me tell you again how excellent a stew you made," he said as he waved her to a seat. "My batman practically wept with jealousy."

Edwina felt herself flush with pleasure at Hampden's praise. "I'm glad you enjoyed it."

"I did indeed. But now that I've stuffed myself, how about another story?"

"You would not rather have a game of chess? Papa said you may keep the board as long as you like."

Hampden shook his head and gave her that warmly intimate smile that always seemed to make her stomach flutter—fool that she was. "No, I'm feeling so lazy after that excellent meal, you'd trounce me for sure. The humiliation of being beaten twice in a row might severely set back my recovery."

Edwina chuckled. "Considering by how narrow a margin I won, I imagine there's little chance of you suffering so horrid a fate. But if you prefer, of course I shall give you a story. Where did I leave off?"

"Prince Rama had been exiled to the forest, where his wife Sita insisted on accompanying him," Miles replied.

"Ah, yes. One day Prince Rama went off to hunt, but first warning Sita to stay inside a protective circle he'd constructed for her. But an evil ogre, ruler of a neighboring land, saw her all alone and was overcome by her beauty. The ogre, who could quite conveniently change his shape, turned himself into a beggar seeking alms. Sita, moved by pity for his plight, was tricked into leaving the circle to assist him, upon which the ogre prince captured her and carried her away."

"Sometimes performing a selfless deed can have unforeseen and life-changing consequences," Hampden said.

Edwina opened her lips to agree, but something focused and fervent in his gaze stopped the breath in her throat. She knew the moment he said it that his comment concerned far more than her story, but was he referring to the sense of honor he felt made it imperative that he not abandon his chance-given wife? Or that the circumstances which brought two improbably matched individuals together had sparked something that was changing how he looked at the situation—and her?

As it was changing the way she felt about him.

She moistened her lips, held captive by the intensity in his eyes, not sure whether to ask him what he meant or to once again ignore his remarks and proceed with the story. Before she could decide, he smiled, easing the tension, and said, "Please, continue."

"N-naturally," she began, her pulse still hammering hard enough to make her stumble a bit over the words, "Concerned when he returned to find his wife gone, Prince Rama became distraught. He could discover neither any trace of her nor find anyone who knew what had befallen her."

"Having one's wife disappear would be most upsetting."

Hampden inclined toward her as he spoke, his voice nearly a whisper, the blue of his eyes deepening with a heat she recognized but could hardly believe she was seeing—in *his* eyes as he looked at *her.*

Her whole body went tense, flooded with a sweet urgency that compelled her to lean toward him even as he leaned toward her. His lips hovered at her cheek, the soft exhale of his breath carrying the scents of ale and spices. Her lips tingled, burned as she angled her mouth up to his.

"Good, you're here, Lady Hampden," the surgeon's voice announced from the doorway, severing the peculiar force that held her spellbound. Feeling color flood her face, Edwina jerked away as the doctor advanced toward them. "You can assist while I examine his wound."

Thank heaven the doctor had interrupted! she thought. The situation—and her emotions—were tangled enough without further complicating them by allowing her attraction to Hampden to have free rein. She'd best keep such urges in check, lest she give the strong-principled viscount greater cause to feel honor-bound not to release her.

Still, she thought wistfully as she helped MacAndrews rebandage the wound he'd pronounced as healing nicely, Hampden had meant to kiss her, she was nearly certain. Much as she deplored the feeling, she could not suppress the warm glow that suffused her at discovering the attraction she felt for him was apparently reciprocated.

Too unsettled by the experience to wish to remain alone with him, she said, "Since your visits always tire the lieutenant, doctor, I shall leave him to rest."

The doctor chuckled. "I seem to have that effect on many of my patients. Rest is a good prescription if you've a mind to be on your way to Lisbon shortly. Which, I believe, you may safely be in a day or so."

Edwina followed in McAndrew's wake. "Can I assist you with any other patients, Doctor? I'm afraid I've not been much use to you of late."

MacAndrews shook his head. "I've had only the odd accident to tend. With winter coming on and the enemy departing, there are few wounded, thank the Lord."

"Lady Hampden," her husband called as she reached the doorway. As she glanced back, he gave her a reproachful look, as if fully aware of the reason behind her hasty retreat. "I'll rest now as you suggest, but please come back soon. If the doctor means to give me permission to travel in just a few days, we have much to discuss."

"I'll return in an hour," she promised, finding it hard to meet his gaze. With a quick smile, she escaped.

At least she'd have a short reprieve in which to regain her composure. If she took up her story immediately upon her return, maybe she could stave off the polite argument about their future she sensed was coming.

She'd been surprised at first to find he truly enjoyed her stories. But, it seemed their minds often ran along parallel paths, just as his dry, understated humor frequently amused her.

Perhaps that was one of the reasons she found herself liking him so much. The deep-seated sense of responsibility that made him beloved of his men spilled over into the rest of his life, whether it be expressed in his feelings of obligation to her, for the welfare of the estate he'd unexpectedly inherited or for his dead brother's dependent family.

While that intense blue-eyed stare affected her in quite another manner. Just recalling it triggered an ache deep within her body that had no prospect of being eased.

She put a hand over the quivering warmth in her belly. Oh, this was bad.

She'd made a special effort to find that chicken and prepare him that stew. She'd wanted him to enjoy it. Worse, she'd wanted to impress him with her resourcefulness, and had derived far too much pleasure from his praise.

There was no point trying to make him think well of her. They were different sorts, and the sort she was did not belong in the world to which he was returning.

Even if, duty-bound, he felt obligated to take her with him, even if he held her in some affection, that would not stop the snide whispers and sidelong glances from his peers, who would look down on so woefully underbred a wife. The affection he felt for her would not change the fact that remaining his wife would mean a permanent exile from her loving, but socially inferior family.

Worse yet, she must face the unwelcome truth that she was already halfway to falling in love with him.

When Daniel had blazed into her life with his fair-haired brilliance and easy charm, she'd thought him a prince as perfect as the one in her nurse's stories. Not until too late had she learned he was but the pasteboard image of royalty, no more substantial than the face cards in a game of whist.

Miles Hampden, however, was showing himself to be the genuine article.

The longer she knew him, the more she admired him. After they'd been apart, she couldn't stop the little jump in her pulse when she walked into the hospital tent and saw him again.

Lest she indulge the increasingly appealing temptation of encouraging him to honor the vows they'd sworn, she'd better recognize the danger her deepening emotions for him would mean, should their temporary marriage of convenience be made permanent.

Quite simply, living with his polite affection could devastate her more thoroughly than the most cold and haughty indifference Daniel had shown her. For Daniel, after a searing view of his true character brought her infatuation to a sudden end, had never truly touched her heart.

The heart that, she realized with a hollow feeling in the pit of her stomach, Miles Hampden had already come dangerously close to capturing.

Chapter Six

AS EDWINA CAME INTO the common room of their billet after a nap, her mother looked up from her needlework. "I'm glad you rested, my dear. How is your husband?"

"Sleeping, at the moment. He must gather his strength, since Dr. MacAndrews said this morning that Hampden may soon be well enough to leave for Lisbon."

"Excellent! You will accompany him, of course."

The pang she felt at refuting that assumption was far stronger than she'd like. "No, Mama, I don't expect so. You know we plan to seek an annulment. I can sign whatever documents are needed here before he leaves. It is better to begin going our separate ways sooner rather than later."

"Why should you separate?" her mother countered. "Only consider, my dear! Hampden is handsome, titled, wealthy, congenial—at your age and in this place, you can hardly expect to encounter a more attractive prospective husband! He married you of his own free will, and I think you should hold him to it."

"Certainly not, Mama! Our agreement was meant to protect his family under very specific circumstances. Should I insist on his honoring the bargain after those circumstances have changed, I am certain he would do so, but he would have to despise me for cheating him of the opportunities a man of his rank should have to choose a more suitable bride. Indeed, I should despise myself should I play him so low a trick."

Her mother raised her eyebrows. "So you say, but I think you have both gone beyond the bargain you made that night. Oh, I know he isn't your beloved Daniel, but I don't believe you would have consented to wed Hampden in the first place if you hadn't, whether you realized it or not, harbored some warm feelings for him. My dear, 'tis time to let go the past and look to your future! Besides, it seemed to me when I spoke with him that he was nearly convinced to let the marriage stand."

"You've spoken to him?" Edwina replied, torn between resentment and alarm. "About me and our—situation? When? What did you say?"

"I've visited him several times while you were resting," her mother replied. "What could be more natural than my looking in on my daughter's new husband? I know your feelings for Daniel may have blinded you to other men's attractions, but truth be told, I find Lord Hampden to be the more engaging. Not that Daniel wasn't handsome and his manners very correct. But your Lieutenant Hampden is much more approachable."

Searching for some appropriate response while she frantically tried to construct a plausible but unrevealing argument, she replied, "He isn't *my* lieutenant, Mama. He never was."

That much was true enough, she thought with a pang.

"I believe he could be, if you'd make but a push to secure his affections," her mother replied. "If you could only hear with what warmth and admiration he speaks of you! And he's been so flatteringly anxious to hear every detail I could relate about your life."

Color rose to her face as Edwina envisioned half a dozen potentially embarrassing scenarios her mother might have revealed. "Oh, Mama, how could you?"

"I told him nothing but the truth," her mother protested. "What a dear child you were, and so brave, like the time you saved your ayah from that snake by bashing it with a club. How kind and sweet you've always been to your mother, who isn't nearly as clever as her daughter and whom you must often find very silly. How deeply you loved your first husband, how long you've grieved over him, and how grateful I am to Lord Hampden for awakening you to a future when I had began to despair of your ever moving beyond the past. You do care for Hampden, don't you, my dearest?"

Her mama had always been able to sense how Edwina thought and felt—which was why Edwina had been forced to distance herself from her parents during her troubled marriage. To admit that her strong feelings for Hampden were the primary reason for insisting this marriage be dissolved might raise uncomfortable questions about how, given her supposedly unshakable devotion to Daniel's memory, she could have suddenly have developed such a deep affection for her new husband.

Facing Hampden now seemed preferable to continuing this discussion with her far-too-perceptive mother.

"I do care for him, Mama," Edwina admitted at last. "I'm sure we'll work matters out to a mutually satisfactory conclusion. But now I should get back to him."

The knowing look in her mama's eye as she made a hasty exit left her feeling distinctly uneasy.

THANKING HEAVEN Hampden didn't know her as well as Mama did, Edwina walked toward the hospital tent. Even if he insisted on talking about their future, she should be able to return the appropriate answers without his suspecting her growing attachment to him.

She halted on the threshold in surprise, however, as she found her husband out of bed, pacing about the tent.

"Are you sure you should be up walking?" she asked.

He gave her the special smile that sent her pulse racing, even as she damned herself for the reaction. "I hope that means you're worried about me, my lady wife. But I need to build my stamina, if we are to ride to Lisbon shortly. I must say, it feels good to be upright again."

Still smiling, he came over and kissed her hand. Feeling her face flush, she tried not to snatch it back. Of course, he couldn't feel the jolt that raced through her at his touch, nor could he know the deplorable rush of joy she derived from that simple, courtly gesture. As if she truly were his lady, and he found pleasure in seeing her.

Edwina, who was usually of a height with the men she encountered, was equally unsettled by having Hampden tower over her. 'Twas absurd to let his superior size make her feel somehow feminine, delicate—and tempted to surrender herself into his care like some spineless heroine out of a Minerva Press novel.

Keep your dealings straightforward and unemotional, she told herself. "Won't you sit?" she asked, anxious to restore the equilibrium between them. "You don't want to chance setting back your recovery. Then I'll continue my story, as you requested."

"Perhaps you are right," he agreed, obediently returning to his cot. "Though I'm anxious to hear what happens next, first I'd rather we talk about *our* story."

Avoiding that too-mesmerizing gaze, she said, "Yes, we should finalize matters. I'm prepared to sign whatever papers you need to begin the annulment process."

For a moment he hesitated, and she thought with a flare of mingled alarm and gratification that he meant to ask again whether she still felt an annulment was necessary. "I suppose you could dictate a statement here, with the chaplain as a witness," he said at last. "But I'd feel more confident of the matter being successfully resolved if you would accompany me to Lisbon. Indeed, the bishop's representative may insist upon speaking with you."

'Twas ridiculous to feel let down. Had she truly expected he would now beg her to continue so unequal a union, simply because she made a superior stew and could match him at chess?

"I expect that would be prudent," she said, relieved that her voice betrayed none of the agitation she felt.

"Good, that's settled. If you would feel more comfortable, I would be happy to have Mrs. Crofton accompany us. With Christmas approaching, she might enjoy some shopping in Lisbon."

The last thing Edwina wanted, on what would doubtless be a heart-wrenching journey, was her perceptive mother close at hand. "I'm sure Mama would be reluctant to leave Papa. I can bring her maid, Juanita, as a chaperone."

"As you wish," he replied. "If you could both be ready to travel in two days, I believe MacAndrews can be persuaded to release me. Now, I should like that story."

He certainly was clever, Edwina thought resentfully as she seated herself. Within a few sentences, he'd surprised her into agreeing to accompany him to Lisbon when every sense warned that bidding farewell to him here, where she had work to throw herself into to ease the pain of parting, would be far preferable. "Where did I stop?"

"The prince's wife, Sita, had been abducted by the evil ogre who ruled the neighboring kingdom."

"Ah, yes," she said, ready to escape from the muddle of her life into the safe realm of fantasy. "The ogre prince tried alternately to woo and threaten Sita into yielding to him, but she refused to think of anyone but her beloved Rama."

Smiling faintly, Miles watched his wife's expression as she wove her story. Strange that when he'd first met her, though he'd admired her fine eyes, he'd thought her otherwise rather plain. Probably because she'd been so shy, her voice low and her eyes downcast. But now, with her face animated, her hands gesturing and the sultry richness of her voice flowing over him, he found her as enchanting as the Indian princess in her story.

Every day spent in her company made him surer that continuing this marriage would be the best solution for them both. Given what he knew of London society, he figured his chances of meeting a lady who would make him a more congenial life's partner than Edwina Denby were slim. In turn, he could offer her respect, friendship, material comfort and a life of purpose overseeing the welfare of his numerous properties and tenants.

Still, when she'd given him a perfect opportunity to declare himself, he'd been unable to take it. Though he sensed in her a growing affection for him, he'd been afraid to ask her to continue their relationship and risk a flat-out refusal. Better instead, he reasoned, to lure her to Lisbon on the pretext of consulting the experts and give himself more time to beguile Edwina into agreeing to make their temporary marriage permanent.

Unease stirred as he recalled her mother describing her continuing grief over her lost husband. An irrational and surprisingly intense spurt of jealousy followed. She was *his* wife now and he wished her to remain so. As his body recovered, so too strengthened the desire to make her his in every way. If he could lure her into his bed and please her there, he could put a stop to this talk of annulment and perhaps loosen the hold her late husband still exerted over her.

Making love to her should also rid her of the notion that he wished to continue their marriage merely out of duty. He certainly hoped so, for sometime over the last few days he'd gone irretrievably beyond that point. He now found himself very fond of his chance-given bride and determined to build a future together.

The sensual possibilities shimmered in his mind. Grinning, he told himself he'd best make sure he was recovered enough by the time they reached Lisbon to seduce her into sharing his vision.

Chapter Seven

THREE EVENINGS LATER, Edwina lounged in the sitting room of the suite her husband had engaged upon their arrival in Lisbon. She was hard put not to pace the room while she awaited Miles's return from the British embassy.

At least, to her relief, their journey did not seem to have set back Hampden's recovery. Though to her discerning eye, he'd been fatigued by the time they arrived, he'd still managed to present quite the commanding figure of the wealthy viscount, awing the staff of the hotel he selected into a flurry of obsequious bowing.

Judging by the sumptuous nature of the rooms they occupied and the lavish meals brought them, Hampden must be dropping quite a lot of blunt. She glanced toward the door, thinking ruefully that the servants hovering outside would treat her quite differently, did they know how soon "Lady Hampden" would become once again plain Mrs. Denby.

By now she just wished to have it done with. It had become increasingly difficult to maintain a calm and disinterested facade when spending so much time in Hampden's constant and engaging company, especially with the landlord and all the world treating her as his wife.

Last night, thinking it best to bring to an end the sort of enchanted intimacy they'd shared while she spun her stories, she declined when he asked that she embellish the shortened version she'd given him of the Ramayana saga. She'd asked instead that, now that he could speak at length without distress, he tell her about his home in England.

She'd hoped an echo of the themes of lineage and duty upon which Daniel had condescendingly pontificated would help distance him. Unfortunately, Hampden had shown he, too, was a gifted storyteller, making her laugh with tales of his exploits as a boy and painting so vivid a picture of Hampden Glen, his friends and family, that she could nearly imagine herself there. Rather than being put off, she found herself filled with a wistful longing to meet his gentle sister-in-law and the niece upon whom he doted. To see the rolling hills and green groves of his home, so different from the India in which she'd grown up.

Perhaps after he returned home, she could write to him, inquire about his own and his family's well-being. They had grown to be friends over these past few days; surely he would agree to them remaining so.

It required little further reflection for her to realize the impossible nature of her wish. His first duty, surely, would be to find a wife, and it would be no more easy for her to envision him with another woman in his arms than it would for that lucky lady to tolerate her new bridegroom's correspondence with a former, if temporary, wife.

No, she could play no further part in his life once he returned to Hampden Glen, even from a distance.

The one topic they'd carefully avoided during dinner last evening was the subject of the annulment.

After visiting the bankers this morning and sending her off to shop, Hampden had gone to his appointment at the embassy. And so she waited with fraying patience to discover what he'd found out about the process of bringing to an end, once and for all, the bargain between them.

Resolutely she swallowed the lump of sadness rising in her throat. Truly, the break could not come soon enough. Each day, as Hampden recovered more of his health and strength, he drew her further into the cocoon of his protective care. Having been forced after her marriage to Daniel to rely completely upon herself, it was far too sweet a luxury to have someone else with whom to share managing all myriad small details of daily life.

More insidious still were the increasing small courtesies he extended her—handing her out of carriage, gripping her elbow as they went up or down the stairs, kissing her fingers when he left her or returned—affectionate touches she ached to reciprocate. She shivered as she recalled how, last evening as he bid her good-night at the door to her chamber, rather than simply kiss her fingertips, he'd drawn her close and rested his lips against her forehead.

Desire had ignited within her at his nearness, heating her belly, making the tips of her breasts tingle, and requiring her to dig her nails into her palms to keep from raising her head so her lips could meet his.

Heat flamed anew in her body, just remembering it. Please, Lord, she prayed, let him bring back papers for her to sign tonight. Let her begin her sad and solitary return to the encampment tomorrow, that she might escape the temptation of his closeness before the ever-strengthening urge to caress him led her to do something that would make him feel honor-bound to make their union permanent.

'Twas pain enough that when he left, he'd take her heart with him.

So on edge were her nerves, she jumped when the door finally opened and her husband walked in. Guiltily, greedily, she offered him her hand, then closed her eyes to savor each touch as he brushed his lips across the knuckles. Her heart rate sped and she drew in an involuntary breath when, instead of releasing her hand, he turned it over and nuzzled her palm.

When he finally let go, she was so giddy she caught only one word in three of the apology for his tardy return.

"I hope you had a…useful meeting," she managed. *Pull yourself together, Edwina.*

"I've asked Manuelo to serve dinner in half an hour, if that is agreeable? We can have a glass of wine first."

A servant knocked even as he finished speaking. The several minutes required for the wine to be poured allowed her to settle her nerves before the footman withdrew, leaving them once again alone.

"Did you have a pleasant afternoon?" Hampden asked. "I'd half expected you to be sporting a new gown, though you look very charming in that one. Did you find what you required in the shops?"

"Yes, the linens here are very fine. I obtained some handkerchiefs for Papa, lacework for Mama and the toy you asked me to purchase for your niece's Christmas gift. I hope it will be suitable."

"I'm sure Beth will love it. But did you get nothing for yourself?"

"I require very little," she replied honestly.

He gave her a reproachful look. "I wish you had purchased at least a few fripperies for yourself. Only imagine the enormous drop in consequence I shall suffer among the hotel staff if they begin to think I'm the sort of nip-parsing Englishman who begrudges his wife a new dress!"

Edwina gestured around the gold brocade and mahogany-appointed sitting room. "I'm quite certain you are already spending enough for this suite to escape so lowering a fate." Resisting the little voice that whispered for her to put off the discussion until after dinner, she made herself ask, "And what did you discover?"

He took a sip of wine before giving her a wry

smile. "Well you might ask, given how patient you've been, even if your anxiety to be rid of me is painful to my self-esteem."

"I'm not anxious to be 'rid' of you!" she protested, feeling as always the unwelcome blush on her cheeks. "It's just that, since we both know a union between us is not...suitable, it would be wiser to terminate it before..."

She made the mistake of looking up into his eyes, as he watched her with a heated intensity she'd found at first astonishing and which, over the last few days, had grown thrillingly familiar. An intensity that set off the familiar ache of need and desire.

She cleared her throat and continued, "Before we grow more...entangled than we already are."

His smile faded. "I'm sorry you think so, for undoing our bargain is proving to be as difficult as I feared. After reading the explanation provided by Chaplain Darrow and expressing his severe disapproval of the haste that prompted the marriage, the bishop's representative declined to judge its validity. I must file a petition with the Archbishop's office in England, he said."

He took her hand and began stroking it. "I'm afraid you will be burdened with me a bit longer."

His fingers traced a lazy pattern from her knuckles up across her wrist to just under the sleeve of her gown. Scarcely able to breathe, her attention captivated by the shiver of sensation he was evoking, it took a moment for his words to register.

"Nothing can be done here?" she asked, conscious

of both dismay and a guilty surge of gladness. He would leave as he must, but the ties between them would not have to be severed just yet.

Even better, she realized, it would have to be easier to say their final goodbyes by letter rather than in a gut-wrenching few moments on the dock. *Thank You, Lord,* she whispered silently.

Then he banished all ability to think by raising her hand to his lips and kissing each fingertip in turn. "'Twill be such a bother to untangle everything. Are you sure we cannot simply leave things as they are?" He raised her chin, forcing her to look into his eyes. "I flatter myself you've grown a little fond of me."

"Y-yes. You've become a very good friend."

"Then don't you think we could rub along well enough together—at least as well as most married couples? I understand you loved your first husband deeply. Knowing what it is to lose someone so dear, might it not be more…comfortable to be married to a 'very good friend'?"

The mention of Daniel conjured up memories bitter enough to dispel some of his sensual sway and stiffen her resolve. Though the inequities in their respective stations would make a union between them uncertain enough, it was precisely because she couldn't live with his "comfortable" affection that she must end this.

Gently she tried to pull her fingers free, but before she could speak, dismay filled his face and he said, "Pray, forgive me! 'Twas presumptuous and insensitive to speak of him, for now I have made you sad again, which was the last thing I wished. Indeed, I was hoping that our…friendship might help you move beyond your grief. We do have much in common, and though I can't offer you anything as wonderful as the stories you've spun me or the exotic appeal of a life on campaign or in India, I can promise you a future of important, useful work. The Hampden lands are extensive and require a dedicated, capable mistress to oversee their well-being. You insist you are not part of the world to which I'm returning, but the truth is, nor was I bred to the role I must now play. You could help me as I learn to assume my responsibilities."

Edwina had to smile. "Yes, but having been neither born to that world, as you were, nor bred to its tasks, I hardly think there is much I could do to smooth your path."

He smiled back. "You could teach my cook to make a superior stew."

In an instant she was transported to the awful afternoon when she'd learned the truth about her appeal to Daniel. Furious upon discovering that she would not receive for several more years the inheritance upon which, it turned out, he'd been counting, he'd snapped, "What other benefit do you think a wife like you could offer me, besides her fortune? I already have a cook and an estate agent to haggle over trade."

That old wound reopened, without thinking she flashed back at Hampden, "Perhaps I could also help your manager barter for a better price on wheat?"

Aghast, she damned her hasty tongue as a look of puzzled distress appeared on Hampden's face. "I'm sorry," he quickly replied, "that was clumsily put. I did not mean to infer that I intended to put you to work—"

"No, of course you did not," she interrupted, casting about for something to soften her remark. "I—I only meant that, what I've learned about directing servants on campaign or in India is unlikely to be of much assistance in England, so I could be of little use to you. That is—your estate is already prosperous, or so I've heard."

Mercifully, the frown left his face and he smiled at her. "The little I've been able to induce my wife to spend should make no serious inroads on my capital."

She smiled back a bit nervously. "That is fortunate. I stand to inherit a large amount from my grandfather, but not until I am five-and-twenty. So at present, I could not even offer you the advantage one would expect to derive by wedding an India nabob's heiress."

"The sole advantage I hope for is to keep close by me the lady who has become my very dearest friend."

As Hampden accompanied that softly voiced rejoinder with a look both heated and tender, fortunately for her sanity, at that moment, a knock sounded at the door. A procession of servants entered bearing trays. While a half dozen attentive footman attended them for the remainder of the lavish meal, their conversation turned to a discussion of the political situation in England and the army gossip Hampden had picked up at the embassy.

After the servants left them to their glasses of port, Edwina said, "I haven't eaten so well since I last visited Grandpapa's compound, where he lives quite like a raja!"

"I thought we would both appreciate a change from rabbit stew and scrounged vegetables. Won't you join me?" Hampden indicated a place on the sofa.

Edwina eyed the spot to which he invited her. Sitting next to him was definitely not wise. But unable to produce a plausible reason to refuse, she came to perch gingerly beside him, all too acutely aware of him so close she could feel the heat emanating from his body and inhale the spicy scent of port on his breath.

"We can book passage on a ship leaving tomorrow," he told her as, senses already beginning to swim at his nearness, she tried to concentrate on his words. "Will you not come with me? Bringing home a bride would do much to restore to a grieving family the joy that should be theirs at Christmas. If you still insist upon nullifying our bargain, I swear I will do all in my power to accomplish that, but I expect the matter would proceed more quickly if you were present to give testimony and sign documents."

The point was valid, and it tempted her. But could she remain in his company and still resist him?

While she pondered that question, he set down his port and slid closer. "It might be prudent to spend more time together. I believe our friendship would only deepen, so if we discovered after returning to England that abolishing the marriage proved difficult, we might grow more amenable to letting it continue. You do consider us friends."

She ought to scoot away from him—but she couldn't. *Savor it,* the little voice in her head whispered. *He'll be leaving tomorrow.*

"Y-yes," she said, struggling to ignore his lips and concentrate instead on his words. "We are...friends."

"We work well together—and laugh together, too. It's important to be able to laugh together, don't you think?"

He began caressing her hand from her wrist down to her fingers. Exhaling a long sigh of delight, barely able to follow his argument, she murmured, "Yes."

He moved his other hand to brush her cheek, then continued down her neck, across the long plane of her collarbone and lower, until the tips of fingers rested at the edge of her bodice, touching the top swell of her breast. "We could share even more," he murmured. "You find me attractive, do you not?"

Without waiting for a reply—which was fortunate, for she was by now beyond speech—he bent his head and kissed her neck. With a wordless gasp, she closed her eyes and focused on the sensation as his lips slowly traced the path of his fingers from her throat down her chest to the edge of her bodice, until she could feel the warmth of his breath against her breasts. Just below where his lips rested, her nipples swelled and burned.

"I could please you," he whispered against her skin.

"Let me show you how well we suit. If I fail to…satisfy, I promise to let you go and implore you no longer."

Please. Satisfy. He wanted to make love to her.

With every nerve aroused, she battled to heed the faint warning in her brain that to yield would mean catastrophe, for she had no doubt that he would please her. And then she would be lost.

"I'm sure you could please us both. But…I cannot."

"Why not?" he persisted, once again closing the distance between them and putting a persuasive arm on her shoulder. "You've admitted we share a deep affection. Why should we not pursue its natural extension?"

It was ludicrous to try protesting that she didn't find him attractive. But she simply couldn't confess that she had fallen top over tail in love with him.

She must invent some excuse to set him at a distance before her senses overwhelmed her judgment and his powerful appeal triumphed over her rapidly weakening resistance.

With her last bits of self-control, she threw off his hand, forced herself up and staggered to the hearth.

Breathing heavily, Hampden leaned back against the sofa. "Again, I must beg your pardon," he said after a moment of fraught silence. "I've repelled you with my forwardness."

"No, it isn't that!" she said, turning away from the fire to face him. "You must know I find you attractive. It's just that acting upon that attraction would be…" *Disastrous. Irreversible.* She thought frantically, trying to hit upon an appropriate word.

Then, suddenly, a means of escape flashed into her mind. "Unsuitable," she finished.

"Unsuitable?" he echoed, frowning. "In what way?"

"You see, though we share a...a fond friendship, you force me to confess that my emotions are already engaged."

She watched his face as he straightened, digesting her comment. "To some other man? Not your late husband?"

"Yes. To someone else," she said, relieved by his reaction and inventing her story as she went.

His frown deepened. "Indeed? Is this a recent attachment? Your mother gave me no hint of it."

"She knows nothing about it. The gentleman in question hasn't made me a declaration yet, and though I am—or I was—in hopes that he might soon do so, until I was sure he reciprocated my esteem, I thought it best not to hint of anything to Mama."

"I see." Eyes narrowing, he regarded her with suspicion. "And who is this lucky gentleman, if I may be so bold as to inquire?"

Edwina took a deep breath. She'd hoped to avoid having to mention a name, but though Hampden seemed to have recovered from the embarrassment of having his attempt at seduction rebuffed, he was clearly not ready to let her off with less than a complete confession.

Uttering a swift silent prayer that both the Lord and the surgeon would forgive her the falsehood, she replied, "Dr. MacAndrews. I've worked closely with him for more than a year now, you see, and a mutual respect and affection has ripened between us that, until your unfortunate accident, I felt might lead to our union."

She made herself stand unflinching under his steady regard.

"You believe yourself in love with Dr. MacAndrews?" Hampden asked.

"I am very much in love with the man I would hope to marry," she replied carefully.

"I see," he said again, rather stiffly. "And he reciprocates your sentiments?"

"I'm not sure. I have hopes that he might."

"And you would prefer to pass up the certainty of the affection we share on the *hope* that MacAndrews might in time reciprocate your stronger feelings for him?"

"I would prefer to retain that option, yes," she replied even more carefully.

Hampden jumped up and poured himself another glass of port before turning back to her. "Why did you not inform me of this attachment earlier?"

"Well, you must remember that, at first, you were not expected to survive until the doctor's return. So under what was, you must admit, considerable pressure from your friends, I agreed to our bargain, anticipating there would be no awkwardness with Dr. MacAndrews that I could not later explain away."

His eyes narrowed. "And when I did not obligingly die? Did you talk with him then?"

"No, of course not. It would not have been fitting to discuss such a thing until the bargain between us was resolved. I thought that as your health improved, you would become as conscious as I of the unsuitability of the arrangement and be anxious to go about dissolving it. Since the matter regarding Dr. MacAndrews is rather delicate, I hoped to avoid speaking of it. I only do so now because you've forced me."

He took another sip and nodded. "With my boorish and forward behavior. For which, once again, I apologize."

He was angry, she thought, stifling the desire to try to mollify him. Well, she'd wanted to put distance between them. With him believing she cared for another man, the honor that had forced him to uphold their bargain would now compel him instead to find the means to let her go.

Silly to feel so dangerously close to tears, when she was near to achieving precisely what she'd attempted. And if the odd scenario she'd invented gave him a disgust of her, so much the better. "I accept your apology," she said with as much spinsterly primness as she could muster, what with her senses still in rebellion and her heart feeling as battered as a shuttlecock. "Perhaps now I'd better retire. You plan to take that ship tomorrow, you said?"

"I said we—I—could do so if I chose."

"You should get some rest, as well. Thank you again for a lovely dinner, and good night."

Abruptly he paced forward and seized her chin in

one hand. "I will see you again in the morning. You'll not try to slip away in the night?"

"No, I won't go away," she answered, jerking her chin free and stepping back before he could notice that her knees were shaking and her hands trembling from the force of the battle raging within her between what she desired and what she knew she must do. So close were the tears brimming at her lashes that she would have agreed to almost anything to escape. "I'll see you in the morning."

He gave her a short, brusque nod, his face now shuttered. "Then, may you sleep well, Lady Hampden."

Chapter Eight

SLEEP WELL. Slim chance of it, Miles thought, watching Edwina walk with her usual calm to the door of her chamber. The door before which last night he'd kissed her, hoping to receive the invitation he craved to accompany her within.

Again tonight, he'd felt her trembling on the edge of succumbing to the attraction that, he felt sure, throbbed in her veins as it coursed through his. Until, clever fellow that he was, he'd brought up the memory of her sainted first husband and spoiled everything.

But that wasn't his worst error—or the greatest surprise. What a presumptuous fool he'd been, thinking he could convince Edwina that friendship was a strong enough base on which to continue their marriage. He should have guessed that, having loved her precious Daniel, she would want no less than a complete commitment if she wed again.

Surely there could be no other reason for her to

prefer a man like Dr. MacAndrews—a man who hadn't yet even declared himself!

Which made Miles twice the fool. He'd come dangerously close to nearly coercing her to accept his advances. Cringing at the memory, he downed his port in one swallow.

If he felt ashamed and angry at having made an idiot of himself, it was his own fault. True, Edwina Denby hadn't repulsed the steadily increasing intimacy of his advances, but neither had she actively encouraged him. He'd thought her major objection to their continued union to be the same farradiddle about the difference in their stations that had concerned Sanbrook. He'd simply never considered the possibility, coxcomb that he was, that another man might have also perceived the qualities he found so attractive in her and made a push to engage her affections.

The fact that her mother didn't know about MacAndrews made him feel a bit better. Prudent lady that she was, it seemed entirely reasonable that Edwina would not have confided in Mrs. Crofton until she'd received a formal offer, since, after arousing expectations in her mother, it would be rather awkward to continue working with MacAndrews if those hopes were never realized.

Of course, the man would have to be an imbecile to earn the affection of a woman like Edwina and not capitalize upon it. No wonder MacAndrews had given him such a strange look when he found they were wed.

As his anger and embarrassment faded, Miles had to

admit that beyond the shock of her revelations lay a deep disappointment—and more than a little jealousy.

As for the keenness of that disappointment, after having considered Edwina *his* for the last few days, it was only natural to feel like a blow the discovery that his plans for the future would be unrealized.

At least he'd had the wit to remain a gentleman, if barely. Upon learning that his lady's heart was set upon another, however strong his dismay—or jealousy, he could not in honor stand in her way. Especially after all she had sacrificed to assist him.

Miles poured himself yet another port, threw himself onto the sofa and glared into the flickering fire. What good was it having survived to return home a wealthy viscount with beautiful ancestral lands if he couldn't compete for the affections of his wife with an untitled, limb-hacking surgeon who offered his bride life in a tent?

Sanbrook and his friends, of course, would say he'd had a lucky escape. He now had a legitimate reason to return to England and petition to dissolve their marriage—which, contrary to what he'd told Edwina, he could probably proceed to do without her accompanying him.

He flinched again, recalling how, if not precisely lying, he'd stretched beyond its original meaning the prelate's simple statement that it might be wise to have Edwina present, should the archbishop wish to question her.

If Edwina remained adamant about the marriage's

dissolution, somehow he must make it happen. He'd then be forced to trade his uniform for the togs of a London Tulip while this year's pack of proud ton mamas paraded before him a procession of overly perfumed, melody-screeching, harp-twanging virgins of impeccable lineage, all eager to acquire his name, title and blunt.

Unlike Edwina—proud, thrifty Edwina—who had disdained a new gown and purchased only handkerchiefs, some bits of lace and the gift for his own niece he'd asked her to buy.

Something uncomfortable twisted in chest. But Edwina had made her choice clear. Despite their friendship and even admitting the physical pull between them, Edwina preferred returning to the army to beguile her surgeon.

While he must go to London, end their marriage and try to beguile a new bride.

An appalling sense of loss welled up from deep within. He doubted he'd find another lady with lustrous eyes like Edwina's, which had never flinched from the pain and horrors of the field hospital. One whose hands could effectively soothe a wounded man's agony, or whose warm velvet voice had kept a dying man tethered to life.

Despite the blow to his self-esteem, 'twas good that he hadn't succeeded in seducing her. For then, despite his pledge to contrary, he'd never have let her go.

Sighing, he sought out the decanter. Time for a good bit more of that port. Though he told himself 'twas his shoulder that ached, he knew in truth that the pain nagging at him was centered lower, on the left side of his chest.

EDWINA CLOSED the door to her chamber and leaned her trembling body against it. She could have no doubt now that Hampden wanted her.

An insistent little voice asked her why desire and mutual affection could not be enough. Why was it so essential that she hold all her husband's heart, as long as she commanded his respect, upheld his name and, in time, bore his children?

If she did not capture his whole heart, she answered, 'twas unlikely she could retain even that affection he now felt for her, once they returned to a world that would disapprove of their union. Even Lord Sanbrook, whom she knew liked and respected her, had made no secret of his opinion that the bonds should be dissolved. She might have entered this marriage without her husband feeling the scorn Daniel had directed at her, but with all his friends and relations ranged against her, in time Miles would come to despise her as well.

Neither her pride nor her heart could tolerate that. Forcing herself to deny the temptation to go back to him, she wandered to the window.

The stars twinkling overhead promised fair skies and a good breeze for the ship that would carry Hampden away tomorrow. She placed a hand over her breast, where she could almost feel the imprint of his kiss still burning against her skin. Never in the worst days of Daniel's casual cruelty had she ached like this.

If only she could have taken his gift and still have been able to set him free! Knowing that if she had succumbed, Hampden would consider them irrevocably bound, did not quell the longing.

She'd experienced physical union during her marriage when Daniel had condescended to take her, no more attractive bed-sport being available. But she'd never been intimately joined with a man she loved, who touched her with affection rather than idle lust.

Now she never would.

A tear slipped down her cheek. It seemed so monstrously unfair that she be denied experiencing that joy just once, when she was already doomed to living the rest of her life without him.

Maybe you can capture joy—just once.

The daring, dangerous thought startled her, made her hand clutch on the rich brocade of the curtain. Though she tried to dismiss it, the idea gained momentum, sweeping through her mind with the irresistible force of tomorrow morning's tide.

If she had the temerity to proceed, Hampden might reject her as she had him. But if he chose not to—they could steal one night together, a night of ecstasy without consequences or regrets.

Of what significance was a bit of humiliation compared to the chance of winning that?

Her decision made, she rushed to the wardrobe.

Already the moon was high in the sky, and if one night was all she would ever have, she didn't want to lose another moment.

MILES WAS SEATED on the bed, shirt off and trousers half-unbuttoned, when a knock sounded at the door. Excitement lanced through him, swiftly smothered by a dose of reality.

It could not be Edwina...or rather if it was, she would doubtless want to consult him about some trifling matter of business—passports or passage money or some such.

She didn't really want him. As husband or lover.

Irritated anew by that truth, he called out, "Go back to bed! We can settle whatever is necessary in the morning."

He didn't like admitting that if he allowed her into his room on any pretext, he knew he'd not be able to let her go without attempting once again to seduce her.

"Please, señor, mistress says I must see you."

The muffled voice speaking in halting English sounded like that of the Crofton's maid, Juanita.

Alarm succeeded his irritation. Had something happened to Edwina?

Snagging his shirt and refastening his trousers as he went, he trotted over to open the door. As he'd suspected, the maid stood on the threshold.

"What is it? What's amiss?" he demanded.

"My mistress sends me," the girl said, dropping him

a curtsy. "She says milord's shoulder gives him pain. She sends me with salve to ease it, to help him sleep."

Only one thing would give him ease, he thought sardonically. "Tell your mistress I'm gratified by her concern, but 'tis unnecessary. My sleeping does not depend on ease for my shoulder."

As he started to close the door, the maid raised a hand. "Please, señor, Mistress will be angry if I do not obey."

The poor girl did indeed appear to be trembling, in addition to having swathed herself in that veil all the local women wore—probably to protect her maidenly eyes from the shocking sight of a gentleman half-undressed. "I promise your mistress won't beat you, child. Go to bed."

Instead of retreating, though, the girl stepped closer. "Please, *señor.* It will bring you…pleasure."

His senses were a bit wine-soaked, but suddenly it dawned upon him that the figure of the girl looked startlingly familiar. Leaning forward, he caught a whiff of jasmine—the scent to which his mind had clung on the awful night of his injury, blocking out the stench of blood and fear.

Edwina! He was certain 'twas his erstwhile wife, not her mother's maid, seeking entrance to his chamber.

She must have changed her mind—so why the deception?

"Please, *señor,* may I come in? It will take little time to soothe you. Then you may sleep undisturbed."

A slow grin formed on his face. Whatever her reasons for this charade, he was more than happy to accommodate her. He'd be a fool if he didn't ensure the "soothing" lasted until dawn—and he had no intention of being a fool twice tonight.

Chapter Nine

"VERY WELL, if your mistress insists." Still smiling, Miles stood aside to let the veiled figure enter, his fatigue and melancholy vanishing in a heat of erotic anticipation. "What would you have me do?" he asked, trying to keep the amusement out of his voice.

"Sit there, on the bed, milord. I will do all."

That sounded promising. The mere thought of what she *might* do made his body harden while he deposited himself as instructed.

She came over to stand beside him, unbuttoned his shirt and carefully drew it off his injured shoulder. Breathing in again her scent of jasmine, Miles grew even surer his midnight visitor must be Edwina.

The flickering light of the single bedside candle outlined the swell of her breasts straining against the too-tight bodice of the maid's gown. He felt himself harden further, his fingers itching to release the taut garment. He wanted to bury his face between the soft jasmine-scented mounds, let his eager tongue tease her nipples to swollen peaks while his fingers delved lower....

Shifting on the bed in his now uncomfortably confining trousers, he bit back a groan and stilled the hands already reaching toward her. For now, he would restrain himself and see what she would do next.

First she folded his shirt—oh, his tidy Edwina—and set it aside. Then she extracted a small bottle from her apron pocket, poured onto her hands a scented liquid and gently applied it to his shoulder.

Warmed by her body, the oil flowed smoothly over his skin. She began massaging it into his shoulders, the top of his neck, down his back. After a few moments, his eyes fell shut and a sigh of sheer rapture escaped his lips. So exquisite was her touch, it almost competed with the desire throbbing in his breeches.

But not quite. Mustering up words with an effort, he said, "Would you rub also...my lower back?"

Her hands obligingly descended, extending the magic of her massaging fingers down his back and flanks. After another few timeless moments of bliss, however, she paused.

As he scraped together wits enough to wonder if her mission had indeed been merely medical, she poured more oil on her fingers and applied them once again to his shoulder. But instead of working the muscles of his back, she inched down his chest, circling closer and closer until her fingers almost touched his nipples, teasing them as he'd envisioned teasing hers. He stifled a groan, his arms going rigid as he struggled to keep himself motionless. Just as he thought he could stand no more, she captured the sensitive peaks and rolled them in her oil-slick thumbs.

A blast of lust roared through him. He wanted to sweep up her skirts, toss her onto the bed and take her that instant. But with his pulse and every other part of him throbbing, he dug his fingernails into the bed linen and made himself remain still.

A mission that became increasingly difficult as her fingers resumed their slow descent, tracing along his ribs and stroking the upper curve of his belly. He thought her breathing grew more rapid and uneven, but it might be only the thunder of his own heart-beat in his ears.

Her fingers paused at the top of his trousers, then dipped beneath, coming oh-so-close to what he badly wanted her to stroke.

Retreating instead, she tugged at his waistband. "Remove these, please," she said, her voice breathless and the accent less pronounced. "Then I can…finish."

Before she had time to step aside, he had the buttons of the trousers undone. In one motion he shucked them and his drawers onto the floor and sat back on the bed.

This time, he knew he was not mistaken about hearing her long, slow exhale of breath, followed by a charged silence as, from behind her veil, she stared at his naked, completely aroused body. Excited by the idea of her watching him, he leaned back to give her a fuller view.

"What would you have me do next?" he asked.

Without answering, she whirled around and paced to the bedside table. "'Tis not...modest for a maid to see you so," she said, and extinguished the single candle.

Miles chuckled softly. Modest or not, she'd taken time to look her fill before remembering her maid-servant's role. What next would she desire?

"Lie down, milord, that I might ease your back."

'Twas the tightness in front he most wanted eased, but again, obedient to whatever fantasy she wished to play out, he lay facedown. "Now that darkness preserves your modesty, will you not remove your veil?" he asked over his shoulder. "So when you... minister to me it does not come loose and become stained by the oil."

To his delight, a faint rustling told him she'd taken his suggestion. Hard as he tried, though, he could make out nothing in the inky darkness that cloaked the chamber.

Then she began massaging him again, and all thought drowned in a tidal rush of sensation.

As if freed from restraint by the darkness, the motion of her hands became frankly sensual. Her fingers outlined his ribs, rounded and molded his buttocks, circled over the tops of his thighs and down between his legs, which he parted, encouraging her to stroke lower still, where his buried cock pulsed in anticipation of her touch.

He groaned when she followed his lead, tracing the juncture of his thigh until her fingers fondled him, igniting another bolt of sensation and ripping a cry from his throat.

As if pleased by his response, she stroked him there again and again, until unable to lie still any longer, he rolled to his back and seized her wrists. "Ease me… here," he gasped, curling her fingers around his swollen length.

For an instant he feared he'd been too bold, for as he released her wrists, she pulled her hands away. Before he could gather enough words for either protest or apology, he heard the faint clink of the glass container, then the sibilant sound of pouring liquid. As he waited, barely breathing, she wrapped her oil-slick hands around him and slowly massaged his entire length.

Sweat beaded on his chest, his forehead as his hands fisted on the sheets and his legs and torso clenched, arching into her touch. She began to stroke him rhythmically and he moved with her, caught up in an erotic trance of her making.

He knew his control was swiftly eroding. As wonderful as this was, he wanted more, wanted his sweat and oil-slick body sliding against her as he buried himself in her warm depths, wanted her bare breasts free to his mouth and tongue, wanted to feel her spasm around him as he exploded within her.

Past reason or speech, he grabbed the material of her skirt, bunching it up to seek the skin beneath. An instant later, she yanked the cloth free and in a rustle of skirts, climbed onto the bed and straddled him.

A single thrust of her hips plunged his oiled cock in to its full length. He wanted her to pause so he could rip loose the bodice imprisoning her breasts, dispose of the skirts that barred his way to bare skin. But she leaned forward and found his mouth, her tongue seeking his urgently, her slippery hands biting into his shoulders as she arched into him and withdrew, arched and withdrew.

And then there was no time for anything but meeting her thrust for thrust as she rode him, her breathing a gasp that rose to a sob and then sharp cry as she tensed and shattered around him. An instant later, keening with her, he followed her into oblivion.

When his brain finally resumed functioning several minutes later, Edwina lay collapsed atop him. A wave of affection swelling his chest, he hugged her close, content to listen to their ragged, panting breaths.

'Twas unaccountably erotic to lie there, still intimately joined, the prim, proper lady who had nursed him so devotedly now stretched against his naked body while she remained almost entirely clothed, her modest maid's gown buttoned up to her chin. Indeed, he could already feel his spent member begin to stir.

Stroking the damp curls off her face, her kissed her. "Thank you for giving me…ease. But I need still more."

She stirred and he felt the butterfly-light brush of her lashes against his chin. "More?" she asked, surprise in her voice.

He chuckled, setting off vibrations in his torso that brought him into pleasing contact with her moist, tight depths. "Yes, more. Soon. But the material of this gown scratches. You must remove it."

He felt her smile against his fingertips. "Mistress said to obey you in all things." With the lazy ease of a cat she stretched and then sat astride him, reaching behind her to undo the bodice, as if unconscious of how each rocking movement made him harden within her.

At last she unhooked the final fastening and tossed the garment aside. Her breasts bounced free into his waiting hands and he moved eagerly to caress them, his mouth thirsting for their taste.

The skirts would have to wait. Quickening his pace within her as he pulled her down to him, he wished he'd not drawn the curtains against the moonlight, for he burned to watch the rosy tips of her nipples stiffen as he licked them. Next time, he promised himself as he fastened his mouth on one and sucked greedily.

A shudder passed through her and she cried out, sparking an answering throb in his cock.

Threading his hands under her disheveled skirts to cup her bottom and pull her more firmly against him, he released the hard pebbled tip and whispered, "Now, sweeting, let us both seek ease."

HOURS LATER Miles woke to find the sun a halo of gold against the still-drawn curtains. Sighing with glorious repletion, he turned over in a tangle of sheets, not surprised to find his audacious Edwina gone.

He glanced about the chamber but, tidy as ever,

she'd left no trace of her midnight intrusion. To be fair, he thought, chuckling, that maid's gown was probably fit now for nothing but to be hurled into the fire.

No matter. He would gladly buy the maid a dozen gowns to replace the one that had emboldened his surprising wife to pleasure him.

After last night, there could be no more twaddle of annulments and unequal stations in life and duplicitous, unworthy surgeons. In her ministering angel disguise, Edwina had bound them inextricably together, surpassing in the bargain his lustiest imaginings.

Suddenly he was filled with the need to see her. Would his mere presence remind her of the bold caresses she'd given him in the darkness and bring that endearing blush to her cheeks?

Too impatient to deal with neckcloths and buttons, he threw on a dressing gown and went out. Surprised at the intensity of the joy that swelled his chest as he walked over to kiss her cheek, he said, "Good morning, dear wife."

Keeping her eyes downcast, she turned her face away while—yes—a blush rose to her cheeks. "Good morning. As it seemed you wished to sleep late, I instructed Manuelo to wait on breakfast. Shall I ring for it now?"

He slipped beside her on the sofa. "Yes, I found last night's activities wonderfully fatiguing. I'm surprised you are not still resting, as well." He picked up her hand, intending to kiss it, but she quickly snatched it back.

"I had much to complete—packing, the disposition of your kit. When must you be at the ship?"

"Mid-morning. We shall have time to breakfast and settle with the hotel before we set off." The faint warning bells in his head rose in volume as she sidled away from him.

"I…I rather thought we would say our goodbyes here," she said, not meeting his glance. "Not on the docks amid a throng of onlookers."

Despite the inner voice warning something was wrong, it took a moment for the meaning of her words to penetrate. "Say our goodbyes?" he repeated, halting in the act of pouring himself coffee. "I understand you wish to inform your family of our departure, but surely they were expecting it. Could you not write a note?"

She shook her head. "I'm not leaving with you."

He set the cup down with a thunk, an odd flutter in his chest, still trying to deny what her words seemed to indicate. "If you simply must see your family again, I suppose I can delay my departure a few more days, though I do need to proceed home as quickly as possible."

"There's no need to delay. I meant I'm not returning with you at all. It may take a bit longer to process the annulment without my being present, but I promise to sign and return the papers the instant I receive them. I thought…I thought we settled all of this last night."

"So did I—when you came to my chamber!" he barked, anger rising in turn with his dismay. Surely she didn't mean to deny what they'd shared!

Her blush deepened. "You are mistaken. 'Twas mama's maid I sent to massage your shoulder last night. I've already chastised her for her...enthusiasm. If you please, I don't wish to speak of it further."

He could almost believe her an outraged spinster whose maid he'd unthinkingly debauched. Almost.

Except for the scent of jasmine that teased his nose and the fact that she would not meet his eyes.

He took her chin and forced her to look at him. "Edwina, what nonsense is this? I didn't understand last night why you felt it necessary to come to me in disguise, but 'twas no maid who spent the night in my bed. Why are you trying to deny 'twas you?"

Her color still high, she shook his hand free and met his gaze calmly, a chill in her eyes. "It most certainly was the maid. After confessing to you my intentions about Dr. MacAndrews, how could you insinuate that I would indulge in bed-sport with a man I did not love? 'Tis a grave offense against my honor."

He could only stare at her, uncomprehending. "You do mean to deny it," he said slowly. "And send me back to England alone, to dissolve our marriage? How can you claim to have honor and do that?"

Her chin rose a notch higher, her gaze growing frostier still. "If we have but a short while longer to be together, my lord, let us not spend it insulting each other." She turned from him to her coffee cup.

A caustic mix of incredulity, outrage, anger and hurt roiled in his belly. "So this is how you mean to end it? We'll break our fast, you'll bid me goodbye and send me to the ship while you return to Torres Vedras?"

"Yes. 'Tis what I expected to do from the first. 'Tis what we agreed upon."

'Twas not what *I* agreed to, he thought, and then suddenly realized she was correct—the myth of her returning with him had ever been solely a creation of his own mind. The sharp edge of his anger blunted against the hard certainty of impending separation.

"You expect me to depart and simply forget the woman who saved my life?" Forget the woman who had surprised and shocked and captivated him through the whole of one long splendid night, he added silently.

"Preserving your life was God's gift, not mine," she countered. "Now I'll go give Manuelo his instructions."

Before he could think how to stop her, she rose from the sofa and went out the door.

Incomprehension turned to frustration and a rapidly reviving anger. Why would she share his bed and complete their union, then turn her back and seek to pull them asunder? It made no sense.

'Twas an insult—almost a betrayal of what he thought they'd shared. A raw sense of loss bubbled up from his gut, stinging like acid on his already flayed feelings. With a curse, he seized the coffee cup and hurled it into the hearth, where it shattered into a hundred fragments.

Rather like his heart.

THREE HOURS LATER, Miles clomped up the gangway of the merchant frigate *Reliant,* scheduled to set sail on the afternoon tide for England. Would that the sharp sea breeze of the journey might succeed in blowing out of his heart and head all thought of Edwina and the pain of her leaving him.

He didn't think it likely.

He hadn't, after a rather desultory effort, managed to persuade her to see him as far as the ship. Instead, after allowing him a single kiss of her cheek, she had bid him goodbye in their rooms at the hotel.

In the hours since Edwina's shocking denial, he'd found himself going over and over last night's incredible encounter. As wonderful as it might otherwise have been to discover so deliciously wanton a side to Edwina, he supposed he should congratulate himself on what now looked like a providential escape from spending his life as a cuckold. A fate that surely would have been his, if Edwina were so free with her favors that she could blithely seduce him while intending to marry another man. Still, Edwina behaving in such a way seemed completely out of character for the woman he'd come to know.

As he reached the main deck, he saw a group of wounded soldiers, some limping, some being carried on litters.

Grateful for the diversion, he thrust his gloomy thoughts aside and went to lend them assistance.

He'd almost reached the small group when he recognized, leaning over one of the litters, the unmistakable figure of the surgeon, Dr. MacAndrews.

Miles skidded to a halt. His first instinct was to change direction and avoid the man. Then again, if he were being forced to relinquish his wife, he could at least discover if the man she preferred returned her regard.

Not that finding out would do much good. But as he hesitated, intending to walk away, memories from last night attacked his senses. The sound of oil pouring into warm palms… The scent of it and her as she massaged it into his skin… The feel of her drawing his length between her fingers and thrusting him deep into her body.

While desire and despair and fury warred for dominance in his brain, his feet began moving. A moment later, he found himself at MacAndrew's side.

The doctor spied him before he could speak. "Going home at last, Lord Hampden? Congratulations!"

"I understand good wishes are due you, as well—if the happy event Edwina hinted about is soon to occur?"

The surgeon stopped short, his face coloring. "Edwina mentioned it, did she? Well, the good wishes are a tad early, but 'twill not be too much longer now, I trust!"

At that avowal, Miles's last, secret hope that Edwina might have been dissembling crumbled. Apparently Mrs. Denby *had* trifled with his affections and lured him to bed, giving him a tantalizing glimpse of a future the doctor's words had just confirmed to be a lie.

He hadn't felt such a sickness in his gut since a

horse kicked him at Talavera. Hurt and fury suffusing him in equal measure, though he'd meant to choke out a goodbye and turn away, he found himself compelled to speak.

Perhaps the doctor needed a pointed, if veiled, warning about the woman he intended to wed.

"I sincerely hope your marriage will be as blissful as you anticipate—given the character of your intended bride."

Dr. MacAndrews stiffened. "Just what do you mean, sir?"

"Only that your prospective fiancée's desire to succor the wounded sometimes carries her to, shall we say, excessive lengths," Miles retorted, glorious memories of Edwina's midnight ministrations again filling his head.

The surgeon's offended look turned puzzled. "Succor the wounded?" he repeated. "Are you still in pain, my lord?"

"No, I am much recovered." *In body, if not spirit.*

"You've not taken laudanum? Your memories must be muddled, then, for you seem to have confused the time you lay wounded with what Edwina told you of my plans. I love my Alicia dearly, but she faints at the mention of blood."

Miles grew still. "Alicia?"

"Alicia," the surgeon repeated, a bit impatiently. "The young lady Edwina told you I intend to marry."

Miles took a deep breath, wild hope emerging

from his initial confusion. "Apparently I *have* muddled it. Your Alicia is not a nurse at the camp?"

The doctor laughed. "Good heavens, no! I'd never allow her within a mile of such a place. No, she's at home with her family in Kent, longing for my return as deeply as I long to return to her, I hope."

"I see. An excellent young lady, Edwina said." *You scheming little minx*, he thought as the doctor rattled on about his beloved.

He didn't know why Edwina had concocted such a Banbury tale, but he did know he wasn't leaving Portugal until he found out. After excusing himself to the surgeon, Miles loped to the gangway.

He'd have to hurry if he wanted to catch his exasperating, infuriating, baffling wife before she left for Torres Vedras.

Chapter Ten

BACK AT THE HOTEL, Edwina paced from her elegant chamber out onto the balcony. Her baggage had been carried downstairs, but still she lingered, gazing over the Lisbon rooftops toward the harbor.

She would wait just a bit longer, until the ship bearing Miles to England sailed by. If he chanced to be on deck, she might catch one last glimpse of him.

Their chilly parting earlier this morning had extinguished the last tiny spark of hope that Miles might declare he truly loved her and beg her to honor their vows, despite her supposed attachment to the surgeon. At which point, she would reveal she loved him as well.

She shook her head. Surely the bitter past should have taught her better than to indulge in such fairy tales.

What was she to do with herself after the end of this short-lived marriage? Despite the desire Miles had awakened in her, the incredible rapture of last night's intimacies had bound her so closely to him she now found it difficult to imagine giving herself to any other man. Perhaps it would be better to hold with her original plan of setting up her own establishment.

Perhaps the indelible memories of that single night with the man she loved would be enough to help her endure a lifetime of emptiness without him.

A knock at the door roused her from her contemplations. Probably it was Manuelo, asking if she were ready to depart. Her eyes still fixed on the view of the harbor, she walked over to open the door. And then stood astounded to find Miles Hampden on the threshold.

"Y-you're not on the ship?" she stuttered.

His unsmiling gaze pinioned her in place. "I found I had unfinished business here. If I might enter?"

She simply couldn't bear playing their parting scene again. "Please, there can be nothing further to say."

Ignoring her outstretched hand, he strode past her into the room. "I thought I could leave, just like that," he said, turning to face her. "But I found I could not. At least, not until I ask you about what I learned this morning from Dr. MacAndrews."

"Dr. MacAndrews!" she echoed, belatedly closing the door and following him to the sofa.

"Yes. I met him just now on the ship, evacuating some of the wounded. By the way, I told him to send our compliments to his fiancée, Miss Alicia Wentworth, who resides with her family back in Kent."

Damn and blast! He'd discovered her deception,

she thought, then realized she should have immediately pleaded ignorance of the engagement and expressed a feigned outrage at the doctor for leading her on. Well, perhaps 'twas not yet too late. "I…I had no idea! To think that he—"

"Edwina, enough. Admit it, you fabricated that story about MacAndrews out of whole cloth."

Edwina hesitated. She might try to bluff her way out of this tangle, but she didn't think she was that good a liar. Perhaps if she served up just a portion of the truth, it would be enough to get him quickly out of this room—before her yearning for him shredded what was left of her good intentions and she begged him to stay.

"I knew you felt honor-bound to uphold the bargain, all the more so as our…friendship grew. I needed a reason for you to release me that would leave you feeling truly free to return home and find another wife, a more suitable lady, of whom your family would approve."

"Perhaps the highest sticklers in society will consider the match between us shockingly unequal, but I expect many will envy me. Snagging an India nabob's heiress for your wife is always good ton."

"Don't you see? It would never suit!"

"But *we* suit, Edwina. Have the last ten days not demonstrated how well-matched we are in preferences, perceptions, wit? Did last night not show how even better we suit in delightfully intimate ways? So why persist in trying to send me away? I think you owe me some better explanation. After all, 'tis an insult to *my* honor that, despite my protestations to the contrary, you seem to think I'm not capable of upholding the vows I made to you."

"'Tis not that!" she protested, trying to come up with some other plausible explanation. "'Tis just..."

"Is it because of what happened between you and Denby? Because he wooed you into wedding him, assuming you were already in possession of a fortune, and was furious when he discovered he had to wait for it?"

For an instant, shock like a dunking in the icy waters of the Douro stole her breath. "Who told you that?"

He shrugged. "'Tis the conclusion I came to just now, on my way back from the docks. It simply wasn't reasonable for you to be so opposed to our union because of the disparity in our stations when you'd already been married to a man of similar standing. Unless, despite what everyone seems to believe, the union wasn't a happy one." His voice softened. "It wasn't happy, was it?"

At that unexpected question, all the aching sorrow she worked so hard to contain seem to burst free of its restraints. For a moment, she struggled to keep the tears back and halt the flow of painful memories.

Perhaps, after all they had shared, he deserved the complete truth—since he'd stumbled upon most of it anyway.

"No," she admitted. "The union was not a happy one."

"Denby dissembled to you about his feelings, didn't he? I cannot imagine you agreeing to wed a man who wanted only your inheritance, no matter how much in love you may have been. But if it was the fortune he wanted so badly, why did he not discover the terms of it before you wed? For neither can I imagine you deceiving him."

After all the half truths she'd fed him, she felt gratified that he still believed she possessed that much honor. "I didn't. The first time he mentioned my fortune, I hastened to inform him of its conditions."

"And yet he wed you anyway, thinking it worth the wait? And in time you discerned his true feelings?"

She smiled, a bitter twist of the lips. "It happened sooner than that." She looked away, the humiliation of the memory making her unable to meet his concerned gaze. "Several weeks after he began courting me, he took me walking in the Queen's Gardens. I was mad for him, too young and stupid to realize what he truly desired of me, and delirious with joy when he kissed me and said he wanted me for his bride—his very rich little bride. His ardor began to cool when I had confessed I wouldn't become an heiress for several years, but just then two of his friends burst out of the shrubbery and caught me still in his arms. Having been found in that compromising situation, my reputation would be destroyed, he told me, if we did not become engaged."

"So you felt compelled to marry him?"

"No—at least, not at first. After he called on Papa and, I imagine, had confirmed what I'd tried to tell him about my fortune, he was furious. He avoided me for days. Having by then had time to realize his true sentiments, when he finally did call, I told him there was no reason to continue the engagement. I would cry off. He informed me that was impossible—for a Denby of Alvaney Court to be jilted by a provincial nobody would make him a laughingstock. Besides, having determined in the interim that my eventual fortune would be all he'd hoped, he knew his papa would agree to pay off his debts—which, it turned out, were massive—and fund him until I received my inheritance. Distasteful as it was for him to marry so far beneath him, he would make the best of it, and so must I."

Miles uttered an oath. "You were still so in his thrall you settled for that?"

"I thanked him for the honor of his offer and told him I considered our engagement over. He warned me if I insisted on crying off and ruining his plans, he would tell my parents he was relieved that honor no longer compelled him to marry the daughter of a man of mediocre family serving in a third-rate regiment, whose mother was the vulgar offspring of a jumped-up Cit. That his friends had seen how I'd lured him into the garden to trap him into making me an offer, and soon the whole cantonment would know I was an ill-bred girl of questionable morals."

"Your papa should have shot him."

"I suppose I should have found another way out, but Mama was so delighted with my excellent match, Papa so proud and happy for me that I couldn't bear to think of the hurt and embarrassment they would suffer if Denby carried out his threat. So I married him."

"Bastard! You are a thousand times too good for him."

Edwina smiled wryly. "'Tis certainly not what he believed."

"How did you endure it?" Miles asked softly, reaching out to stroke her cheek.

She closed her eyes at his touch, the painful memories somehow eased in the telling. "As one does anything unpleasant. And by vowing I would never allow myself to be placed in so untenable a position again. I hope now you understand why you must let me keep that pledge."

"I understand why you've been so insistent on ending our agreement. But do I have no say in a matter that concerns me so nearly? Am I not permitted to plead to keep the companionship of a woman whose courage, intelligence and resourcefulness fill me with admiration? Who has come to occupy such a central place in my life that I cannot imagine living without her? Do you care for me so little?"

She opened her mouth, closed it, that last, most dangerous confession trembling on her lips. The one she dare not make. "I do care for you," she said instead.

"How much, Edwina?" he demanded. Then, before she could imagine what he meant to do, he pulled her close, his mouth coming down hard on hers.

She might resist his words, but to pull away from the touch she yearned for so desperately was beyond her power. With a moan of despair and need, she clutched him fiercely, opened her lips to the invasion of his tongue, pursued it with her own, putting into the last kiss she would ever have from him all the passion she'd been denying, and the love that consumed her soul.

When at last he broke the kiss and cradled her against his chest, she could not bear to look at him. Knowing she was close to losing the battle to restrain her tears, she tried to pull away.

He refused to free her. Tilting her chin up, he demanded again, "How much do you care for me?"

It was too much; her nerves and will were worn past resisting. "All right, I admit it—I love you! And so I cannot subject myself to the misery of remaining wed to a man who holds me in a merely familial affection. Please, let us keep the bargain we made. Take the freedom I offer you and find a woman you can truly love."

His gaze grew fiercer, more insistent. "If that is how you feel, let me propose a new bargain. It may have taken a French sniper's bullet to get my attention, but I've now had two weeks to discover what a treasure was waiting right before my eyes. I love you, too, Edwina. Will you agree to remain my wife—not for my title or fortune or even to bless my family with your caring presence—but so that I may hold forever the woman who has completely captured my affections? I must warn you, I'm not prepared to let you go unless you swear to me that you cannot give me your heart, as I have yielded you mine."

For a moment she forgot to breathe as she took in

the enormity of the declaration he'd just made. "Oh, Miles, I gave you mine long ago."

"Then let us share our first Christmas together, my dear wife, while we plan for our future. The Lord gave back me life—you offer me freedom. Now I would freely pledge my life and love to you. And is love not the greatest gift of all?"

He loved her, loved *her* with the same passion she felt for him. Though she could still scarcely believe it, she had no doubt how priceless was that pledge.

Miles let her go and dropped to one knee. "Edwina Denby, will you do me the honor of remaining my wife, to love and to cherish until we are parted by death? Oh, and I promise to furnish an endless supply of scented oil."

Over the burst of joy swelling her chest, Edwina could feel the blush suffusing her cheeks. "When you phrase it thus, I suppose I must say yes."

With a whoop of triumph, Miles bounded to his feet and captured her in a hug. "Excellent!" he cried as he released her. "Now, what with nearly forcing the man who loves you to sail out of your life, you've had a distressing morning. I believe it must be time for some *soothing*—at my hands." With a wicked grin, he tugged her toward his chamber.

Edwina couldn't help but smile back. "Let me place myself in your hands, now and forever, my dearest love." And with that, she willingly let him lead her away.

STEEP/LIST/1-4 V2

A young woman disappears.
A husband is suspected of murder.
Stirring times for all the neighbourhood in

THE STEEPWOOD *Scandals*

Volume 1 – November 2006
Lord Ravensden's Marriage by Anne Herries
An Innocent Miss by Elizabeth Bailey

Volume 2 – December 2006
The Reluctant Bride by Meg Alexander
A Companion of Quality by Nicola Cornick

Volume 3 – January 2007
A Most Improper Proposal by Gail Whitiker
A Noble Man by Anne Ashley

Volume 4 – February 2007
An Unreasonable Match by Sylvia Andrew
An Unconventional Duenna by Paula Marshall

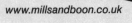